PUBLISHING GROUP

Printed in the United States of America
First Printing, 2023
ISBN 979-8-9879668-0-8
Red Thread Publishing Group
Hartwell, GA 30643
www.kaybratt.com
Cover Design by Elizabeth Mackey Graphic Design

This book is a fictional dramatization that includes one incident inspired by a real event. Facts to support that incident were drawn from a variety of sources, including published materials and interviews, then altered to fit into the fictional story. Otherwise, this book contains fictionalized scenes, composite and representative characters and dialogue, and time compression, all modified for dramatic and narrative purposes. The views and opinions expressed in the book are those of the fictional characters only and do not necessarily reflect or represent the views and opinions held by individuals on which any of the characters are based.

ALSO BY KAY BRATT

All My Dogs Go to Heaven

Standalone Books:

Dancing with the Sun

Wish Me Home

Chasing China; A Daughter's Quest for Truth

A Thread Unbroken

Wish You Were Here

Wishful Thinking

Caroline, Adrift

Willow Duology:

Somewhere Beautiful

Where I Belong

Sworn Sisters duology:

A Welcome Misfortune

To Move the World

Children's Books:

Mei Li & the Wise Laoshi

Eyes Like Mine

IN MY LIFE

HART'S RIDGE BOOK 3

KAY BRATT

CHAPTER 1

*S*econd chances should be stronger than secrets, or at least that was what Taylor chose to believe and had spent the last six months practicing. It wasn't easy, but anything worth having took work, and she firmly believed the merit of a person had a lot to do with their capacity to forgive.

Getting to know Cate was interesting. She was nothing like the mother Taylor remembered.

The forgiveness wasn't quite a done deal, but she was working on it. There she sat, waiting in the truck with her eyes on the door of a gift shop in town, instead of at home taking Diesel for a long walk by the lake, as she'd prefer to do on her day off.

He must've read her mind because he turned and shot her a disappointed look before he returned to staring out the window, waiting for one of his new favorite humans to return.

Taylor was still a bit shaken from her conversation with Lucy earlier that morning. After catching her sister once again glued to the national news, she'd asked what she was watching for. Lucy had taken insult to the 'line of questioning,' as she'd called it, and told her to mind her own business. Something big happened when Lucy was out of town—when she'd had the baby. Taylor hoped it wasn't something that was going to come back and bite her sister in the butt.

Lucy also had some money. Taylor wasn't sure how much, but Lucy had returned the thousand dollars she owed Taylor, bought an old car, and didn't seem as desperate for the things she'd once scrambled to buy. Baby things were costly, and Lucy was being careful, but little Johnny had everything he needed and then some. It couldn't be done on what she was making at the Den waitressing.

Taylor noticed the little things, and something didn't add up.

The second Cate emerged from the building; Taylor could tell she didn't get the job. It was in the way she hung her head with her shoulders slumped.

"Didn't get it. I'm sorry," Cate said as she opened the door and got in. Diesel immediately picked up on her disappointment. He nuzzled under her elbow until she lifted it and put it around him so he could lean into her for a hug.

"Thanks, boy," she whispered.

They'd been to four places, but the one they just left was the only one that had called Cate in for an interview.

"Don't say you're sorry," Taylor said. "You have nothing to apologize for. They're idiots and, believe me, you don't want to work for idiots. "You need to see this rejection as a re-direction. So where to now?"

Cate sighed as she looked at her phone. She sounded so tired. "Only one more on my list, then we can call it a day. I found a Christmas tree farm on Google. They might need some help."

"Hart Valley Farms. That's a great idea. Amos and Beverly Higgins own it. They run it with their sons, and they are the nicest people. With your horticulture experience, I'm sure they could use you somehow, especially around the holidays, but I'm not sure what they do in May."

"May is when the new growth begins on the trees. They call them candles. They'll be fertilizing saplings. If they grow Fraser

Firs, the cones should be removed by hand about this time." She stared out her window.

"Alright, then. Let's go. Since it's a family business, it would be a good place to work. Think positive." Taylor pulled onto the road, turned right, then headed toward Gator's Gap. She thought she heard a skip in the truck's motor, making a mental note to ask Sam to take it for a test drive the next time he came over.

Cate had worked a few jobs in the months she'd been home, but they were customer-service related and hadn't worked out. She needed something where she didn't have to deal with strangers, or that was what she said. It wasn't that she was unpleasant to anyone. It was that strangers made her nervous, resulting in small mistakes that made her feel stupid.

"You would've been great in there, so their loss," Taylor said.

"Yeah, I guess."

Taylor hated seeing her look so dejected. Cate had been through a lot, and she was still paying for the crime she didn't commit. The felony popped up on the background checks employers did, making it hard to gain enough trust to be hired. Getting it expunged would take a lot of time and even more money.

"It's just another ten minutes," Taylor said, notching her speed up to just two over the limit. The time on the radio said the afternoon was getting away from her. She had a lot to do when she got home. Keeping house was a lot more labor intensive now that people other than Diesel and she lived there.

Cate hadn't wanted to move in with any of them upon exoneration, but other than going to Florida to live with Adele, she'd had no other choice. Until she could get a stable income and save enough for a deposit, the first month's rent, and enough to set up the utilities, she'd been forced to move in with Taylor.

Now that made three and a half of them—plus a dog—all trying to make things work within what had once been a quiet home.

Taylor had hung on to the master bedroom by a thread, but Lucy and the baby were in the next biggest room with Cate taking the small one. Jo and Levi had moved back to town. Thankfully, they had managed to scrape up what they needed to rent a small apartment close to Levi's school.

No one wanted to live with Anna and her family, even if there had been an invitation, because although Anna was coming around more, it was still awkward to be around Pete. It felt like he looked at them as though they were specimens under a microscope, their family drama something to be studied or enjoyed like a sideshow at the circus. She'd love to know what secrets his family tree held, but like most people who thought themselves in a different league than those on the struggling side of life, he was better at keeping them to himself.

"Oh, did you get to see Johnny trying to crawl last night?" Taylor asked.

"No, I missed that." Cate smiled wistfully.

"He was rocking back and forth on his knees next to Diesel. He knows something exciting comes next, but he hasn't figured out what yet."

Taylor had to admit she was enamored with the baby, too. She'd spent many nights rocking him to sleep when she wasn't working late, soothing him with soft singing to take his mind off his teething. Usually, though, his sunny personality and joyful babbling brought them all a lot of smiles, helping to cover the uncomfortableness of getting to know each other again.

Lucy remained closemouthed, not only about where she'd been hiding out for months, but also about Johnny's paternity, making Taylor nervous that some street thug might show up one day, demanding visitation. She agreed a father should have rights, but, hopefully, he'd be a better-caliber person than some of her sister's past boyfriends.

"He's smart for six months old. Just like Robert was. I bet he walks before he's ten months old."

That was new, too. Now that they knew their little brother hadn't suffered in the fire that took his life, they could all speak about him more easily.

Her dad was the most obsessed with his new grandson. Taylor had never seen him try so hard to stay sober, though she wasn't completely sure it was only for Johnny and not for Cate, too. Taylor had seen his name pop up a few times on Cate's phone screen for some text messages, though she wasn't sure about the content.

So far, it appeared Cate wasn't ready for anything more than being cordial to him, and some of that was because, over the last months, she'd learned more about how he'd let them all down in her absence. She hadn't said as much, not with words, but Taylor could read her pretty well now.

Diesel was taken with Johnny, too, and wanted to be near him all the time. He laid close to him for protection, and even hesitated when it came time for him to leave to stay with Sam on weekends, not sure whether he should leave or not.

"Here we are," Taylor said. She drove alongside the mile of farm fencing until they got to the big gate, then turned in. "Amos and his sons grow the nicest trees in Georgia. It's Amos' dream to have one of his trees on display in the White House before he dies. They've taken third place in the national competition three years running. He and the boys are obsessed with winning."

"Well, it's pine heaven around here, so they probably have a great chance," Cate said.

"Yep. So far, a farm in North Carolina is their biggest competition, but Amos is going to win this year, you watch. He's got a lot of support. Everyone in town loves him and his wife, Beverly. They do a lot for the community, especially veterans. Oh, I just remembered… last year, Beverly opened a small shop in her barn to sell trinkets, and a better setup for the coffee and hot chocolate. Maybe they'll need you there."

"Maybe. But I'd rather work on the farm. I enjoy the open air and working with plants and trees."

Suddenly, a man on a four-wheeler emerged from the tree line and waved at Taylor. She pulled up beside him, then put down her window.

"Hey, Danny."

"Taylor! What're you doing up here?" He grinned through the mud splatters on his face. At barely twenty-four, he was the youngest of the Higgins boys. He had made a name for himself with the sheriff's department back when he was a teenager. All the boys had their moments, but Danny had taken a bit longer to outgrow his rebellion.

Taylor was glad to see him working on the farm and looking healthy. That meant he'd repaired things with his family. At one point, Amos swore to give him tough love and escorted him off the land, telling him to come back when he was ready to be respectful. Danny had struggled badly back then, getting nothing from his parents. Amos was old school. He firmly believed parents couldn't enable bad behavior and call it love. Taylor agreed, but it was something she had struggled with, too.

She gestured at Cate. "This is my mother. She's new in town and looking for a job. She's got a lot of experience with plants and stuff."

He nodded appreciatively. "Gotcha. I don't know if we're hiring. That's not my area, but I need to check on them anyway. No one's answering my calls, and I sent Carlos to bring me some gopher traps. I'll lead you up there."

Taylor waited for him to pull out in front, then she followed him up the driveway to the main house that doubled as their office.

"He's the youngest of three sons," she told Cate as they drove. "Danny, David, and Doug. But they lost Doug to a motorcycle accident a few years back. Beverly still hasn't recovered from that. He was a good one."

"You never recover from the loss of a child," Cate said. "No matter how old they were when they passed."

Taylor's eyes were still on Danny when they got up to the house. He jumped off the ATV, screaming, then ran around a small truck parked in the driveway.

"What's wrong with him?" Cate asked, leaning closer to the front window.

Diesel's hair rose on his back, and he started barking.

"I don't know. I can't see him. Diesel, no! Hush!" Taylor parked behind the truck and cut her motor. She wasn't even out her door before Danny ran toward her, his face pale with shock.

Diesel quivered with nervous excitement.

"Call an ambulance! Quick! David's been shot," Danny yelled.

Cate climbed out of the truck, seeming confused.

Taylor beckoned for her to get back in and to hold onto Diesel. "Stay down and call emergency. Tell them we've got one man down, gunshot wound at Hart Valley Farms, up at the home office. Don't get out of the truck."

Taylor pulled her gun from the glove compartment, then shut the truck door. When she approached David, it was obvious an ambulance wouldn't be needed. He stared at the sky, eyes blank, unmoving. He'd been shot in the forehead.

Danny cried out, dropping to his knees beside his brother. "No. No, no, no. David... no!"

There wasn't anything Taylor could do for David, but she needed to see if the killer was still there. "Danny, you stay with your brother, but don't touch him again. I'm going in."

The rest of her day off had officially been canceled.

CHAPTER 2

*T*aylor had secured the scene the best she could by the time Sheriff Dawkins and Sarge arrived, with Grimes and Penner as backup. She'd found another victim in the garage, then one more in the house. She had cleared every room. After confirming no one else was there, she'd backed out and closed the garage door, then stood guard and waited.

The sheriff pulled in, lights and sirens blaring.

Behind the police tape Taylor had pinned around the best she could, Cate held onto Diesel. She looked worried. She and Danny, along with a smattering of family members and employees, stood watching.

The ambulance had left, no passengers to take with them, and the coroner was on his way. A forensics team from Alpharetta was also en route.

Taylor had covered David's body with a blanket she kept under her truck seat. A few feet from him lay a pair of men's slippers, seemingly discarded in a hurry.

Amos' wife, Beverly, was on her way home from a supply run to Atlanta, but they hadn't told her what awaited her. Taylor hoped no one there would be cruel enough to tell her before she arrived, but even Danny didn't know there were two more of his loved one's dead inside.

"What the hell is going on?" the sheriff belted out as he got out of his cruiser and slammed the door. "Grimes, Penner, you keep them out." He pointed at the people huddled together, then joined Taylor next to the body.

"It's bad," she said. "A triple. I didn't want to say it over the radio. First victim down from a shot to the head."

She sounded professional, but she was quaking inside. This was the worst crime she'd ever seen happen in Hart's Ridge.

And to a good family, at that.

The sheriff and Sarge squatted next to the body, then pulled the sheet back.

"Son of a bitch," the sheriff said. "It's David. This is going to kill Beverly and Amos."

"Not Amos," Taylor murmured so the crowd wouldn't hear. "He's already dead. Shot execution style in the garage. Danny doesn't know yet. I kept him outside with Cate."

Slowly, the sheriff stood. His eyes found Danny's first, then he looked away and locked on hers. She saw confusion, sadness, and a flicker of rage. Amos was a good friend of his. He and his wife went out for dinner with the sheriff and Diane often. Sometimes, they even vacationed together. Their oldest son had gone to college with the sheriff's daughter.

"Who else? You said a triple. Please don't tell me it's Beverly."

"No. She's on her way home, but she only knows there's an emergency. It's a male. I can't tell for certain, but I think it might be Carlos, Danny's best friend. Danny doesn't know that, either. I didn't let him enter the house."

"Damn it," the sheriff said, shaking his head. "Let's go look. Where's Weaver? He needs to be with us."

He glanced at the slippers and then at David's feet, which stuck out of the bottom of the sheet. They were clad in worn work boots, mud caked on the bottoms, showing that only a short time ago, he was living, breathing, and putting in a good day's work.

Now he was just dead.

"So, the slippers aren't his," Sarge said, following the sheriff's visual line.

"They belong to Amos," Taylor said. She'd never get the vision of his bare feet out of her head. Or the expression of panic frozen on his face.

Shane pulled up, screeching tires on the concrete as he slammed on his brakes. He got out and joined them, his face grim.

Taylor did a double take.

He'd told her the sheriff had approved a new detective uniform, but she hadn't expected such a drastic transformation from his usual polo shirt and slacks. Now he wore olive-green tactical gear. His snug-fitting cargo pants were paired with a long-sleeved black shirt that hugged his muscles and had the Hart County Sheriff's department logo on his chest. His badge was hooked to his belt, and he wore a ballcap pulled low over his eyes. Gone were his shiny dress shoes. In their place was a roughed-up pair of tactical boots.

He looked ready to jump out of a van with a team of heavy artillery special-ops guys.

"Gray, you were first on the scene?" he asked, his notepad already out.

"Yes. I was bringing Cate here to apply for a job. I met the youngest son, Danny Higgins, on the way up the driveway. He led us here. Once we saw this one—it's David, Danny's older brother—I secured the area and went into the garage to access the house. Victim two is Amos Higgins, Danny and David's father."

"I know how they're related," Shane said solemnly. "I came here dozens of times when I was a kid."

Taylor nodded. "Me too."

She had to give it to her dad. Although they rarely had much money for gift-giving at Christmas, they'd always managed to get a tree. He loved the ceremony of finding the perfect one, then cutting it down. There at the farm, people could cut their own or have it cut for them, then end the excursion with a cup of Beverly's famous hot chocolate. She always gave it to them free of charge. She'd somehow known that was the only way Taylor and her sisters would get to have it.

"I bagged Danny's hands until we can do the GSR test," Taylor said. It had been brutal telling him why she had to wrap his hands. He'd looked at her like she was the devil, but he'd complied.

The sheriff led the way to the garage, and they followed. Inside, he held his arms out, keeping them back.

A set of wooden wind chimes hung in the window at the back of the room, tinkling a peaceful yet eerie melody as a soundtrack for the carnage inside.

Amos' knees were bent. His body lay forward, his forehead touching the cement floor. There was a small hole in the back of his head. A rivulet of red ran from it, down his neck, and then onto a large pool of blood next to him. A few carpet squares had been put over the blood, but they weren't big enough to completely cover it.

In the corner stood a huge gun safe, at least five feet tall and three feet wide. The door to it was open, the key still in the lock.

"Execution style," Shane said, moving around the sheriff to get closer. "Couldn't even look him in the eye when the sonofabitch killed him."

"This just ain't right," the sheriff said. "Amos never hurt a soul. Was the kindest man I know. He would have given the shirt off his back for anyone who needed it."

Taylor could hear tears in the thickness of his voice, and it cut her to the quick. She had to swallow hard to get past it.

"Large-caliber handgun," Shane said, peering at the entry point. He turned to Taylor. "Did the other son hear gunshots?"

"Yes, but he said he figured it was someone hunting. They hear shots all the time out here."

Shane grimaced. "Look for casings."

Taylor saw one casing on the floor next to a stack of firewood, only two feet from Amos' body. She pointed at it.

"25. automatic," she said. "The one on the driveway was from a 44."

"Two different killers," Sarge said. "Leave it for the team to collect."

Items in the garage were in disarray, showing either a scuffle or someone working in a hurry. They scrutinized the area from where they stood, careful not to disturb any DNA that could be collected.

"Let's go look at the third victim," the sheriff said.

"Yeah, I want to get in there before forensics," Shane said, starting for the door. He passed out black plastic gloves before opening it. "If y'all are coming, be careful. Glove up and don't touch anything you don't have to."

They followed, entering the kitchen. The body was just inside, sprawled on the floor next to a shattered cell phone. Another shot to the back of the head, though this one left a huge hole.

Taylor felt sure it was Carlos. She'd seen him around town with Danny a lot. The dark hair and lean body combined with the fact Danny said Carlos hadn't returned from the errand he'd sent him on had added up.

"He ran in to call for help," Shane said. "They got him before he could dial."

The sheriff bent to pick up a casing. "This one's from a 22-magnum rifle. So that's three guns. Must be three suspects."

Taylor surveyed the kitchen, noting items on the floor that had probably been knocked off the countertop. On the dining table was an open laptop with stacks of paperwork around it. A chair was pulled out like someone had gotten up from it abruptly.

Shane took the casing from the sheriff, dropping it into a clear evidence bag before scribbling on it. "Know anything about this victim?"

"I'm pretty sure it's Carlos Rodriguez, Danny's best friend," Taylor said, then explained her reasoning. "He's married and has a baby. They brought him in as a field supervisor when his construction work dried up for the winter and he needed to provide for his new family."

At least that was the gossip around town. If Taylor didn't get the juice herself, she could always depend on Dottie in dispatch to fill her in. More than she'd like, to be honest. Taylor wasn't a fan of rumors.

"Could he possibly be involved in a gang?" Sarge asked.

"Why do you ask? Because he's Mexican?" She glared at him as she answered his question. "No—he's not involved in gang activity. From what I hear, he's a good family man now."

"Three different guns means three suspects." Sarge raised his eyebrows. "You sound a bit sensitive today, Gray."

"You said *now*. That he's a good family man *now*." The sheriff turned to her. "What are you leaving out?"

Taylor fought to keep the annoyance out of her voice. "I just meant he's settled down. He and Danny used to get into some small-time trouble. Teen stuff."

When she glanced at Shane, he looked sympathetic. He knew that when it came to her townspeople, she was protective. And yes, sensitive. It would take a monster not to be upset that a man, his son, and his son's best friend were gunned down in cold blood. Even if they weren't friends.

"Okay, then give us your best shot at what you think happened here," Sarge said, putting Taylor on the spot.

She hesitated, getting her thoughts in a row so the three men didn't shoot her hypothesis down from the get-go.

"We haven't investigated enough to know who the suspects might be or what the motive was for sure, but from what I can tell, it could've gone like this—a suspect, or multiple suspects, snuck into the garage to rob the safe, thinking no one was home. Amos was inside—"

Taylor's theory was cut short by the sound of a high-pitched scream outside the house.

"Beverly," the sheriff said. "Let me go."

When he hurried out, Taylor followed.

Beverly and Danny had somehow made it past the deputies into the garage. They stood over Amos' body, eyes wide and disbelieving. Danny held his mother, supporting her when she went silent, then completely limp.

Just outside the driveway, a news van from an Atlanta station was setting up. The first of many, most likely.

"For Pete's sake," the sheriff said. "What an astronomical shit show. Get them out of here!"

CHAPTER 3

Taylor felt like a complete jerk, but she had to do her job. After they'd pulled Beverly away from her husband, Cate had stepped in to help calm her down, but even after an hour or so, the poor woman was still incoherent and couldn't even form a complete sentence.

Her interview would wait until morning, but Danny had to be questioned while everything was fresh in his mind. He was first on the scene and could hold vital clues, even if he didn't know it yet.

Shane was lead, but he requested her help. The move was probably to make up for how he'd betrayed her months before, but it was one she was glad to take. She wanted to be a part of getting the filth who had murdered three good men in cold blood.

"Did you handle a firearm at any point yesterday?" Shane asked.

"No. It's not usually a tool we use when working with Christmas trees," Danny said, his tone sarcastic. "You should know... you did the gun-residue test. Not only on me, but also on Jenny and Mom. I mean, c'mon, guys. Did you *have* to do that to them?"

"Standard procedure. Okay, close your eyes and think back to the exact moment you saw David lying there," Shane said. "What else did you see?"

"I've already told you at least four times. I don't know what else to say," Danny said. "Taylor saw exactly what I did only seconds later."

He looked exhausted, eyes red-rimmed and skin as pale as paper.

"Please refer to her as Deputy Gray," Shane corrected. "This is an investigation, not a neighborhood cookout."

His scolding was uncalled for, but Taylor kept her mouth shut. For each interview, Shane had his technique and she had hers. Sometimes, he was the bad guy—and sometimes he was so nice it was nauseating.

"Fine, but why did *Deputy Gray* have to take my clothes? Of course you're going to find David's and Pop's DNA on it. I bent over them both. Is that a crime?"

"No, it's not, Danny. Taking your clothing is police procedure. What about the gunshots? Can you pinpoint what time you heard them? And how many?" Shane asked.

"No—sometime this morning. I didn't even think twice about it. We hear gunshots around that area all the time. Hunting and target practice. It's like background noise to me." He slammed his hands on the table.

"Can you tell us who all knows about the safe in the garage?" Taylor asked, her tone much gentler than Shane's.

Danny threw his arms in the air, making the blue paper suit he wore crackle. "Who doesn't? Pop paid the employees straight from the safe. They line up in there every Friday. Why are you in here wasting time with me instead of out there trying to find who did this?"

"The investigation is going in many different directions as we speak," Shane said. "But we also need to eliminate the people closest to the victims as being suspects. Can you tell us where your mother went shopping today?"

"I can't tell you where all she went, but I know her main task was to pick up our order at the wholesale supply store we use in Atlanta. Sometimes, she gets her hair done while she's up there. Or goes shopping. I don't know, you can ask her. Dad wasn't even supposed to be home today. He came in early from out of town." Danny ran his hands through his blond hair, then bent over his knees and sobbed, hiding his face as he rocked back and forth.

"So, it's possible someone thought no one would be at the house today," Taylor said, jotting a note down.

That could point to someone close to the family who knew where everyone was supposed to be.

"And David's wife? Do you know what she was doing today?" Taylor asked.

He shook his head. "I guess what she does every day. Takes one kid to school, but keeps the other at home. Shops. Cleans. Mom stuff, I guess. I don't know."

"So she doesn't come up to the farm?" Taylor asked.

"Yeah, but not all the time. I usually only see her at Sunday dinners. Lately, they've been coming earlier, so Jenny can help Mom cook."

"What about you? Dating anyone?" Taylor asked.

"Nope. Haven't dated in a long time. Got too much going on with work and trying to stay out of trouble."

Shane raised his brows at that. "Do you have a hard time staying out of trouble?"

"It's a phrase, man. I didn't mean it literally."

"What about you and David? Did you have any recent arguments?" Shane asked. "I know it must've been rough working under your brother's supervision."

Danny glared at Shane. "I haven't argued with my brother in ages, and I didn't kill my brother. I haven't argued with my father, and I didn't kill him either. I haven't argued with Carlos, and I didn't kill *my best friend!*" His words started softly before ending in a bellow and another sob.

Taylor caught Shane's eye. She nodded toward the door, then got up.

"Danny, I'm going to get you a cup of coffee. We'll be right back."

They went out, letting the door shut behind them. Shane leaned against the wall in the hall, crossing his arms. "A bit melodramatic, don't you say?"

"He's done. We can't keep him here," Taylor said. "Let him be with Beverly. She needs him."

"But what do you think? Is he being for real? I didn't see a single tear with those sobs."

"It looked real to me. You can't fake that kind of despair."

"You can if you did something horrific and now wish you hadn't."

Taylor shook her head. "I know we have to consider him as a viable suspect, but don't jump to conclusions before we get something solid."

Shane shook his head. "Don't you think it's coincidental that you pull up the driveway and he just so happens to pop out of the tree line right at that moment, tells you he's going up to the house, and then you both find the scene? C'mon, Taylor. That's a stretch. Danny knew exactly what was up there. He was hiding until he figured out what to do, but when he saw you, he jumped on the opportunity."

"Maybe. But what's the motive?"

"Money, of course. That's what it usually is."

"But he was already going to inherit the place once Amos and Beverly retire."

"Not all of it. He would have had to split it with David. But not now. His dad's gone. Brother's gone. Danny gets to step in, take care of Mama, and run the farm."

"He hasn't worked there long enough to know how to run it." Taylor wasn't going to give credence to those suspicions. It was a sick theory. But she had to at least consider it. Money was the root of all evil. It could make good people go bad. She'd seen it time and again.

"I want to see what else the forensics team digs up," she said. "And I want to talk to Beverly. See if there was any discord between Danny and his dad that he's not telling. Or with him and his brother."

"She'll protect her only surviving son. We'll get nothing from her."

Taylor shook her head. "Not if she thinks he killed the love of her life and her other son. I don't believe that for a minute. Beverly is a kind woman, but she's also a fair one. She'll want someone to pay for cutting those lives short, even if it is Danny."

"I hope so. When we go back in there, I'm going to ask him about anyone who holds a grudge against the family. Has anyone recently been fired or passed up for a promotion? That farm is one of the largest employers in the state, both for locals and seasonals from other areas. I want to interview as many as we can, past and present."

"Agreed. And Danny said they usually pay the seasonal employees in cash. That's going to make it hard as hell to track them down. Many are Mexican migrants, traveling from state to state, picking up whatever jobs they can until it runs out and they must move on."

Shane sighed. "I forgot about that. We're going to need an interpreter."

"And for all we know, this could've been done by some random stranger passing through," Taylor said.

"Nope—someone passing through wouldn't know about that safe in the back of the garage."

"True, but lots of people know that farm is raking in cash, and they'd need somewhere to hold it. People from all over come to buy their trees. The possibilities are endless." Taylor let out a long breath, trying not to allow the stress to overwhelm her thinking ability. She needed to be sharp.

After the conversation drifted off, Taylor excused herself, then went to the breakroom for the coffee she'd promised Danny. She'd already had a few cups herself, but it was going to be a long night and she needed more.

She'd sent Cate home with Diesel. She should call to make sure they'd gotten there safely. Cate had finally jumped through the hoops to get her driver's license, but she wasn't comfortable behind the wheel yet.

To Taylor, it felt like Cate was always nervous, like she was afraid she was going to get in trouble. They couldn't even walk through the grocery store without Cate constantly looking around. Once, she'd told Taylor to stop putting her hands in her jacket because it made her look like she was shoplifting.

"I doubt anyone in this town is going to accuse a sheriff's deputy of shoplifting, Cate," Taylor had said. They'd both laughed, the tense moment diverted.

Cate needed counseling—that much was clear to Taylor—but the one time she'd mentioned it, Cate had gone quiet for the rest of the night. The next morning, she'd asked Taylor if she felt safe there with her and said if she didn't, she'd find somewhere else to go.

Cate didn't have anywhere else to go. Jo didn't have room in her new apartment, and Anna's place wasn't an option. Cate didn't seem interested in rekindling her relationship with Jackson. They were awkward with each other, so that was a dead end. But it didn't matter because Taylor felt safe enough around Cate, and the subject had been dropped.

However, it didn't feel like a mother-daughter relationship.

Not to Taylor.

Lucy and Anna were having a harder time than Taylor was. Lucy never trusted anyone, so that wasn't a big shocker. Anna was standoffish at best, and her kids acted frightened around Cate.

Jo was more at Taylor's pace, cautiously optimistic that it would all work out but not being too friendly yet.

Levi—well, he was just Levi. He had embraced his newfound relationship with a grandmother he hadn't known he had. It was nice having him around as much as possible to smooth out the rough edges.

It was all so complicated.

Taylor lifted the coffee pot to find it empty. She fixed up another filter and slid it in, cussing under her breath. The men at the station only knew how to drink it. They rarely made it, acting as though it was a woman's job.

"Hey, Gray," Penner said as he burst through the door.

"Hey yourself. What's it looking like up there?" Taylor leaned against the counter to wait for the coffee. She didn't want to go back into the interview room without it.

"Not good. Word has spread. There must've been two hundred people standing around out there. I had to threaten them with a disturbing-the-peace citation if they didn't disperse. The rookie helped, and most have cleared off now. The forensics team is only about halfway done. I bet they are there until midnight."

"It takes as long as it takes," she said. "What did you find regarding surveillance? Anything more than cameras on the fields?"

"Nope. You'd think that Amos would've at least put one at the front gate and one at the house since they do business from it, but I guess his only concerns were the critters wiping out his trees. The rookie is going to do another sweep of the property tonight, just to be sure, but both Jenny and Beverly said that was it."

"Does Kuno know you're still calling him the rookie? He's got more than five or six months under his belt, doesn't he?"

Penner laughed. "Yeah, he knows. Told him he's the official rookie until a new one comes in."

"From what I hear, he's banned you from wanting to pick his wife's brain about writing a book. Thinks you're trying too hard," she teased.

Taylor hadn't met her yet, but Kuno's wife, Emily, was a writer. She had published a novel centered around a woman and a dog.

Word was she'd made a lot of money off it and was working on a series now.

Penner laughed. "You just wait. One day, I'll have my name on the cover of a true-crime novel."

"Gotcha. Anyway, didn't you know David? You're about the same age."

Penner nodded. "Yep. He was a grade ahead of me. I knew him, but we didn't hang out. He was a nice guy. Played basketball and football. That's a shitty way to go out. I know his wife, too. Jenny. They were high-school sweethearts."

"Man, I'm glad I didn't have to see her."

"Yeah. It was bad. She got there right before I left, so I had to give her the news. Sucks. Thank God she didn't have the kids with her."

Taylor felt for Penner. No one wanted that task, especially him. He was more comfortable writing up blotters for the town paper than he was informing kin of deaths or investigating murders.

"Did you tell her to come here as soon as she could? Weaver wants to talk to her before we finish tonight."

He nodded. "I did, but I don't know if she will. She was with Amos' wife, and they were holding each other pretty tightly."

"I can't even imagine what they're going through. What a nightmare for the entire family. Poor Danny is back there sobbing his guts out. He just wants to go home and be with his mama."

"Oh, that reminds me," Penner said, lighting up. "Jenny said there's a truck missing. It belongs to Amos, but Carlos was driving it. It's gone."

Taylor slapped her forehead. "Of course! We hadn't even considered the fact that Carlos had to have come to the house in some sort of vehicle. Even though Danny was on a four-wheeler, that doesn't mean Carlos would be, too. Did you get the stats on the truck?"

"Yep. Already put it out on the system, but I guarantee those wheels are hundreds of miles away by now. But the good thing is that we might find the killer if we find the truck, right?"

"Or killers, plural." Taylor felt a surge of hope. Having a vehicle missing was big. She maneuvered a cup under the dripping coffee, holding it there until it was full.

She couldn't wait to get back there to tell Shane they might have a lead.

CHAPTER 4

𝒾t was nearly dark, but Cate continued to sit on the porch swing, letting the gentle motion take her back and forth, her bare feet grazing Diesel's soft fur at each pass. She wondered what time Taylor would get home. This was the latest she'd worked since Cate had moved in, and she was worried about her.

She wondered if Adele had felt the same during all those years she'd tried to do her best for Cate in prison, not knowing if her daughter was alive from one call to the next.

Jackson had reached out to Adele in desperation, which had to have shocked her socks off. Cate wasn't the one her parents had thought would end up in jail. Jackson had raised their suspicions, and they'd tried to call out his future. Never in a million years had they thought the daughter they'd brought up in a nice home, put in a good school, and had all the bells and whistles of a normal life would be the one who carried her stack of meager belongings into a cell, crawled up on the top bunk as her surly cellmate had ordered, then spent the next twenty years trying not to lose her mind.

Cate had to give it to Adele, though. Her mom had stepped up to be the only human on the outside connecting Cate to the life she'd known before.

Her lifeline.

Adele had been the only stable connection Cate had in the concrete jungle of loss and violence, which was filled with the desperation of those who carried guilt and regret with them like nooses around their necks. Desperation had filled the eyes of young mothers, old mothers, and everything in between. Many were there only for doing whatever it took to feed their children. Some had been talked into crimes by the men they thought loved them, but who'd tossed them aside as soon as they received their sentence. Thousands of women had acted as drug mules—so many hearts broken, and futures shattered.

Cate hadn't known what to expect when she'd arrived at the women's prison. The constant drama had surprised her. It felt like everyone around her got their period at the same time. The women had always competed for sink time and their share of the limited supplies of pads or tampons.

The love affairs, too… They'd been more intense than the Spanish novellas that sometimes played on the TV in the rec room. The relationships would start sweet—almost childish—with friends setting one another up, then love notes being passed back and forth. Soon, though, it progressed to intense obsession, which always went hand in hand with jealousy and cheating.

God forbid a long-term couple had to be split up by one getting released. The one left behind moped around for months, looking forward to letters and waiting for phone calls, until it all dwindled away. At that point, the one left behind usually sank into a deep depression—at least until she found someone else to fill her hours.

Cate hadn't been involved in that nonsense. She hadn't been gay when she arrived there and a few lonely years hadn't turned her, though she didn't judge anyone who chose differently. She'd stayed out of the drama as much as possible—meaning other people's relationships as well as thwarting every pass she got herself.

Years ago, she'd heard some of the prisoners had an ongoing bet—with a cache of hoarded chocolate as the prize—for anyone who could tempt her into a love affair.

That had sealed the deal. No one would profit from her private life.

Some women had husbands, boyfriends, or so-called fiancés—those who visited and those whose only contact came through words scratched out on letters from a men's prison to theirs, full of empty promises about the new life they'd lead once both were free.

Cate had thought about Jackson often. She'd hoped that with her out of the picture, he'd put the booze aside and step up to be a good father. The few times they'd had contact, that was what he'd *said* he was doing. He'd sent her money almost every month, too. Not a lot, and she hadn't wanted it, but it had come in handy to get her a few necessities she couldn't live without.

And she hadn't needed much. Too much comfort would only remind her of what she'd lost.

She'd spent most of her time in her bunk—it had been her only safe place for years. Her oasis before she had enough clout and trust to earn her way into the dog program, then the nursery to work on the prison's growing food program. Her quiet ways had also earned her the respect of her peers. There'd been a few times, in the beginning, when she'd been approached by someone with a reputation to prove, looking to jump her for no reason at all. Each time, Cate had stood her ground, fixing them with a steely glare and daring them to make a move, which would give her an excuse to exile some of her internal anger at the injustice done to her.

Something in the set of her shoulders and the steel in her eyes had always diffused the situation.

Eventually, she'd started to make friends. She'd been picky

about who she let into her circle of silence, but the first one just sort of happened.

Gwendolyn—or Gwendy—was paralyzed from the waist down. She'd been transferred in after receiving a life sentence for killing her husband in a failed murder-suicide. The shot to her head hadn't killed her. Instead, it had traveled in a downward trajectory right through her neck, exiting from her spine on the other side.

Her husband had been a champion bronc rider who had taken home the buckle, but when she'd caught him in the saddle with a rodeo cowgirl, the girl had escaped, but he hadn't been able to get his pants up fast enough.

Considering her circumstances, Gwendy had a fairly optimistic attitude. Assigned to be her pusher for the first month, Cate had assisted Gwendy with getting to the canteen for meals and to pill count for her medication. Gwendy had been able to do it herself for the most part because the buildings were handicap accessible. During winter, when the snow piled on the ramp outside, it had been harder to get her chair up it. It had still been Gwendy's responsibility to be there at pill count. The times she hadn't made it to get the medication she needed, she'd spent miserable nights wide awake, as well as received disciplinary action.

No one had been allowed to take the medication to her, either. If Gwendy hadn't been there herself, no meds.

Cate had made damn sure Gwendy got her meds.

One time, Cate had to recruit three others to help carry the chair up the ramp. Gwendy had a great sense of humor, though, and she'd constantly cracked jokes. That day, she'd said she felt like a queen on a chariot.

Something about her pulled at Cate's heartstrings. Perhaps because she'd been near Taylor's age, or maybe she'd made Cate feel needed. Either way, they'd become best friends. Cate still felt guilty about leaving her behind.

Typically, Cate got along with everyone. At least until they'd found out Taylor was a cop. Gwendy had tried to warn her it was coming, but Cate never thought they'd do anything. Most women who pretended to have power had been all talk.

Cate touched her jaw, not wanting the memories of that beating to resurface. She breathed deeply, trying to expel the flashbacks.

The night air was unusually brisk for May, and it felt amazing on her skin. Across town, Beverly Higgins was living one of the worst days of her life, trying to come to grips with losing both her husband and son in one day.

The entire ordeal made Cate pensive and keen to think about her own family and the miracle of them being reunited. Tragedies happened every day, as she knew so well herself, and the fact that all four of her daughters were still alive and well was a blessing Cate would never take for granted.

She'd never take the small things for granted again either: the feel of the wind in her hair or the sun on her face; the comfort of sinking into a warm bath; or even something as simple as total privacy on the toilet.

Music... Not what she'd been forced to listen to in prison, but anything she chose.

She hadn't appreciated the little things before her freedom had been stolen, but she would now.

Life wasn't perfect, though.

With the girls and her, there was an awkwardness Cate didn't know how to smooth over. It was expected after so many years, but a part of her had hoped the mother-daughter bond she'd established with them when they were children would've held fast. She felt like she was starting over with strangers. Strangers she knew much better than they thought she did.

Also, crowds now made her so nervous that she felt nauseated and broke into a sweat each time she had to be in one. In her head, it felt like everyone in town knew her story and thought she was a murderer. It wasn't true, of course, but when had insecurities ever made sense?

Choices were a blessing and a curse.

While she enjoyed choosing when she ate, what she ate, or even what she listened to on the TV or radio, other decisions proved to be too overwhelming.

Taylor had taken Cate to Walmart for necessities, but the excess of choices in the shampoo aisle had left her paralyzed. She'd left without buying anything, scurrying out of the store and into the truck like a frightened child where she'd had to wait for Taylor to take her home.

She was also having a hard time sleeping. For the last few decades, she had slept with loud noises stirring her every so often: a cell door slamming shut; an argument between inmates continuing late into the night; the jangling of keys as the guards did their routine checks.

Quiet had been something she could only occasionally find— like moments in the greenhouse where she worked, her fingers reaching into the rich, cold soil as she pretended to be a regular person working a normal job, instead of someone who was being watched nearly every second of her life.

Taylor had cameras set up around the property, too. She said it was something she'd done recently because she felt like someone had been snooping around, but they'd showed up at about the same time Cate did. Coincidence? Cate didn't think so.

Inhaling deeply, she forced her shoulders down, then willed herself to relax and stop thinking about it.

But late at night, when the house was quiet, it was all she *could* think about. She'd toss and turn for hours until she could no longer make herself lie there, then she'd get up and slip out the door, where at least the sounds of the night brought her comfort. If Diesel were there instead of with Sam, he'd follow her, suddenly alert and on guard as he slipped into the role of her protector.

"You're such a good boy," she murmured to him, then used her feet to push the swing a bit higher.

The cedar swing was a nice addition to the porch. She needed to find a cushion for it, but it was still much better than the hard chairs she'd been using. Jackson had installed it earlier. Cate wasn't sure she believed him when he'd said he picked it up at a yard sale. She'd also noticed he sported a new shirt and some sort of outdoorsy cologne.

Diesel glanced up, checking to see if she was ready to go in.

"Not yet. Give me a few more minutes."

Lucy was trying to get Johnny to sleep, so Cate had escaped with the excuse of taking Diesel for some air, though he surely knew that was only the first of their outdoor treks for the night.

"Your mama should be home soon," she told him.

At least Cate hoped she would be. She hadn't seen her since Taylor had sent her home from the Christmas Tree farm. But it hadn't been before Cate got a good look at the young man lying dead in the driveway. Now, she couldn't get that image out of her head.

She also couldn't forget Taylor's instant transformation from regular citizen to law enforcement officer. All business and professionalism, she'd not hesitated to jump out and put her safety at risk for everyone else's well-being. It had been impressive, but it wasn't surprising. Cate's most selfless daughter, Taylor had always given everything she had from the very depths of her soul, sometimes to her own detriment. Even as her mother, Cate didn't know whether she'd ever be able to make Taylor believe that it wasn't her responsibility to carry everyone else's burdens or fix everything.

Lucy had filled in the details about their childhood after Cate had left them. It hadn't been a big revelation that Taylor had taken on a protective role in Cate's absence. Even as a child, Taylor acted like a mother hen toward her younger siblings, always making sure everyone had what they needed.

As her mother, though, it was disheartening to realize Taylor wasn't pursuing a personal life. Sure, she had a career she excelled at, but what about love? Marriage? Children of her own?

There was more to life than just work.

From what Cate could tell, Taylor had two men in her life who were just waiting for a sign that she was interested.

Shane and Sam were both good catches. Completely different from each other, but Cate could picture Taylor with either one. Shane was quiet, but he had a way about him that made her think he'd always be able to handle anything. He seemed protective of Taylor, even if she didn't see it.

Sam was boisterous and affectionate. An overgrown boy in a man's body, but still capable and dependable. One man was tall, dark, and handsome while the other was a golden boy. Either would make pretty babies with Taylor if that was something she wanted.

Which was why Cate needed to find a job quickly—to get out of the way so her daughter could have one less person to worry about.

Then there was Lucy and Johnny—it might be a while before they could make their own way in the world. Lucy hadn't changed much over the years, either. Cate's youngest child would always be somewhat of a free spirit, bypassing the norms of society in the search for something—what that something was, Cate has no idea.

Lucy might be the most damaged from not having a mother, but she wasn't completely turned off. She talked to Cate, though not about anything important. She'd put a boundary up, but what Lucy wasn't expressing worried Cate. There was bound to be pent-up feelings she needed to get out, but she kept them locked up inside herself instead.

Cate wondered why Johnny's father wasn't in the picture. Lucy wouldn't even discuss him, so it must've ended badly. Because Lucy had never seen what love between a couple was supposed to look like when she was a child, Cate figured the description of love Lucy held somewhere deep inside was something dramatic and chaotic. Probably painful.

Then there was Jo, who'd become a mother when she'd been barely more than a child herself—a teen mom. Her son, Levi, didn't have a father to speak of either. He was at the age now where he desperately needed one. Anna's kids *did* have a father, but Cate didn't consider what Anna and Pete had to be a normal relationship, though she tried to pretend otherwise. There was some sort of underlying uneasiness there, which Anna tried to hide.

Cate would never get over the guilt of what she'd done to her children.

First, they'd been unwilling participants in a toxic home environment. Then, they'd lost their mother and brother in one fell swoop. She hadn't wanted to leave them, and it hadn't been her fault, but, as a mother, it still felt like there'd been something else she could've done. In hindsight, she should've stayed involved in their lives from prison. Maybe they'd be healthier adults now if she had.

When the screen door creaked, she glanced over. Lucy had slipped out the door, carrying two mugs.

$\sim$

"Hot chocolate," Lucy said, handing a mug to Cate before she sat beside her. "You shouldn't be out here alone with a crazed killer on the loose."

"Oh, I'm fine with Diesel. He watches out for me. Thank you for the cocoa."

"Don't get too excited. It's instant," Lucy said softly. "I finally got my little booger to sleep. He fought a valiant battle, but I won."

Cate smiled. "It will get easier. Once he's walking, he'll be so tired from all the activity that he'll conk out early every night without a fight."

"I sure hope so. This is getting ridiculous. If Taylor isn't here, he gives me fits. I don't know what magical powers she has, but I need them. He just about knocked my tooth out when he tried to head-butt me to keep me from laying him down. I feel like I'm doing everything wrong."

"Don't. He's teething, too. His little mouth hurts. How has he been doing with Margaret?"

"So far, so good, but it's only been a month. I worry he's too much for an older woman, but Sissy says Margaret enjoys it. Sissy's daughter loves having a playmate, even if it is just a baby. She likes dressing him up."

Cate smiled, imagining the little girl using Johnny as a human doll. "That's good, but are you making enough at the Den to pay for childcare and still make a profit?"

Lucy shrugged. "Sort of. Some days, I get good tips. Others, I don't. I can't stay there forever, so I need to think about what I'm going to do in the future. I can't raise a child on a waitress income."

"I'm glad you're thinking ahead," Cate said. "Some do make it on that type of income, but it's hard. Always a struggle."

"Right. Sissy can because Margaret keeps her daughter for free. Plus, they split the household bills down the middle. I won't have that, so I need to make more money. Oh—" She winced. "I didn't mean that as an insult. I know you need to work, so you can't keep Johnny. Margaret doesn't have anything else to do."

"I didn't take it that way. Believe me, I'm not that sensitive."

"Good. So, are you okay? Taylor called earlier. She told me what happened—and that you stuck around with Beverly for a while. How was she when you left?"

Cate hesitated. It wasn't easy to describe. "Not good. She asked me to come back tomorrow to help her get through some of the arrangements."

"That's strange, considering she just met you," Lucy said.

"I think it was because I was the calmest one there, probably since I don't know her family. She said her sister, Pauline, who is hard to deal with and will try to take over, will be there. She wants me to be a buffer."

Lucy nodded. "That's the South for you. Meet you one second, and the next you're their best friend. Are you okay with doing that?"

"Yes, I'm fine. It feels good to be useful for a change. After this is over, I'm going to ask her for a job, too. I'd like to work out there."

"I'm sure you'll get it, too," Lucy said. "You're welcome to use my car. I'm off tomorrow. No plans except catching up on the laundry. Forewarning—it's not the most dependable vehicle in the world, but for four grand, beggars can't be choosers. It does the job, and it's safe for Johnny."

Shocked that Lucy would let her use the car, Cate thanked her, touched at the offer.

"Hey—have you talked to Jo today?"

"No, why? Is something wrong?" Cate was instantly anxious.

"Nothing's wrong. I just wondered how her job at the ranch was going. And how Levi's doing in his new school. That's a big change for a kid his age."

Diesel got up and wandered off the porch. After he lifted his leg against a bush, he sauntered back and dropped down.

"I think he'll be fine. He's a resilient kid."

"Because of Jo. She makes being a single parent look so easy," Lucy said. "I wish I didn't look like a walking disaster in comparison."

"You don't, Lucy. You're doing just fine. Give yourself some grace. Having a baby is hard. And I'd be glad to watch him any time. Even when I get a job. If I'm not working, I can help."

She wanted to add, *if you'll let me*. So far, Lucy hadn't accepted any of Cate's offer to keep Johnny. Lucy hadn't left him alone with Cate even once.

"Have you thought any more about suing the state of Montana?" Lucy asked.

"No, not really. Right now, I'm just trying to put it behind me." Cate tried for a matter-of-fact tone, hoping Lucy would get the hint. Cate didn't like it when the subject of her incarceration came up.

"I'd sue. I read about a man who served eighteen years for a murder he didn't commit. He was awarded five million dollars from Sanders County in Montana. Evidence was withheld in his case, too, and he got them for abusing his civil rights. His team was able to prove the misconduct contributed to his wrongful conviction."

"Yes, I read that, too. Richard Raugust. They thought he killed his best friend. But, Lucy, I don't know if I can handle more legal stuff right now. I need to heal a bit first. Catch my breath."

"Millions of dollars could help you heal fast. They owe it to you. They stole your life, Mom. They stole our childhood."

Lucy sounded so angry. It made Cate sad. Money would never be able to replace what they'd lost. It could potentially make things worse. She knew a lot of women behind bars who'd ruined their lives just to make a dime. Not only that, but Cate just wanted to be free from that life and try to forget it had ever happened. She had to if she wanted to heal.

"Maybe. We'll see."

They sat in silence. Cate wished she dared to start a meaningful conversation—something not about work or the case. It was a beautiful night, they were alone, and it couldn't be more perfect timing. She wanted to ask Lucy so many things: about her first kiss; her first prom; her driver's permit; her first puppy love.

All the things a mother should know without having to ask.

Everything she wanted to know about all her daughters... but was too afraid of being shot down to ask. She'd lost so much.

They had *all* lost so much.

Yawning, Lucy stretched one arm above her head. "You coming in? It might be hours before Taylor comes home."

Cate nodded. "I know. I'll be in soon."

Once Lucy had returned inside, Cate stared up at the stars and dreamed of a day when she could have easy relationships with all her daughters, and one day, possibly, just be their mom again.

CHAPTER 5

"We've got to nail down a timeline for David as best we can," Shane said. "Start from that morning when he got out of bed."

They were recording the interview, which Taylor would then transcribe into notes later. For now, she wanted to watch Jenny's expressions and mannerisms.

"I got up at seven to get Nora ready for school," Jenny said, her tone low and extremely slow. "David was still outside, which was usual for him. He gets up earlier so he can feed the animals before he goes to work."

Two murder notebooks sat on the table between them, and Taylor thumbed one of the hard plastic covers. Every step of the investigation would be recorded inside them—witness statements, forensic reports, and crime scene photos. Since she'd taken owner-ship of them, every tiny detail would be included. She knew from all the research she'd done over the years that sometimes a cold case was solved years or decades later because of one tiny name or note scribbled in a murder book by the initial investigators.

"What kinds of animals do you have?" Shane asked.

Jenny used a tissue to wipe her nose. "Goats. A donkey. A

dozen or so chickens. We had two peacocks and a peahen, but the males got into a fight. Now, we just have one male and a hen."

David had chosen well. Even with her blonde hair pulled up in a messy bun and makeup streaked around her bloodshot eyes, Jenny was pretty. She'd showed up in the usual young-mom attire of yoga pants and a stretchy shirt, her feet shoved into canvas sneakers. She was fit and looked smart.

Day two of a murder investigation was usually even worse than the first. By now, the surviving family members had usually gone from shock to anger—sometimes to pure rage—demanding that law enforcement use any means possible to find the suspect and throw justice on his head.

That wasn't the case with Jenny, David's wife.

At least not yet.

As Taylor watched her talk, the word that came to mind was *subdued.*

Resigned.

That didn't seem possible. How could a woman be resigned to the fact that her husband, the father of her two young children, had been gunned down in cold blood?

"I helped Nora get dressed, then guided her to the bathroom where I washed her face and supervised her while she brushed her teeth. I put her hair up in a ponytail, then we went to the kitchen. She sat at the table, and I'd just started fixing her some instant grits when David came in."

"How did he seem to you?" Shane asked.

"Fine. The same as always. He kissed Nora on the top of the head then before he sat at the table. I served Nora the grits, then fixed him eggs and toast while he joked around with Nora and asked her about having a boyfriend."

"How old is Nora?" Shane asked.

"Six, but he always joked that she was his girl and could never date anyone," Jenny said. A fresh round of tears welled up her eyes, overflowing to trail down her cheeks

"Oh. Okay. Did he say if he had to do anything different that day? Meet anyone new?"

Jenny shook her head. "No. He said Amos would be coming back from out of town early. They planned to go over the monthly report that afternoon. He said something about labor and production—I don't really remember."

"Was he nervous about the meeting with Amos?" Taylor asked. "Tense, maybe?"

Jenny looked up. "Well, maybe. But he always dreaded their monthly meetings, especially the last year. Amos was putting more on him, giving him more administrative responsibilities. He always said, 'I'm not going to be here forever, and you have to figure this stuff out'." The last few words were barely audible over the sob Jenny released.

"I know this is hard, Jenny," Shane said. "But did he say that kind of stuff in front of Danny?"

Jenny nodded behind her tears.

"And how would Danny react? Was he jealous?"

Taylor wanted to kick Shane under the table for leading the witness.

"They're brothers," Jenny said. "There has always been some sibling rivalry there, but Danny knows he can't handle that kind of stuff. Danny is great with his hands, and he's getting better at supervising the workers, but he's not one for managing the books or dealing with our mass-quantity customers."

"Is that your opinion, David's, or was it one Amos held?" Shane asked.

"Everyone knows it. We tease Danny all the time that he can't stand to be inside for more than fifteen minutes before he paces a hole in the floor. He hates to be in the office, and it was understood by all that David would take Amos' role, and Danny would take over David's role in the management part."

"But the company would be split down the middle regarding profit?"

"We assumed so, but Amos never came out and said that. I do know it doesn't go to either of them until after both he and Beverly are gone."

Shane scribbled a note, then glanced up. "Does your husband have a life insurance policy?"

Jenny gave him a cold stare.

"Yes. After Nora was born, Amos insisted it was necessary. I was not for it, because we've been saving to build a bigger house and needed every dime, but David always did what his father told him to."

"Do you remember how much the policy pays out?" Shane asked.

"No, I don't. Please forgive me if that wasn't the first thing on my mind when I saw my husband's crumpled body in the driveway with a bullet hole through his head."

The tension rose between them.

"Take us through the rest of the morning before David left," Taylor said. She had to get them back on track.

"There wasn't anything else. He ate, put his dishes in the sink, then he and Nora left," Jenny said, turning her body in the chair so she pointed more toward Taylor.

"Oh, he took her to school?" Shane asked.

"Yes. He always did so I didn't have to get Ella out of bed. She's a night owl. If I don't let her sleep late, she's grumpy all day. Next year, I know I'll have to start getting her up earlier to prepare her for kindergarten, but I'll cross that bridge when I come to it."

"Did he call you or text you from the time he left home until after he dropped Nora off and got to work?" Taylor asked.

"No. He would only do that if it were really important because he knows when he leaves, I only have about an hour or so to clean up and take a shower before Ella wakes up and has to have my total attention."

Shane nodded. "Okay. Have you and Danny ever had any sort of relationship?"

Taylor visibly winced. He'd sure brought that one out of nowhere.

Jenny stared at him coldly for a second or two before answering. "Yes, we have a relationship. He's my brother-in-law."

"You know what I'm asking," Shane said. He tapped his pen on the wooden tabletop. In the sudden silence, it sounded like a sledgehammer with every plunk.

"Never," Jenny said. "Never had and never will."

"Has he come on to you? You're a beautiful woman. His brother's wife. That's always a taboo that can be tempting to a man."

Jenny scooted her chair back so suddenly that it hit the wall behind her.

"My husband—his brother—has barely been dead twenty-four hours... and you want to ask me something like that? You're disgusting."

"Jenny, we have to ask these questions," Taylor said, trying to soothe her. She didn't want her to suddenly lawyer up, which would end the interview.

"Not today you don't," Jenny said. "I'm done."

She stood, grabbed her purse, and stomped out the door, letting it slam behind her. The echo reverberated through the small room.

Shane raised his eyebrows at Taylor.

"I guess that didn't go well."

CHAPTER 6

$\mathcal{C}$ ate gripped the steering wheel with both hands, hoping Beverly and her daughter-in-law, Jenny, didn't pick up on her nervousness about driving. She'd done well so far that day, but tension was starting to set in as she grew tired. She reminded herself repeatedly that she was not a criminal, that she knew traffic laws, and nothing was going to happen.

They were headed to the Den now to discuss catering the memorial.

"I appreciate this, Cate. I just cannot do all this with my sister, and Danny isn't able. We need someone not emotionally connected to our family to help guide us through," Beverly said, gazing out her window instead of looking at Cate.

The hand Beverly held her phone with shook. She looked like she'd aged a decade in the days since the murders.

"I'm glad to help," Cate said. She meant it, too. It felt good to be needed, even if it was by a stranger. It was a bit strange Beverly had gravitated to her and was treating her like a best friend, but people did weird things during tragedies.

Jenny, the daughter-in-law, sat in the middle. She had barely

47

said a word since Cate had picked them up and taken them to the funeral home to make the decisions for the burials. Because Amos has been a good planner, there wasn't much to decide, but everything still had to be confirmed. It looked to Cate like the hardest part had been picking out the caskets and deciding what photos and poems they wanted in the funeral programs.

Mundane little details—like whether to use flowers, doves, or even tractors as decorative items—made it feel surreal. They had chosen to go with fir trees on the covers, an ode to their lives on the farm.

They'd moved on to discussing a memorial website where friends and family could pay their respects online and could order a memorial tree planted in Amos' and David's honor.

The meeting had stuttered when the time to decide between burial and cremation came.

Beverly had insisted on burial for both Amos and David, but Jenny claimed she and David had discussed it and he said he would prefer to be cremated.

"But we've already got a place for him in the family plot," Beverly said. "He'd want to be next to his dad."

"No, he'd want to be with me. If he's cremated, I can take him with us if the girls and I ever leave this town," Jenny replied.

"Not to be crass, Jenny, but you might eventually remarry. You're so young."

"I will never marry again," Jenny said, her voice tinged with heavy emotion.

They'd remained civil, but it was tense for a bit. The funeral director had stepped out of the room to let them have a private discussion.

After Beverly broke down in sobs, Jenny relented.

Cate pulled into the parking lot of the small restaurant. After she glided into a spot, she cut the motor.

"I can't go in there," Beverly whispered.

"Me neither," Jenny said. "There're too many cars out here. They'll all want to talk to us."

Cate glanced from Beverly to Jenny. They weren't budging.

"Okay, I'll go in to tell Mabel we're here. I'll see if she'll let you come through the back door." She started the car again. After she drove around back and parked, she got out and walked around to the front door.

Cate had been to the Den a few times with Taylor, and once with Lucy, but she didn't like walking in alone.

The door opened just as she approached. Two deputies walked out it, then held the door for her. She hadn't met them before, so she only thanked them and went in.

"Hi, Cate," Sissy called from behind the bar. "You bringing Lucy in with you, I hope? We've got a crowd for lunch today!"

"No, I'm here to talk to Mabel," Cate said.

"Okay, I'll get her. Let me fix you a glass of sweet tea first." Sissy quickly grabbed a glass and dunked it in the ice bin, then held it under the tall tea canteen's spigot.

She perched a lemon on the edge, then brought it over and put it in front of Cate.

"Thank you," Cate said, sliding onto the only open bar stool.

"You're welcome. Lucy told me you are helping Beverly and Jenny with the funerals. That's so nice of you."

"Well, I wasn't busy, and Beverly wanted someone not attached to the family. It's nothing."

Sissy leaned over the bar. "Between you and me, everyone is scared. We aren't staying open past dark until this is over. I can't believe this has come to our town. Makes a mama scared to raise her children in this world, it does. If I didn't have my mother to keep Hayley, I'd have to quit my job to protect her myself."

Cate nodded. "Yes, it's scary. I hope they find out who did it."

Cate felt awkward. Sissy talked to her like she was a long-lost friend, but they'd only met a couple of times. Cate also didn't want Taylor to find out she'd talked about the case, even innocently.

"Let me tell Mabel you're here," Sissy said, then disappeared into the kitchen.

Relieved, Cate took a long swig of tea, then winced at the sweetness. She'd never get used to the syrupy taste.

"You must be Lucy's mom."

She searched out the voice, spotting a handsome guy at the end of the bar. He wore a short-sleeved shirt with a fire department emblem on the left side of the buttons.

"Yes, I am."

"Finally came on over from Montana, huh?" he asked, winking conspiratorially. "Glad that all worked out in your favor."

Cate froze. He acted like he knew something, which made her want to throw up. Taylor had assured Cate that no one in town knew her story.

"Sorry, I didn't get your name," she finally said.

"Alex. I'm the fire chief," he said, his chin proudly thrust higher.

"Oh. Well, tha—" She started to thank him for his service, but couldn't recall if that was only meant for veterans or if it was said to firemen, too. Thankfully, Mabel bustled out of the kitchen then, wiping her hands on her apron.

"Hi, Cate. Where's Beverly?"

Cate waved her closer. "She doesn't want to see anyone. Is it okay if they come through the back door?"

"They?"

"Jenny is with us, too."

Mabel smiled. "Oh, of course. I should've thought about that. Yes. I'll go open the door right now. Come on, just follow me. We'll get all the details sorted out—make sure Amos' and David's final shindig is one for the books."

Cate purposely avoided looking in the fireman's direction as she went around the bar and followed Mabel. If their gazes met, he'd see a scared woman. As she walked, she felt like every eye in the room was on her back, judging her and wondering if she *had* killed her child.

She hoped they could get through this as quickly as possible so she could return to the safety of her home.

Soon, Mabel popped her head out the back door. "Come on in, y'all."

After they came in, they sat at a small table in the corner. It was piled with Styrofoam boxes for to-go orders, but Mabel pushed them out of the way.

Through another doorway, Cate could see the kitchen. Sissy picked up a few full plates, arranging them up one arm to carry out. The short-order cook stood at the grill, flipping pancakes. Mabel offered breakfast for lunch to her customers.

Cate only realized she was hungry when the aroma of the bacon and burgers sizzling on another grill assaulted her senses.

"Okay, what did you have in mind for food?" Mabel asked, pulling a notebook closer to her.

"Whatever you think Amos and David would like," Beverly said.

"BBQ," Jenny said. "They both loved it. And your famous potato salad and baked beans."

"I think that's a good idea," Cate said. "Keep it simple. Let everyone else bring the baked goods for dessert."

"I wonder if the sheriff and his team will stop investigating long enough to attend the funeral and the after-event," Beverly said, her brow furrowed with worry.

"Oh, of course," Mabel said. "Amos and David were both like family. No one is going to miss sending them off in style."

"Did you know Amos was the one who gave the sheriff his nickname, Mad Dog Dawkins?" Beverly asked.

"No, I didn't," Mabel replied.

"They were such good friends. They played football together in high school. Matt was the linebacker. Amos said when they lined up out there, Matt got a look in his eye that reminded him of a dog getting ready to fight."

"I had graduated by then, but I still went to every game," Mabel added. "I do remember that look. Amos was pretty good, too. And quite the lady's man until you nailed him down and stopped the chase."

Cate could tell the last comment was meant to lighten the mood, but no one laughed. A tear trickled down Beverly's cheek, hitting the table in a dramatic splash.

"He was a good man, Beverly," Mabel added, reaching over and patting Beverly's hand.

"Yes, he was. And I know Matt will do everything possible to find out who did this." Beverly stared over Mabel's head through the window, out into the parking lot. "He'll get them."

"I'm sure he will," Cate said. She didn't mention that Taylor was also giving the case all she had.

"I'm getting their fingerprints imprinted on charms. I'll wear them on a necklace to keep a piece of them with me always," Beverly said. "It was Cate's idea."

"I'm getting David's," Jenny said.

"What a wonderful idea," Mabel said. "Are they going to be buried or cremated?"

"Buried," Beverly said, her voice firm.

Jenny bit her lip, keeping her eyes averted. Cate didn't think Jenny was happy with that decision.

"We're going to plant a few new trees that will stay on the farm and be decorated every Christmas in their honor," Beverly said. "I'll have benches and a plaque there for people to pay their respects."

"That's a lovely idea," Mabel said.

Beverly stood. "Thank you. Do you mind if I go out for some fresh air? Jenny, do you want to take a walk?"

Jenny nodded, rising to join her. It warmed Cate's heart to see they were fighting to keep their bond solid during such a tragedy.

"Take your time. I'll work out the rest of the logistics with Cate," Mabel said.

Beverly waved a hand in the air. "Fine. The church is putting on a small luncheon after the funeral, so let's do this tribute the evening after that. You two can figure out the rest of it."

CHAPTER 7

*D*ying was imminent for everyone, but no one wanted to face that truth. Yet, it was never clearer than at a funeral with grief thick in the air. Considering the struggles and pain that most people had to deal with to get by in life, Taylor thought some would be more welcoming about seeing it all done with.

To finally rest in peace, as people said.

Not like this, though—not with people being brutally struck down for no apparent reason.

May seventeenth would forever be branded in her mind—and in the townspeople's—as the day of the Hart's Ridge triple murder.

She felt sorry for anyone who had a birthday or anniversary that fell on the date.

At the front of the church, the three sisters from the Dixie Dillard's band harmoniously sang *May The Circle Be Unbroken*. Taylor was amazed at the way they blended their voices perfectly in melody to the organist playing behind them. Amos would have wanted the old-fashioned Southern funeral expected for a man such as himself, and whether David would've wanted it or not wouldn't matter.

Cate had told her about the differences in wishes between

Beverly and Jenny. Taylor felt sympathy for both women. She was glad they'd ultimately agreed and were able to have the services together, so Amos would not be separated from his son.

At the wake, there would be a huge cookout with pulled-pork BBQ and hush puppies—brought in by Mabel and her crew—and plenty of potluck dishes brought by everyone else. A bonfire, a Southern bluegrass band, and a ton of fireworks would round it out.

A few kegs of beer and some moonshine would surely be there, too, for the last celebration of two of Hart's Ridge's finest.

Taylor just hoped people would have sense enough not to drink and then get behind the wheel.

She sat in the back of the church, in the second-to-last pew, with her dad and sisters, chosen for the vantage point of being able to observe almost everyone. Levi was with them, too, looking so grown up in his new suit. Jo had an even bigger fondness for Amos than Taylor had, and her sister also had somewhat of a crush on David long ago. Jo had been devastated at the news. She constantly bugged Taylor for updates on the case, which, of course, she couldn't give.

Anna had chosen to leave her two kids at home with Pete, saying they weren't old enough yet to understand death.

Taylor didn't think that was true, but it was just as well. She didn't have time to worry about anyone else. While paying her respects, she was simultaneously doing her job, but she also couldn't stop her gaze from continually straying to the two caskets at the front. It was still a shock that something so awful could happen to such a good family.

Speaking of family, it had made Taylor proud that hers had shown up. Her dad had even pulled his old suit out for the occasion, and he appeared to be clean and sober. Cecil was there, looking smart in a perfectly pressed suit. He sat on their pew, as Taylor had insisted, but, so far, she hadn't seen him or her dad speak to each other.

So many of the town's finest had gathered. Della Ray sat next to her daughters, using a fancy linen handkerchief to swipe at her eyes. Sissy, Margaret, and Mabel sat on the same pew, with a few of the other kitchen staff from the Den. Sissy's little girl, Hayley, played quietly, distracted by the coloring book and crayons in her lap.

A few townspeople had nodded to Taylor as they passed by, like Horis Hedgepeth, the pig farmer, and Boone. She'd heard Horis talking to Boone about how big he was getting as they walked in.

"You're so big that it looks like you ate your brother," he'd joked.

The joke was on him because Boone didn't have a brother. She hoped Horis would behave himself for the service. It was a funeral, not a pig-picking.

Dottie from dispatch was there, quietly sobbing from the moment she walked in and sat. She and Beverly were friends from way back in high school.

Taylor hoped the girl filling in for Dottie could handle any calls that came in. She was a part-timer while she attended college for a degree in Criminal Justice Administration, but she had little experience. With any luck, nothing major would be called in while most were away. It would be a great time to commit a big crime since most of their force was otherwise occupied. Hopefully, though, the town's criminals would be too dumb to think of it.

Since family and friends had come in from several other states, Taylor didn't know everyone there. No one immediately stood out as suspicious, but she still wondered if the killer were in the room with them, listening to the fond stories about Amos and David from their loved ones. Mostly stories about Amos, who she was learning was even more of a legend in Hart county than she'd already thought.

So far, three of his old buddies and two brothers had spoken about him. They talked about his sense of humor, and the way he had always been there if anyone needed him. Another friend came up and spoke about Amos' charitable ways and his recent activities to help the needy.

Now Amos' sister, Gladys, was up there. Her chubby chin quivered as she talked about their childhoods. Currently, she reminisced about when she'd been bitten by a copperhead snake and her big brother had carried her through nine acres of woods to the nearest house.

Amos was starting to sound like a saint. So far, David paled in comparison to his father. *That* was something to chew on.

Could David have had enemies that no one chose to speak up about?

Taylor heard a beep. In her peripheral view, she caught someone scurrying out the door. Across the back wall, uniformed first responders from Hart's Ridge formed a line, the town's finest, all solemn and respectful. It included the sheriff, the sergeant, and the rest of the deputies. Then there was Alex and his firefighter crew, both paid and volunteers. Several times already, she'd seen one or two go out the doors, pushing through the dozen or more people who stood in the foyer because there were no seats left. She presumed they'd left to check their radios for emergency calls.

In the most peculiar of situations, Cate sat in the front pew between Amos' widow, Beverly, and her daughter-in-law, David's widow. Danny sat on Beverly's other side.

After Gladys finished, an elderly Mexican man slowly made his way up the aisle to the front, turning to observe them.

"Sixteen years ago, I came to Georgia to look for work. We were down to our last five dollars and an empty gas tank, with four children to feed," he started. "It wasn't the farm's peak season, so he didn't *need* to hire anyone, but Mr. Higgins gave me a job anyway and then helped us find an affordable place to rent. Amos was my first friend in this town, and he remained one until the day he died. I will never forget his kindness."

Beverly dipped her head close to Cate's, whispering something.

Taylor wished she could hear what was being said.

Over the last few days, Beverly had clung to Cate like she was her lifeline, asking for help in organizing all the arrangements— from the funeral to the graveside gathering, including the open celebration afterward at the farm. Taylor still couldn't figure out how that had come about, but Cate said it had something to do with the stoic way she'd comforted Beverly at the scene.

Pauline, Beverly's sister, sat several people down from them. Even from the slight view Taylor had of her, it was easy to tell she was put out at having been demoted in status because of Cate. The woman sat stiffly, her nose raised so high that she would drown if it rained.

Preacher Haddon was an old school minister and didn't believe in wasting the opportunity of some people visiting his church for the first time in ages.

Fire-and-brimstone preaching was his specialty, and his volume —along with his blood pressure if the reddening of his face was any indication—climbed as he dove into his spiel to save souls.

Taylor wondered if he'd invite them up to the altar. If so, what would they do—gather around the coffins? The Southern way of using death as an opportunity to win souls had never set well with her. Obviously, it didn't with Danny either because he stood and went to the podium.

Impatiently, he gestured for Haddon to move over.

The room fell deathly silent. No one upstaged a preacher at a funeral.

Danny looked terrible. Pity washed over Taylor. He wasn't ready to take either place, not his dad's or his brother's. It was a lot of pressure, and he didn't seem like he was holding up well.

He cleared his throat before lifting his chin. "My dad laughed easily, and he made others laugh, too. He and David were two peas in a pod. My dad and my brother liked to go hunting together. Fishing, too. Even to Charlotte to watch the races. I used to be so jealous of their relationship. I know I should wish at least one had survived, but, at this moment, I don't. I'm glad they are together for one last adventure. In my heart, I have no doubt they are entering the gates of Heaven as we speak. As good as they were, they have to be."

People nodded. A few murmured, "*Amen*".

"I also have no doubts," Danny said, his voice low and fierce, "that we will find out who did this. We won't stop until we do."

A few people turned to glance at Taylor and her team, who were behind her. She felt her neck flush, hoping he was right. It had been three solid days of following leads and interviewing people—from farmhands to family, she alone had probably talked to at least a hundred—but nothing had helped clarify the case. She and Shane had divvied up their list, as well as handed over the least important ones to Penner and Kuno. The sheriff hadn't wanted to bring the State Police in for help, so they'd found a bilingual college senior to translate as they questioned the Mexican segment of the farm, or at least those who hadn't fled yet. Many feared anything to do with the legal system. They had taken off as soon as they'd heard about the murders.

The missing truck had been a dead end. They'd located it, only to find it had been borrowed, with Amos' permission, by a foreman who'd had to drive a few hundred miles away to pick up some discounted hay at another farm.

The CSI team assigned had relayed some odd information, though. Between Amos and David, there were only four bullet wounds, yet a total of nine shell casings had been recovered from the scene.

Taylor thought maybe the suspect, or an accomplice, had been shot during the crime, but after checking every hospital within a hundred miles, she'd only found one patient admitted for a gunshot wound. That had been a young man who'd taken a bullet in his hand, but he'd checked out. Just an idiotic kid who didn't know how to handle a pistol.

When Danny finished, the preacher took over. He started with a short sermon about getting right with God, ending with a plea for any lost attendees to accept Jesus Christ as their Lord and Savior. When he had no takers, he closed it out in defeat.

Taylor watched as Beverly, Cate, and the family left first, with each pew of people following. When the last few were out, Taylor exited. Once everyone had gathered at the gravesites, she could observe the attendees again.

In the foyer, she passed a large funeral wreath on a stand. It had a tiny pink toy phone attached to it. Curious, Taylor lifted the tag to read it.

Jesus called, and Paw-Paw answered. Love, Ella and Nora.

She dropped the tag, embarrassed at intruding on something so personal.

Outside, the onlookers lined each side of the walkway from the church to the parking lot. Taylor waited with them. There were tears and sobs all around as the pallbearers made their way down the ramp to the hearse.

The sheriff would lead the procession to Amos' and David's final resting places at the cemetery. Every car they passed had better pull over and put their lights on, or step out and bow their heads, or they'd hear about it later from the townsfolk. Funeral processions were still serious business in their county, and probably would be forever.

Taylor had never seen this particular hearse before. She guessed the funeral home had acquired a new one. A young man she didn't recognize stood outside the car—the driver, she presumed. As the pallbearers approached with the coffin, he fumbled with his keys, seemingly confused about how to open the rear hatch.

Danny and Beverly waited, too, flanked by Cate and other family members.

The somberness of the crowd was palpable. Taylor could feel the tension rise while they watched, but, just in the nick of time, the driver managed to get the door open so the pallbearers could gently slide the coffin in.

The driver closed the door firmly behind it.

Suddenly, the car alarm went off, a loud *whoop-whoop-whoop* that stunned everyone.

The young driver jumped in and out of the vehicle a few times, frantically pressing every button on the key fob he held. As he turned white with panic, Taylor stepped up to help him.

"Here, give it to me." She took it out of his hand. When she pressed the off button, the alarm silenced. "Just a technical glitch. Don't worry."

After she handed him the key and turned around, she saw Danny shake his head. Beverly put her hand on his arm.

"It is just like your dad to do something like this, Danny," she said, then smiled slightly.

When he smiled back, she chuckled.

Which made him laugh.

Gradually, the giggles moved through the crowd until all Taylor could hear was laughter—tears of sadness turned into tears of mirth.

Apparently, the driver didn't know what to do. He seemed taken aback, as though everyone had lost their minds.

"Okay, Dad, you got us," Danny said loudly toward the hearse.

People nodded and laughed. Finally, the driver got into the car and shut his door. The click hushed the crowd. Everyone began to disperse after Beverly led the way to the family car.

Taylor hoped the graveside ceremony wouldn't have any surprises.

CHAPTER 8

*T*he days after the funeral passed both excruciatingly slow and shockingly fast. Before Taylor knew it, they were a week out from what the town now called *'The Christmas Tree Murders,'* with no primary suspects to note. The funeral, graveside attendance, and the celebration-of-life cookout for Amos and David had all gone as well as could be expected, at least until a few of Amos' old buddies started shooting their guns in the air as a final sendoff.

The sheriff had just shook his head and said to let them do what they needed to. Luckily, no one had been hurt, though it was a miracle considering a few barrels of moonshine had been carted in after the church ladies retired to their homes for the night.

Taylor and Penner had stayed until the last person left, just to make sure no other tragedy could happen.

Despite some of the high moments, the events had been heavy with grief and disbelief. Taylor had gone back to the investigation with a renewed commitment to find the murderer.

"It's crazy," Shane said. "With the way Amos did business, the suspect pool is massive."

"I think we've interviewed everyone at least once," she said.

They had cleared out the canteen, setting up tables in formation to lay out every piece of evidence they'd found. Food was either being called in and ate at their desks, or outside when they had a chance for a break. Though she and Shane were leads, this was an all-hands-on-deck investigation, and they had permission to make anyone help if needed.

Beverly had been the hardest to interview. Thinking about it made the blood rush to Taylor's face. Sometimes, it was tough to make people realize that detectives had to start with the closest family members in a homicide investigation, then work their way out from there.

The poor woman hadn't given them much to go on, other than providing the current employee list. That had been helpful. Although, as they'd suspected, many had taken off either because they didn't have the papers needed to work legally, or they didn't trust law enforcement and feared being accused. Finding those to question them would be a slow process.

They'd assigned Deputy Kuno the task of tracking down as many of the seasonal workers as possible. They also had Amos' itinerary from the trip he'd just returned from, but nothing had jumped out so far.

Carlos' wife had been cooperative, but she'd had no idea who could've committed such a heinous crime, and she swore her husband had no enemies. Other coworkers agreed. Carlos had been a likable guy.

The canteen door swung open, and the sheriff stomped in.

"A fifty-thousand-dollar reward to anyone with any information that leads to the arrest and conviction of the murderer has been offered up to the public," he announced. "Penner set up a tip line."

"That should get some new leads," Taylor said.

"And a thousand dead ends." Shane rolled his eyes. "Everybody and their brother will be trying to solve the case… or just throwing out all kinds of bullshit lies to try to get the money."

Taylor was exhausted, but she couldn't complain because Shane and the rest of the department were, too. They'd put in more hours this week than they usually did in a month, and the sheriff wasn't easing up. He was incensed that someone had gotten away with killing one of his best friends, and he stomped around with red-rimmed eyes, his complexion gray with fatigue as he barked out orders.

Taylor was worried about him.

The sheriff leaned against one of the tables, arms crossed. "What do you two have?"

"The GSR tests on Danny, Beverly, and Jenny came back negative," Shane said.

"Same for Carlos' wife. Danny's clothes came back, too. There was no blood spatter to suggest he was in on it, only transfer from leaning over his brother's body," Taylor said.

She hadn't realized how relieved she'd been when that one came back. Taylor didn't want Danny to be a monster.

"So, not only do we have nothing, but we also don't even know who the target was supposed to be," the sheriff said. "It could've been Amos or David, with the robbery an afterthought."

"Or Carlos," Taylor said. "Though we haven't found even a shred of evidence to suggest he'd been involved in anything unsavory, despite a few of the guys who worked under him claiming he was always up to something or on his phone."

"The whole damn town is getting paranoid," the sheriff said. "The Shoppes At Franklin have cut their hours and close at five now. Mabel won't stay open past six. Walmart has hired extra workers just to watch videos and look for anything out of the ordinary with their shoppers. Greg, the manager, said his sales have plummeted. People are afraid. We gotta solve this case and get this town back to normal. Get closure."

She and Shane nodded solemnly.

"We should get phone records today," Shane said.

It always took a while for the phone company to help in an

investigation. Even though the wives had handed over the phones so they could look at call logs and text messages, they needed to know what cell towers the phones pinged on in the days before the murders. That could tell them if any of the men had gone anywhere unexpected.

"I want a list of every damn place their phones put them at from a week before to the very day of," the sheriff ordered.

"You'll get it," Shane replied.

"Beverly told me their farm harvests more than a hundred thousand trees every year. They have tons of employees coming and going, and they move a lot of money in and out for payroll, sales, and supplies. This was a bigger venture than I ever dreamed of," Taylor said. "Who knew we had someone making that kind of money in our small town?"

"I'm sure some knew or at least suspected," the sheriff said. "Especially the ones who stood in line at that safe every Friday."

"Working with cash like that puts a real target on their backs," Shane said.

"Obviously," the sheriff agreed.

"From what I understand, only the migrant workers were paid in cash, but that's the bulk of their employees," Taylor said.

Shane's phone rang. He excused himself, heading into the hall to take it.

The sheriff turned to Taylor. "I don't have to tell you how important this is to me."

"I know. Amos was your friend."

"He sure was. Hell, the whole damn town loved him. We gotta make this right. Get justice for him and David. And Carlos, too. I don't want you doing anything else but supporting Weaver on this. You're officially off traffic."

"Ten-four."

Shane returned. "I have a lead. My guy at the casino in Cherokee said Danny has been there several times over the last few months, burning through money."

Taylor's heart sank.

"How much money?" the sheriff asked.

"Not sure yet, but there's video of every visit. Mostly slots."

"Tell him we want the footage," the sheriff said.

"Already did. He's emailing it to me."

"Great lead, Weaver," Taylor said. "But let's not jump to conclusions. It's a big leap from playing slots to killing your dad and your brother."

"It's been known to happen. Mark Goudeau. Remember him? He killed nine people. Before he went on his killing spree, he'd been heavily in debt with a casino."

"I don't remember that one," Taylor said. "But Danny isn't a cold-blooded killer."

"That's what they thought about Goudeau. He was the kind of person you'd sit next to at a bar and buy a drink. Clean-cut. Attractive. His neighbors said he was a nice guy who worked hard. He was often seen tending his yard with his wife."

"That's called a psychopath," Shane said.

"Come to find out, he had done prison time earlier in his life, but had been granted clemency. Got out and started a quiet life with his new wife, then decided he couldn't help himself," the sheriff said.

"Danny has a record, too," Shane said.

"Small stuff from a long time ago," Taylor said. "No prison time."

"That doesn't mean he hasn't done some bad stuff. Just means he didn't get caught."

"I'll call the judge, start working on a search warrant for his place. Does he still live in the studio apartment on the farm?" the sheriff asked.

"Yep." Taylor nodded.

"I'll send Kuno out there while you have Danny here for another interview," the sheriff said. "You two get to work."

CHAPTER 9

*C*ate stood with her arms crossed over her chest, shaking her head at Jackson. He looked proud of himself as he practically pranced around the monstrosity he'd pulled up in.

"It's a Chevy Express. Extended cab. She's got a lot of miles, but she's clean as a whistle. Come on, Cate, look inside!" He opened the sliding door, throwing his arm out in a grand sweeping gesture.

"First of all, Jackson, providing me with a vehicle is not your responsibility. I'm not your wife anymore. And I don't want to hurt your feelings, but it looks like the epitome of a kidnapper's van—a white box with dark-tinted windows. I've seen that one in every bad movie." She laughed.

"Nah—kidnappers are smarter these days. They come at you flashy with all sorts of fancy stuff. I know this isn't the sexiest ride, but it didn't cost me anything except that old camper I had rotting back in the woods. Even trade."

He was like a little boy in a candy shop. Despite her reluctance, she smiled.

According to Anna, he had made a complete transformation since Cate had returned home, though Taylor wouldn't confirm or deny it. Taylor and Lucy didn't have anything bad to say about their dad. Jo wasn't around enough to talk about it—not that Cate needed more details. She was already disappointed that he hadn't come through for the girls to give them a decent childhood.

They were both guilty, so she couldn't throw stones.

To appease him, she went to the van and ducked her head in.

It was in good shape for the miles and age. There was only one saddle seat in the back, with the rest open space.

If she were a caterer, it would be perfect.

"I won't be able to afford the gas on this thing," she said.

"Sure, you will. You'll only be using it around town. It's not like you'll be road-tripping in it. I wouldn't advise that."

"I don't even have a job yet, Jackson. I can't pay you for it."

"I told you, the guy did me a favor by hauling off that old camper. The van was a bonus. You don't owe me a penny. Not only that, but the girls also said they were going to pitch in and pay to get it registered and insured for the first six months. Just until you get on your feet."

She turned to him. "They know about this?"

"Sure do. Cate, we're a family."

Cate headed back to the porch. After she sat on the swing, she said, "Jackson, I think you and I need to have a conversation."

He took a seat in a lawn chair against the window.

"I know what you're going to say," he said. "It's going to take time."

She shook her head. "I divorced you more than ten years ago. You signed the paperwork, too. If you think we are somehow going to rekindle our relationship, then I need to stop you right now. I'm not the same woman you married. Twenty years is a long time, and I do not intend to be part of a couple ever again. I've been alone too long, and I don't mind it."

"You don't know that right now, Cate. You're still reeling from what happened to you. You have trauma." He studied his hands.

"Don't you remember how good we were together? We had some fun times."

Cate sighed. "Don't you remember how toxic we were together? The arguments? The fighting? How you abused me?"

He visibly flinched before he met her eyes. "I don't do that stuff anymore, Cate. I'd never hurt you again."

"I believe that. I do. But over the last twenty years, something died inside me. I know I'll never have a happily-ever-after kind of life, and I'm fine with that. I just want to earn my way back to being a mother to our girls and a grandmother to the babies. I want peace. Solitude. I am better alone now. I'm sorry, but you need to know that. You need to work on yourself, too. Get and stay sober. If not for yourself, then for your family. And if you don't want to give me the van now, I completely understand."

He stood and tossed her the keys. She caught them midair.

"I still want you to have it. I also want to do whatever I can to help you get your life back on track. No strings attached. Just friends. Can we at least be friends?"

When he opened his arms, she went into them. They embraced, but she pulled away quickly.

"Friends. And thank you, Jackson. I'll accept the van until I can get something else on my own, then I'll give it back."

He nodded. "Great. Oh, one more thing. I heard the animal shelter is looking for a kennel technician. They don't pay much, but with your experience, it might be something you'd like doing."

Cate felt a rush of energy. "Wow, thanks. I'll put in an application right now."

He smiled broadly. "Since you're going that way, can you give me a ride home?"

~

After Cate dropped Jackson off at his house, she rolled down her window to let the wind flow in. She hadn't noticed it until their hug, but he'd smelled like alcohol. It was disappointing, but she reminded herself that she wasn't responsible for his choices, and she had enough on her plate getting her own life on track.

She turned off the radio, glad it worked but craving silence. Jackson had talked nonstop, narrating as they passed houses and businesses, telling what he knew about their histories—who had married who, who had lost their job or gotten better ones, and what businesses were shady or the best to go to.

It had been information overload, and she wouldn't remember any of it other than the rumor he'd spilled about a high school girls' volleyball coach who had groomed and then molested a player, causing her to take her own life, but who still hadn't faced justice.

That one would stick in her memory.

She wouldn't repeat it, though. She remembered something her mother had told her once, and Cate had almost said it to Jackson.

"Make your words sweet. You may have to eat them someday."

This was the first time she'd been alone in a car in decades. Though a bit nervous, she felt truly free for the first time since being released from prison.

The van was perfect.

She didn't even care that it looked like a kidnapper's van.

It was all hers.

She thought of the possibilities having a van could bring. She could do deliveries for Amazon. Or a flower shop. She could be a caterer!

Well, she didn't love cooking.

Hopefully, she'd get the job at the shelter, but at least she had other options now. A vehicle was her first step.

Soon, she'd have a place of her own.

She could feel it. Things were starting to happen. It was scary but exciting, too.

Jackson had cleaned the van before he'd brought it over. He'd even put in an air freshener. The armrest was missing, but that was okay. A few rips in the driver's seat had been covered with duct tape and the carpet piece over the console was soiled, but it was all fine. She could put a tea towel over the console. Maybe even get new seat covers eventually.

Not too long ago, she would've never imagined how happy staring at a black Christmas tree dangling from her rearview mirror would make her.

Then she remembered Beverly.

The farm and their gift shop were closed for now, with no idea when they would open back up. Beverly had told Cate she'd love to have her work there one day, just not now. Hopefully, the animal shelter hadn't already hired for the position because Cate needed a job. If she could snag something working with animals, she'd be on cloud nine.

She followed the directions from her phone. When she spotted the sign for the Humane Society, she turned in and parked the van.

It wasn't anything fancy, just a clunky white building with a chain-link fence that ran along the sides and then back into the property where she couldn't see. She assumed the kennels were back there, but it was quiet.

Before she got out of the van, she closed her eyes and recited a short prayer. She wasn't overly religious, but she did believe in God. She hadn't asked him for much, so a few things here and there she felt could be considered.

Let's do this.

When she got out and slammed her door, it started a cacophony of barking from behind the building, which had mostly quieted down by the time she reached the entrance. Just hearing their barks gave her an instant good feeling.

Dogs understood her. And they never judged.

She took a deep breath, pulled her shoulders back, and went in.

Immediately, she could smell animals. Not in a bad way, but in a warmly familiar one. She longed to go straight back to where they were to get to know them.

"Hi, can I help you?" Behind the counter, a girl, her hands full of file folders, smiled at Cate. She looked like a college student. A smart one, too. Her glasses were sensible, yet pretty. She had on a name tag sticky label with *Sarah* written across it.

"Yes. I'm here to apply for the open kennel tech position." Cate clutched her hands below the countertop where the girl couldn't see them tremble.

"Oh, okay. You can apply for that online. Here's our card with our website address on it." She picked up a card and held it out.

"I-I… can I just apply here? I mean, since I'm here?"

"Oh, yeah, that's fine, too. Let me get you an application." After she fumbled around in a file drawer, she pulled out a piece of paper, handing it over with a clipboard. "Do you have a pen?"

"I do. Thank you."

"You can sit over there to fill it out if you want to." She pointed at a few chairs set up against the wall.

Another young woman came in from the back hall. She started telling the first girl about a festival that was coming up, but said she didn't know if she could go because of finals.

Cate sat, pulled a pen from her purse, and began filling in the questions. The first parts were easy—name, address, phone number, etc—but she felt her anxiety start to build when she got to the section about previous employment. Technically, the jobs she held in prison were actual jobs, though. She put them down, expanding on the duties she'd held as a dog trainer.

Then came the dreaded question.

Have you ever been convicted of a felony?

She held the pen poised over the paper. If she marked *no*, she would be lying, but based on her experience with dogs, she might get the job.

If she marked *yes*, she probably wouldn't get the job. Especially with the fresh-faced young girls they had working there. They needed to be protected from bad elements. From negative influences.

Cate *needed* this position.

More than that, she *wanted* it. Badly.

Covertly, she studied the two girls. They had their entire lives ahead of them, probably had no past baggage to hold them back. They had no idea how lucky they were.

Quickly, Cate finished filling everything in, signed it, and rose to return it. The second girl saw her coming, retreating out of the front area.

"Here you go." Cate handed it over to Sarah.

"Okay, great. I will say, though, that you should probably also do one online because Angela usually goes through those first. We're trying hard to go as paperless as possible to stop polluting our earth, and she encourages using the website."

"Whoa there," a woman said as she came through the door the other girl had exited. "I consider every application, online or in person, Sarah."

Sarah looked embarrassed. "Oh, I'm sorry, Angela. I thought you preferred online."

"*If* it's convenient," Angela said, frowning at the girl. "But online isn't always available to everyone. I don't want to miss out on any good applicants by only choosing from that pool."

She came to the counter, then held her hand out. "Hi. I'm Angela Zimmerman, the director."

Cate shook her hand. "Catherine Gray. I applied for the kennel tech job."

Angela picked up Cate's application and started reading. "I see you have experience in dog training. Why aren't you doing that now?"

"I-I just moved to Hart's Ridge to be near my daughters. Right now, I need a stable paycheck. If I go back into training, it will take a while to build clientele."

Angela nodded. "True."

She read a bit more, her expression changing. When she looked up and locked eyes with Cate, she knew it was over.

"I'll just show myself out," Cate said, backing toward the door.

"Wait. I want to talk to you in my office. Follow me."

Cate felt sick to her stomach, wishing she didn't always have to be so damned honest.

Angela showed her into a small room that held an old-fashioned metal desk and a few chairs, all shoved between several tall metal filing cabinets.

"Take a seat," Angela said.

Cate sat.

"Do you go by Catherine?"

"Cate, actually."

"I'm sorry about Sarah up there, Cate. She's majoring in environmental science, and her parents were hippies back in the day. Still are."

Cate chuckled. "No problem."

"What were you in prison for?" Angela asked, getting right to the point before she sat in the chair behind the desk.

"Arson and murder. But I was recently exonerated," Cate said, nearly choking on the words. She could feel the heat running up her neck to flush her face and ears.

Angela sighed. "Who died?"

"My son."

"I'm so sorry."

"Thank you."

"But I can't give you the job just because I feel sorry for you," Angela said.

She set the paper down in front of her.

Cate tried to keep the quaking inside her still. "I don't want you to. I want you to give me the job because I'm good with dogs. I work hard, and I keep to myself. No drama, complaints, or asking for extra time off. I'll be here when you tell me to, do what I'm supposed to, and cause you no stress."

"That sounds great, but you wouldn't be training dogs here, Cate. This position is not a glamorous one. You'd feed them, make sure they have water, and clean up crap all day. Maybe give baths. Once all that's done, then you'll help walk the dogs and rotate them out in the play areas if there's time."

"Sounds perfect to me," Cate said, holding her breath.

Angela studied her for a moment, then stood and headed toward a black box in the corner. When she fed the application into it, Cate realized it was a paper shredder. Her heart sank.

When it finished, she turned toward her. Cate held her breath, not sure what to expect.

"If you work with me, you come with a clean slate. Nobody needs to know your past because you'll only be judged on the present," Angela said.

Cate couldn't believe it. She felt hope tentatively stir in her heart. "I'd like that," she murmured.

Angela put her hands on her hips, exhaling a long sigh. "We have a free vaccine clinic this Saturday at Tractor Supply. I need some extra hands."

Cate bit her lip so hard she tasted blood, anxiously waiting to hear more.

"Consider it a trial run. Do well, blend smoothly with the rest of us, and you'll get the job. If you aren't a good fit, no hard feelings. Okay?"

Cate nodded, still holding her breath.

"Deal, then. Get some rest beforehand and dress in your oldest jeans. It will be messy. You can show yourself out." She turned and walked out of the office, leaving Cate staring after her.

Thankfully, the tears held off until Angela turned her back.

CHAPTER 10

*T*aylor ate the last chunk of country-fried chicken, then sopped up the gravy with the remainder of her biscuit before popping it in her mouth. Under the table, she felt Diesel's muzzle land on her knee and heard him sigh with longing. She discreetly passed a stray morsel to him.

When she pushed her plate away and leaned back, she looked up to find Sam watching her with a grin.

"What?"

"Nothing. I just like to see a woman eat—one who doesn't pick at her food like a skinny bird."

"She can cook, too," Lucy said. "Especially chili beans."

"I know. I've had them," Sam said, making Lucy gasp dramatically.

Jo laughed. "Oh, we need to hear details. When were you here for Taylor's chili beans?"

"Y'all stop," Taylor said.

"Anyone for banana pudding?" Cate asked. "Full disclosure, I'm not a banana pudding kind of girl, but I did my best. I know it's a Southern thing, so I hope it tastes okay. I used the Paula Deen recipe."

"Me," Levi said, raising his hand high in the air.

"A small bowl," Jo warned him. "The sugar will keep you up all night."

"None for me," Taylor said. She already felt like a bloated seal. Sam obviously thought she was a hog, too, so she was sitting dessert out. "But you've seriously outdone yourself on everything, Cate. Thank you for doing this."

"You're welcome," Cate said.

"Yes, thank you," Sam said. "I haven't had a meal like this since I went to Cracker Barrel with Pop a few months ago."

Cate laughed. "Good to know my cooking compares with Cracker Barrel food since I'm so rusty. But you might want to hold that compliment until you taste the pudding."

"I'll scoop," Lucy said, getting up from the table. "That way, I won't have to do dishes, which means I might have time for a bath before Johnny wakes up for his before-bedtime energy surge."

"I don't mind cleaning up," Cate said. "Makes me feel useful."

"I'll help," Jo said.

Taylor was so tired she could barely keep her eyes open. The sheriff had insisted she take half a day off after he caught her at the department after midnight three days running. He'd sent Shane home, too. Told them not to come back until eight o'clock the next morning.

Shane and Taylor had picked the case apart repeatedly until it felt like a never-ending loop. Her brain needed a break. The phone records hadn't showed any surprising detours on any of the phones. Everyone appeared to have been where they were supposed to be, other than Amos coming home earlier than first planned.

Despite canvassing the area and talking to people again, there was nothing new. It was upsetting, but the investigation had stalled.

To make it even harder, Danny called every day, accusing them of not doing their jobs and taking out his anger on them. He said his mom couldn't eat or sleep, and they needed justice. Jenny had called a few times, too.

All the leads had turned out to be dead ends. Even the reward wasn't bringing in anything substantial, which was surprising. Many people would turn their own child in if it meant a big payday.

Taylor was glad Sam had brought Diesel home, but she hadn't expected Cate to ask him to stay for dinner. Cate, Lucy, and Jo seemed to adore him, and he treated them as though they were belles of the ball, so it wasn't any wonder.

Diesel was funny.

When she and Sam were together in the same space as him, he was so happy and frolicked like a puppy. It was good to see him that way, and Taylor wondered if that was how he was at Sam's house.

"Well, I have some good news," Cate said.

Taylor blinked to clear her blurry eyes. "Oh?"

"What is it?" Lucy hollered from the kitchen. "Wait for me."

"Is that why you bought groceries *and* cooked tonight?" Taylor asked. She had also noticed Cate was in a better mood than she'd ever seen her in.

Cate nodded. "Yes… My little celebration might be presumptuous, but I couldn't help myself. I wish Anna were here, but I can call her tomorrow."

Lucy returned, balancing the small bowls of pudding. She handed them out before taking her seat.

"We already know about the van," she said.

"I know you do, and I wanted to thank you for helping with that. It was very kind. I'll be sure to thank Anna, too. But the news is that I might have a job."

"Great!" Taylor said.

"Where?" Jo asked.

"Congrats," Sam said, digging into the dessert. He dramatically rolled his eyes with an appreciative groan. "This is amazing banana pudding, by the way."

"Thank you, Sam. Wait until I tell you the best part," Cate said. "It's working with animals at the Humane Society. If I get the job, it will be as a kennel tech. But first, I have to help with a vaccine clinic they're doing at Tractor Supply this Saturday. Then she's going to let me know."

"Oh, a test," Taylor said. "Interesting. So, Beverly didn't offer you anything at the farm?"

"No. She said things are at a standstill right now and she doesn't know when she'll need someone again, but she'll consider me later. Jackson gave me the lead about the job at the shelter."

Taylor wished Cate would talk more about Beverly, wondered at how close they were getting. Maybe Cate knew details Beverly hadn't shared with anyone else. Taylor needed something new. Anything to get the investigation going again.

"That was so nice of him," Lucy said. "He's trying so hard."

Taylor didn't comment on that. She knew her dad was doing anything he could think of to get on Cate's good side, but Taylor didn't think it would end well. If he got his heart broken, he would probably return to drinking himself into oblivion, then her life would be more complicated again. She'd been enjoying her respite from supervising his life.

"Would you be training dogs as you did at—um, at—oh God, Cate, I'm sorry," Sam said, eyes on his bowl as he put his spoon down.

She waved a hand in the air. "It's fine. Please, don't worry about that. No, I'd just be doing the dirty jobs for the most part. But you never know—maybe I could work myself up to some sort of dog-training position once I get my foot in the door."

"Well, congrats, Cate. Or good luck, I guess," Taylor said. She stood and stretched. "I'll help with the kitchen, then I'm off to bed. I'm beat."

"Me too," Sam said. "Thank you so much for dinner. I have to get up early tomorrow to work on a tractor, so I'd better get going."

"For Horis?" Taylor asked.

He nodded.

"Make sure he pays you. He's been known to skip a bill or two," she said.

"Taylor, you see Sam off and take Diesel out while you go," Cate said. "Jo and I have kitchen duty under control."

Taylor wasn't going to argue.

"Levi, if you're done, get your homework out and start on it, please," Jo said. "When we get home, you need to get right in the shower."

Levi groaned.

Taylor and Sam headed out, Diesel following them.

"Want to sit for a minute?" Sam asked.

She didn't. She was exhausted, but he looked so hopeful that she nodded.

"Just for a minute or two. I might try to do some work before I take a shower. See what I can dig up." She planned to do another deep dive into Danny's and Jenny's social medias. Amos and David didn't have any. Beverly did, but she only ever posted about the Christmas Tree farm. Taylor had gone through it all several times, but there had to be a clue she'd missed somewhere. She would go back to looking at their friends, and their friends of friends.

Sam held the swing steady until she sat, then he joined her. He kicked off, sending them into the air. Diesel jumped off the porch, disappearing around the side of the house.

"I like Cate," Sam said. "I can't believe what I almost said. I was so embarrassed."

"She doesn't take offense to anything. My mother is the most low-key person I know. She won't hold that against you. I promise."

"Good. I don't want her to hate me." He smiled.

"I can't imagine anyone hating you."

He pretended surprise. "What? No, really. I had some haters in school. Mostly because I stole all the pretty girls and kept them for myself."

She laughed. "Now *that* I'll believe."

He flexed his muscles and winked. "Oh, I forgot to tell you. I moved. Now I'm only a few miles from here, out on Olivet Road."

"You did? Why? When?"

"Geez, Taylor. One question at a time," he teased. "Less than a month ago, I saw a little two-bedroom house for rent. Last week, I put the deposit down on it. Yesterday, I moved in. It has a garage where I can work on cars and a small yard with a few trees and some grass. I'm going to put up a fence so Diesel can sit out there with me without chancing he'll end up lost by chasing squirrels."

"That's great. I'm sure he'll love that."

"Yeah. At the apartment, he was always pouting on the balcony while I worked on cars in the parking lot. Made me run my legs off taking him up and down the stairs. He loves to be outside."

"What's the address? I probably know the house."

"1309."

"Oh yeah. That's the Langstons' house. It's old, but it has good bones. They moved to Florida a while back. I wondered if they were going to sell."

"Yep, that's them. They aren't sure yet, so they let me have a year lease."

"Good. I mean, I guess that's good. Is your dad still okay about you being away from him?"

"That's something else I was going to tell you. He's thinking about moving in with me for a while. Now that I have two bedrooms, I told him he needs to see what he thinks about Georgia and Hart's Ridge. I think he'll like it here, but he's going to keep our house, too. Just in case."

"Probably a good idea. This town isn't for everyone."

"Yeah, well he's supposed to let me know by the end of the month. I'll need to set up his room."

Diesel came back. He flounced down on the porch slabs, staring up at them with his dark brown eyes. He was so gorgeous.

"One more thing," Sam said, sounding suddenly nervous.

"What?"

"I was thinking. Since I have a house and a yard now, and you're always working…"

She didn't like where this was going.

"…that maybe it's time for Diesel to live with me full-time."

Taylor's stomach dropped. She'd known this day would come, and it was her fault. She'd been the one who'd hunted until she'd found Sam, then confessed to having his dog. She'd agreed to give him back.

Eventually.

She stared at Diesel. He must have felt it because he looked up at her, a smile in his eyes. He thumped his tail on the porch, thrilled to have her attention. He was such a good boy.

"Taylor?"

"I hear you. I just don't know what to say. Right now, I'm in the middle of a triple murder investigation, so yeah, I'm gone a lot. At least for now."

"And when that's over, there will be another investigation, right?" he said quietly.

Taylor had a couple of options. She could play dirty—turn herself into a whiny female, crying and begging him to not take Diesel. He'd probably fall for that because he was a Southern gentleman.

But she wasn't that kind of woman.

Or she could pull up her big-girl panties and admit Diesel would be better off with a stay-at-home dad.

Doing the right thing was going to be brutal.

"I don't know how to answer that, Sam. Officially, I'm not a detective."

"But you want to be." He kicked at a plank below his feet.

"Yeah, I do. Since the sheriff allows me to assist, I never really know what my workload is going to be."

"I know. And I wouldn't even ask if you were still out here alone, Taylor. But you have Lucy and Cate. I've seen your dad out here several times. Someone is always around."

He was right about that, though she didn't know how long Cate and Lucy would be living with her. Both claimed it was temporary. Occasionally, Taylor grumbled about her space being invaded, but, deep down, she enjoyed having her family around.

Taylor didn't fear being alone, though. She hadn't found any more cigarette butts since she'd put up a few cameras, but she still didn't know where they'd come from and that made her nervous, not afraid. There was still a man out there who had gotten to her once when her defenses were down, and she didn't want it to happen again.

"I have an idea. You could get another dog. When I bring Diesel to visit, they could hang out. We could take them on hikes together."

He was such a guy. Next, he'd suggest Diesel and his new fictional doggie-best friend could have guy's night or beers on the dock. Sam had no clue about the emotional attachment she'd already formed with Diesel. It couldn't simply be replaced or healed by getting another dog.

But she just couldn't say the words to agree with Sam.

"Do I have to decide tonight?" she asked. "I'm exhausted and not thinking clearly. I might have questions."

He stood. "For sure! I wasn't planning to take him right now. I want you to be comfortable with it. I just miss him when he's not with me. You know how it is."

Yes, she did. Sometimes when Diesel was with Sam, she couldn't sleep.

"Yeah."

Sam bent to rub Diesel's ears. "I'm going to take off, buddy. See you tomorrow."

Diesel tilted his head at Sam. Taylor could tell he didn't want Sam to go. She felt a ripple of guilt at what they were doing to him.

"So, see you tomorrow?" Sam asked.

The air between them felt heavy and sad.

"Maybe. Not sure what time I'll be here. I'll text you. Drive carefully," Taylor said. "That curve a mile from here has seen some tragedies over the years."

"Gotcha." He nodded, then went to his jeep and climbed in.

The screen door opened, and Lucy stepped out. She came to the swing and sat beside Taylor. Sam took off.

"Ouch. I heard the tail end—no pun intended—of your conversation. You okay?"

"I guess. I don't know. But I need to get to bed. I'll digest Sam's request tomorrow when I've had some rest."

Lucy put her hand on Taylor's thigh. "Wait. Can you give me a few minutes? I have something important to talk to you about."

Another wave of fatigue washed over Taylor. She wanted to tell Lucy it would have to wait, but that was something she still couldn't do. Cecil—who she missed dearly lately—often told her she always put everyone else's needs above her own. She agreed, but saying *no* just wasn't in her vocabulary when it came to her family. If it were, they'd probably fall over from a stroke the first time she said it. Then she'd have to take care of that, too.

"What's up?" she asked.

Lucy took a few breaths, inhaling in and out like she was about to jump off a cliff and needed courage.

"I need a favor. A big one."

"And do you want to tell me about it?" Taylor wished her sister would get straight to the point so she could go to bed.

"Yes. Okay, you probably don't know this, but it's always been my dream to live on a houseboat."

Taylor couldn't even imagine where this was going.

"I found one, but I need you to buy it for me," Lucy said.

Taylor laughed.

"No, I'm serious. I need you to put the boat in your name," Lucy said.

"How am I supposed to buy you a boat? I can barely keep up with *my* bills. I think I have—*maybe*—a thousand dollars in my savings account."

Lucy smiled smugly. "I have the money. I just need it to be in your name."

Alarm bells started ringing in Taylor's head.

"You have enough money to buy a houseboat? Is that what you're telling me? If you do, Lucy, then you'd better start telling me how you got it. Are you in trouble?"

"It's not a lot of money, Taylor. The houseboat is used and very old. But it's nice. I already looked at it. It's perfect for Johnny and me."

Taylor felt a headache starting behind her right eye.

"Let's skip over the money part right now—we'll circle back to that. Why would you think living on a boat with a baby is a good idea? You do realize that a boat is usually on water, right? Or is this boat on land?"

"It's on water. I know it sounds dangerous, but the boat is at a marina. Not the fancy one up at Harbor Light, but the one they call the Redneck Yacht club up on Beaver Dam. I met a couple there who live on their boat with their teen son, but they were there when he was a toddler, too. There are security measures I can put in place to keep Johnny safe. And the slip rent is so cheap. There's also a little park there for Johnny, and a bathhouse in case I need it."

Taylor had never heard Lucy sound so enamored by anything. She was off and running, babbling like a child telling Santa everything they wanted.

She continued. "I'd call it vintage, but it's clean as a whistle. They kept it covered any time it wasn't in use. It's a Myacht Tracker —thirty-four feet with a twenty-five horsepower Yamaha motor and an upper deck for sunning. The utilities run on gas or electricity, but it also has solar panels. It's furnished. There's a kitchen and a stateroom with a queen-sized bed, plus the dining nook can be made into a bed. Kitchen has an oven and microwave, and there's a full bathroom with a tiny tub, too. Even has a nice little covered porch with chairs and a table. You have to see it, Taylor."

"Staterooms?"

"Well, that's what they're called. But they're tiny."

"How much is this fantasy boat?"

"Twenty-two thousand dollars."

Speechless, Taylor swiveled to stare at Lucy, eyes wide with shock.

"Now you've got my full attention. Lucy, how the hell do you have that kind of money? You're going to tell me right now so I can figure out how I'm going to get you out of whatever mess you've gotten yourself into."

"You don't need to worry about how to get me out of any messes," Lucy said. "This time, I figured it out on my own. The money is mine—I earned it fair and square."

"How did you earn it?"

Taylor didn't trust her. Lucy had never made any significant money in her life. None of them had ever had that kind of cash. They were all paycheck-to-paycheck kinds of people, like most Americans.

The door opened. Jo came out with Levi behind her.

"Bye, old aunties," Levi said, laughing as he rushed past them and took a running leap off the porch.

"We're leaving," Jo said.

"Drive safe. The deer are always more active at this time," Taylor said.

Jo gave her a thumbs-up, said her goodbyes, and they got in her car and left.

Lucy stood and went to the door. After she peered in, she returned to the swing.

"Look," she said. "I don't ask for much, Taylor."

That wasn't true. Lucy had a short memory. Taylor was going to have to question her carefully if she wanted to get anything out of her.

"If you have the money to buy the boat, you don't need credit, so why do you need me to put it in my name?"

"For safety. In the past, I'll admit I've run around with some questionable people. I would rather have the boat title and the slip rental agreement in your name. That way, no one can look me up online. For safety—now that I have Johnny. I don't want to go back to that life."

"Is that life how you got this money?"

"No, Taylor. I told you; I earned it."

There was only one way Taylor could think of where Lucy could earn that much money. The thought sickened her.

"Lucy, please tell me you didn't—"

"Whoa," Lucy said, quickly interrupting. "If you are thinking I was prostituting, you need to back up. I'd never do that."

Taylor let out a long breath, feeling her shoulders relax. "Okay, but listen, Lucy—all these secrets we all keep? They are killing this family. Can't you see that? At some point, you're going to have to trust someone. I want to help you, but I can't while you continue to be so evasive."

Lucy hung her head, staring at her feet.

"You want to tell me," Taylor said. "I can feel it."

"You'll hate me." She didn't look up.

"I'd never hate you."

Lucy raised her head, locking eyes with Taylor.

"I sold Johnny."

CHAPTER 11

*I*t was shocking how three little words could turn the world upside down. In the past, Lucy's problems had never been solved, but they'd been dealt with. But this one hit Taylor with the reality that anything Lucy had ever done before was nothing compared to her confession about selling her child.

Taylor struggled for something to say, but Johnny's sweet face swam in her mind. Lucy had given Taylor so much trouble over the years, but this—this was unforgivable.

"You better tell me what you mean by that," she finally said, doing her best to keep the anger from her voice.

Lucy began to lay out a story so unbelievable, yet so detailed, that it had to be true. All Taylor could do was hang on for the ride because now that her sister had decided to talk, the dam had burst.

"I was only going to be the dog walker," she said. "Everything was fine with me staying in their home to take care of two French bulldogs."

"Who were they?"

"That part you don't need to know. Let's call them Jack and Jill."

"Jack and Jill. Got it. Now get to the part about selling your child."

"I was promoted to an assistant. Taylor, I was good at it. I hadn't known I could do so much on the computer—website stuff, scheduling, emails. And I was learning all about art."

"Go on."

"They didn't know I was pregnant. I had planned to terminate before they found out, but it didn't happen like that. When Jack realized I was pregnant, he asked if he and his wife could adopt the baby."

Taylor felt relief rush through her.

"So, you didn't *sell* him—you planned to give him up for adoption in a private arrangement. They were going to pay you as if you were a surrogate, right? Not legal in your circumstance, by the way, but go on."

Lucy sighed. "Well, to be honest, it felt like I was selling him. I agreed to it. At first, it didn't bother me. I didn't want to be a mother. Couldn't imagine myself dragged down by a kid. I felt like that until I held him in my arms. I still didn't admit it at the time, but, down deep, I knew I couldn't walk away."

"This was all in New York City?"

"At first. Then Jack moved his wife and me to their home in Hudson Bay. Once there, it was like being in prison."

"A luxurious prison?" Taylor asked.

"Luxury means nothing if you aren't allowed to leave the property. Or if someone dictates every move you make and every bite you take."

Lucy continued, explaining the strict rules she'd been forced to comply with concerning exercise and her diet, rehashing her attempts to make friends with the wife, who'd been controlled by "Jack," too. She left out real names, but Taylor didn't push her on that. For once, she was getting information about one of Lucy's exploits, so Taylor let her talk.

"Then I found out that his wife was his *sister*."

Taylor leaned forward, mouth dropping. "What?"

"Yep—they're from Ukraine, and Jill was posing as his wife. Their family had ordered her to participate in the sham. Johnny was meant to be a part of the charade, except Jack actually *did* want him to be his son."

Taylor was suddenly wide awake.

"Charades like that are usually meant to cover up illegal activities. What was going on?"

"I'm not sure, Taylor. He was an art dealer. Other than that, I'm still in the dark."

Lucy was lying. Taylor could tell when her sister wasn't being truthful.

"You said *was*."

"He's dead," Lucy said.

Taylor's stomach dropped. "Oh my God, please tell me you didn't kill him."

Lucy laughed. "No. I wasn't there. I got her and the baby out of the house earlier that day and we checked into a hotel. A plan was in place for Jill to start over with the baby somewhere else, away from Jack—until I heard her on the phone through the bathroom door. Jill had called her brother, apologizing for leaving. When I heard her ask him to pick her up, I grabbed my stuff, along with the money she'd stashed in her suitcase, and I got the hell out of there. I took Johnny with me. On the news the next day, I saw a news report about an armed robbery at their home in Hudson Valley. Jack was killed and Jill was beaten, but survived."

"That's some very suspicious timing."

"I know, right?" Lucy said, then looked away.

"Is her family in Ukraine aware of everything that transpired?"

Lucy shrugged. "I don't know. I haven't had any contact with Jill. She could've gone back there, or maybe she's still upstate. But I damn sure don't want her to know where I am."

"You think she'd try to kidnap Johnny?"

"No, I don't think so. Then again, I never would've thought she was cold-blooded enough to kill her brother, so I can't say for sure what she's capable of. She never seemed genuinely enthused about being a mother, either, but I imagine she's furious about the money I stole."

"I bet you're right. She paid for a baby but ended up with nothing."

Lucy put her finger up. "Technically, her brother was supposed to pay me, but he never did. I found the money in her suitcase, and I stole it. For what I went through, I felt like they owed it to me. Besides, she has plenty of capital to play with after her fake husband died. Believe me."

Taylor put her head in her hands. This was bad.

No, not bad. It was a catastrophe.

Taylor raised her head, locking eyes with her sister. "Lucy, swear to me that you weren't involved in a murder. Swear it on Johnny."

Lucy held her hand up. "I swear. I've screwed up a lot in the past, but I'd never take someone's life. I had nothing to do with it. Everything I told you is just my hypothesis about what happened. I don't know anything for sure. Still, I'm afraid that if Su—I mean, Jill's—family in Ukraine pressures her, she might try to find me."

"Did you tell her about Hart's Ridge?" Taylor's mind spun, wondering how to best protect Lucy and Johnny.

"No. Absolutely not. She doesn't even know my real last name. Her brother supplied my phone, so it wasn't linked to me."

"But she could use your fingerprints to find you if it occurs to her to try. It'd be easy to lift some from your old room in their house," Taylor said. "You have a record. You're in the system."

"I know." Lucy bit her lip. "But she doesn't know that."

"Lucy, you do not need to live alone on a boat. You need to stay here—where I can help protect you and Johnny."

Lucy jumped to her feet, hands thrust angrily on her hips.

"No, Taylor. I don't *want* to stay here. I want that houseboat. They can't find me if you'll put everything in your name."

"You *have* to return that money. It's the only way to be sure that Jill and her family won't come after you."

"I am not giving the money back, Taylor. *Hell no.* They owed me," Lucy said, shaking her head. "They are filthy rich. What I took would be considered chump change to her."

"Damn it, Lucy! How do you always get mixed up in crazy trouble?" Taylor yelled.

The door opened. Cate stuck her head out, glancing between them.

"Everything okay out here?"

Taylor and Lucy responded at the same time. "Yes!" Both their tones were laced with anger and bitterness. Cate's eyes widened, but she didn't comment. She just retreated, quietly shutting the door.

"Great. Now we've hurt her feelings," Taylor said. The adrenaline suddenly drained from her body, making her dizzy. "Look, Lucy. I'm exhausted. We aren't going to figure anything out tonight. Let's sleep on it. We'll try to come up with a plan tomorrow."

"You won't be here tomorrow," Lucy said, her voice rising. "What if someone else buys the houseboat before I am able to?"

"There will be other boats." Taylor rubbed her temples. A headache had instantaneously manifested, warning her a migraine wouldn't be far behind if she didn't close her eyes and try to rest. When she opened her eyes, she could see that a storm was brewing behind Lucy's eyes.

"You know what, Taylor? You can stick it where the sun doesn't shine. You've always acted like you're the boss of everyone, but I don't need you. I will be out of *your* house by the end of the weekend."

Lucy stomped into the house, letting the screen door slam behind her. Caught off guard by her sister's words, Taylor could only stare after her.

CHAPTER 12

Saturday flew by. From what Cate could tell, the vaccine clinic was a huge success. A lot of people in and around the county couldn't afford to take their animals to vet clinics, and they appreciated the discounted rate and ease of not having to make an appointment. With Angela overseeing the event, the doctor administering the vaccines, and she and Sarah assisting them both, they'd efficiently finished at least three dozen exams with only one incident during that time.

Sissy had brought her mother's calico cat in to be vaccinated. When Angela opened the carrier, it had freaked out, leaping out of there like a jack in the box before scrambling to hide under a parked car.

"Callie, *no*," Sissy screamed.

Sissy and the vet staff had surrounded the car, trying to urge the cat out, but it had been a nine-year-old little girl who had saved the day. She'd crawled under the car and befriended the cat, then coaxed it to come out with her. They'd had a good laugh when Sissy informed them that if something had happened to her cat, her mother would've hung them all out to dry.

Cate couldn't help but overhear some of the conversations

between the people who waited with their pets, and they usually centered on the murders. Their worry was tinged with a hunger to exchange rumors and armchair detective the case. Some threw out ridiculous hypotheses—jilted lovers, mafia, and other crazy scenarios.

Others claimed Danny, the youngest son, had committed the murders. Their reasoning seemed to be based on Danny always being a troublemaker.

Cate also heard a lot of people expressing disappointment in the sheriff's department, since they couldn't even name a suspect yet.

She didn't let on that she had any connection. Before long, everyone would know anyway. In a small town, secrets were never secret for long.

John Dellory, the manager of Tractor Supply, was thrilled with his decision to loan out the parking lot because it had manifested into the vet clients coming into the store and making impulse buys. To thank them for the business, he'd ordered Subway sandwiches to be delivered for their lunches. They took turns taking lunch breaks to keep their momentum going. Before Cate knew it, it was four o'clock and they'd just finished with their last patient.

Being busy had helped her keep her mind off what was going on at home and the tension between Lucy and Taylor.

Lucy had said she was moving out, but she hadn't given a reason why.

In Cate's opinion, Lucy needed to stay right where she was, especially since she was a new mother and somewhat unsure about how to be one. If she moved out, what was she going to do on the nights Johnny wouldn't fall asleep without Aunt Taylor? And how would Lucy sleep in when she needed to without Cate around to babysit Johnny for a few hours?

Cate treasured those times with her grandson, quietly bonding with him away from everyone else.

No one had asked Cate's opinion about the issue, so she wasn't about to weigh in uninvited. She still felt like a guest—not their mother.

"Great job, everyone," Angela said, high-fiving Cate.

Cate was tired, but it was the welcomed kind that resulted from a good day's work.

She was confident she had the job, too. She and Angela had hit it off. Cate felt like she might just have gained a friend along with the position. They were the same age. Like her, Angela possessed a laid-back and somewhat quiet personality. She wasn't one to giggle or chatter meaninglessly as some women were prone to do. When she did speak, her words were worth listening to.

Cate was the same, if not quieter, but Angela made her feel at ease. She'd assigned Cate to help calm the nervous animals, distracting them with soothing cuddles and rubs while their vaccines were administered.

The tending veterinarian, Dr. Ruthie, had also expressed her appreciation for the way Cate had handled some of the more nervous animals. She'd said she could spot an animal lover right off.

Cate hadn't known how to respond. She wasn't used to compliments. In prison, she'd been lucky to land the jobs she had. She'd been grateful, doing the jobs to the best of her ability, but keeping her head down. Getting attention in prison was never a good thing.

Their last customer, a nice high schooler named Jarret, was helping them take down the tent while his dog rested near a bowl of water. After the dog had received his vaccines, he'd acted a bit woozy, so the vet wanted to watch him for a few minutes.

An old pickup truck pulled into the parking lot. Cate watched it, realizing it was heading toward them.

"Looks like we have one more," she said, alerting the others.

Sarah looked up, then groaned. "That's Weldon Gentry. He's probably bringing in some of his hunting dogs."

Confused, Cate cocked her head. She'd thought the goal was to vaccinate as many dogs as they could in Hart County. Why were they dismayed to see him coming?

"Don't pay attention to Sarah," Angela said. "She gets upset at 'ole Weldon for the shape he lets his dogs get in, but I'm glad he's here. It's usually impossible to get him to comply with the state's vaccine laws."

"Weldon Gentry is exactly the kind of local we need to get through to about spaying and neutering his dogs," Dr. Ruthie said. "At least now the door is opened to where we can give out vaccines."

The man parked and got out of his truck, slamming the door. Letting out a string of profanity when it didn't shut all the way, he jammed his shoulder against it until it did. In a muddy pair of brown Carhart coveralls with a Nascar ballcap pulled low over his eyes, he was an imposing figure.

Cate had expected a dog or two to jump out of the cab. Instead, Gentry went to the truck bed and opened the tailgate.

"Come on out, you chicken shit. Ain't no one gonna hurt you," he muttered, leaning in and disappearing from view.

Cate heard a growl and a snap, then an even angrier Gentry reappeared.

"If you bite me, I'll drag your ass behind this truck all the way home, you little bitch."

"Uh-oh, he must have a new one," Angela whispered. "Cate, why don't you see if you can help him?"

"I'll go with you," Jarret said. "Gentry can get right ugly sometimes. I deliver wood out to his farm. He pays me to stack it, too. If it's not perfect, he gets all worked up over it."

It felt like an initiation, but Cate headed over with Jarret behind her.

Gentry turned around. "Can you just do the shots here in the truck bed? She ain't cooperating."

The dog was a Wired-Haired Pointing Griffon, a breed that was bred to be good hunting dogs. Brown and white with a perfect chocolate nose, this one had the deepest brown eyes she'd ever seen. The dog sat huddled under the rear window at the front of the truck bed, a heavy chain around her neck securing her to a metal hook and weighing her head down. She bared her teeth, growling out a low warning. Cate could tell it wasn't anger that made her both growl and tremble—it was fear. Her sad brown eyes begged for someone to understand—to treat her with compassion.

"Hey, Weldon," Jarret said. "Whatcha got here? I don't remember seeing this one at your place."

"Just picked her up a month ago. She's turning out to be a right pain in the ass," Gentry grumbled. "I have to break her, but I haven't had enough time lately. You can't get lard unless you boil the pig."

Cate had no idea what he meant about the hog, but she cringed when he said the dog needed to be broken. *Breaking* a dog was never a way to get them to adjust. Usually, it only brought on more trauma-related behavior. But she wasn't there to counsel.

"I wouldn't have her here today if that jackass from Animal Control hadn't been out at my place last week, checking rabies tags." He called the dog again, but she didn't move.

"Let me try," Cate said. "I'll get up there with her."

"You think that's a good idea?" Jarret asked.

Laughing, Gentry motioned her forward. "Let her give it a go, Jarret. I'm due for some entertainment. Just remember, I'm not liable. I warned you."

Cate ignored his barb, climbing into the bed of the truck.

The dog shrank back even farther, baring her teeth again. She growled low in her throat.

"It's okay," Cate said, edging closer. After she unfastened the chain from the eyehook, she laid it down. "You sure are a pretty girl."

"She damn sure ought to be," Gentry said. "Cost me a fortune because of her bloodline."

"What's her name?" Sarah said.

"Moxie," Gentry answered. "And she's sure got some."

"It's all about your energy," Cate said quietly to her growing audience.

The veterinarian, Angela, and Sarah had come over, too.

"She's afraid. She needs to know she's safe. You can't come at her with fear or anger. Relax, then show her that you're confident and able to protect her."

Gentry snorted in derision.

Moxie let out a warning bark, her fur standing on end.

"Come on, Moxie. We just need to get you taken care of," Cate soothed.

"We don't need any dog bites," Dr. Ruthie said. "Let's just wait a bit."

"I got it," Cate said. She took a deep breath, letting it relax her muscles, then she confidently closed the distance between her and the dog, picked up the chain, and pulled it taut.

Frantically, Moxie looked everywhere but at Cate. When she growled again, Cate gave the chain a little jerk and made a sharp noise by pushing her tongue against the back of her teeth.

"Relax," she said, then began leading a suddenly quiet Moxie toward the truck bed opening.

"I can't believe it," Gentry said.

Jarret gave an appreciative whistle.

Cate jumped down first, then handed the chain over to Gentry to guide the dog down.

He didn't even hesitate before he jerked it violently, pulling the dog off the truck tailgate and onto the concrete where she fell on her side. She immediately jumped up, trembling again.

"What are you doing?" Cate said, glaring at the man. "You just ruined the trust I built with her!"

"My dog don't need to trust anyone but me."

"Let's get her over here and done with," Dr. Ruthie said.

Everyone else was shocked speechless.

The tent was already down, but the table and chairs were still set up. Gentry sat, took the pen and paper Sarah handed him, and started filling out the permission form.

He kept the chain wrapped around his left hand. At the end of it, Moxie huddled into herself and trembled violently.

Cate could see that the dog was malnourished. Although she was still pretty, her coat was dull and overgrown. She could barely see out from under the hair that grew in front of her eyes and her claws were long, too.

It was very apparent she wasn't being properly taken care of.

Gentry handed over the form, holding the chain tightly, not giving the dog any slack while the doctor readied the vaccines.

"What do you think about spaying this one, Weldon?" Angela asked. "I have some vouchers so you can get it done at a discount."

He shook his head. "Nope. If she don't hunt, maybe her pups will. I aim to pair her up when she goes into her first heat."

Moxie flinched when the first shot went in, then she looked up and found Cate. They locked eyes. Cate felt her heart break because she could see the dog wasn't happy.

When Moxie yelped and jumped again on the second shot, the man kicked her in the ribs with his muddy work boot.

"*Sit*," he growled.

Moxie yelped.

"Hey," Sarah exclaimed. "Don't do that."

"Aww, Weldon. Come on, she's barely more than a puppy," Angela said.

"She has to learn," Gentry said.

Cate was steaming mad. She wanted to kick the man's ass halfway to the moon, but she didn't. She needed the job, and today was a test. She doubted assaulting clients would get her the job.

Dr. Ruthie finished up with Moxie.

"What about your other dogs?" she asked Gentry.

"Got them taken care of by a mobile vet that came through a month ago," he muttered.

"You sure they were licensed? If not, it's not legal," she said.

Gentry rolled his eyes. "Yes, he was licensed. I ain't stupid."

Cate would have to disagree, but she'd do it silently.

Sarah handed Gentry his bill. After it was paid, he led Moxie to the truck, yanked her up into the bed, and shut the tailgate.

"Later," he called out, then got in his truck and started it. After revving the engine, he took off.

"I'm out of here, too," Jarret said. "I've got to mow my grandma's lawn."

"Thanks for your help," Angela told him. "Tell her I said hello."

"Will do."

When he was gone, Angela turned to Cate.

"You did a fantastic job today. I was especially impressed with your skills with Gentry's dog. Have you worked with a lot of reactive dogs?"

"A fair share," Cate said. "But most were scared more than anything. It truly is about the energy of the handler. It can change a dog's behavior instantly."

"Do you watch "The Dog Whisperer"? Cesar Milan?" Angela asked.

Cate laughed. "No, but I've heard of him."

"There's a new one now," Sarah said. "A young guy they call the Dog Daddy. He's spectacular."

"I'll have to see if I can get that," Cate said. But she probably wouldn't. Watching TV wasn't her thing.

Angela began throwing paperwork into a box. "Well, just make sure you're at work Monday at seven AM sharp. Bring your ID and social security card for the paperwork."

She said it so nonchalantly, barely even looking up. But she did see the huge smile that crept across Cate's face, because she matched it with one of her own.

CHAPTER 13

*T*aylor and Shane followed the sheriff into the garage. The crime scene had been released but was still intact because Beverly claimed she wasn't coming back to stay until the murderer was caught. She was still staying with Jenny.

Danny claimed he wasn't coming near it either.

The farm was shut down until further notice.

Taylor had something she wanted to talk about with both Shane and the sheriff, but she needed to wait until the sheriff got out everything he wanted to say.

"Damn shame, I tell you," he said, shaking his head as he stared at the floor.

The bloodstains had faded to a dark rusty brown color, randomly spattered around the concrete. Taylor cringed internally, instantly visualizing Amos as they'd discovered him. The man had been so full of life, and that life had been snuffed out too soon and so viciously.

"I still don't get the carpet squares," Shane said.

Half-a-dozen squares were scattered on top of the trail of dried blood. The safe was at the back of the garage. It still set askew, as though someone had pulled it away from the wall and then left it there.

They went around it, noting a few dents and some scratch marks. It was an old safe, but like anything older, it was surprisingly heavy duty. It stood at least five feet tall and was a few feet wide. Taylor pointed out the scratches on the side, gouged in the burgundy paint.

"Not a single fingerprint," Shane said. "Someone wiped it down."

"No doubt," Taylor agreed. "I think we're dealing with more than the average low-IQ criminal here."

"Stop wasting time wishing. Both of you take a side of this garage and walk every inch of it, see if forensics missed anything," the sheriff said.

Taylor went to the far-left corner where an old washer and dryer took up most of the space. On top of the washing machine were a garden hose and a canister of ant killer. On a shelf above it were several boxes marked 'front porch xmas'. She swept the space from top to bottom, finding nothing out of place.

She moved to the left, toward the garage doors.

It was a cluttered garage just like most others she'd seen before. Garden tools, tennis rackets, and some ancient lawn chairs with the webbing ripped up had been thrown in one corner.

She continued, moving past several boxes marked 'camping gear' and a couple of spare tires. She noted a few kerosene space heaters, then saw the stack of carpet squares the others had been plucked from.

"I saw more of these squares put down in the kids' area of the shop where Beverly serves hot cocoa," she said.

"Yeah, I saw them, too. Those must be the worn ones they've pulled out." Shane kept his attention on what he was doing. He had the tool side of the garage—pegboards, hand tools, and a bench with skill saws and drills scattered about. Nails, screws, and other odds and ends made it harder for him to check every inch.

They'd already been to the big shop, but they were sure nothing had happened there. The day of the incident, there'd been a small team of workers inside, and they hadn't seen anything. The shop was located too far from the house to be able to hear anything, either.

Taylor spotted an old dollhouse on another shelf, dusty and outdated, and wondered if it had belonged to Beverly when she was a kid.

One thing piqued Taylor's curiosity—the fact they were sure the Higgins were pulling in a ton of money through the farm, but they lived as though they were regular working-class people. Neither the garage nor the house was what she'd call fancy, nothing like the expensive lake houses that had been built around Hart county in the last few years. Built to impress, inside and outside, with all the latest trims and finishes.

Everything that Taylor had seen in the Higgin's house and garage was well-worn and not of high-end value. Except for the kitchen. It had been made over not too long ago. It now had top-of-the-line appliances and a huge marble island to sit at.

Taylor could just imagine Beverly and Amos in there, working side by side to put together a holiday feast for their extended family. Maybe a Christmas Eve breakfast.

That was the kind of couple they were, the kind who hosted the big events and was where everyone wanted to be. They probably held the church family events and boy scout stuff, too, right there in that kitchen or living room.

During Christmas, they'd come to pick out a tree. Lucy had been a child. She'd refused to use the portable potty meant for customer use, then begged Taylor to ask Beverly to use hers.

Beverly had agreed and led them inside. As soon as they walked through the door, the delicious aromas had hit Taylor— pine and cinnamon, everything she'd expected their house to smell like, only better. Then they'd continued through the kitchen and living room to the hall bathroom, and it had been so beautifully decorated that Lucy had stopped in place, her mouth dropped in awe.

Just like now, it hadn't been fancy at all, but beautiful and cozy. Flames flickered in the fireplace, and deep couches with colorful coverlets for snuggling had been artfully arranged around it.

"Taylor, why can't our house look like this?" Lucy had asked.

It was embarrassing because Beverly had to have heard them, though she'd pretended not to. Taylor had pushed Lucy into the bathroom. When they'd finished and she tried to slip them out unnoticed, Beverly had caught them and sent them out with a pecan pie and a plastic gallon of her holiday juice recipe.

Lucy had carried the jug, her arms wrapped around it as she held it to her body, so proud of it as she'd pranced outside and taken it to their dad. He had tried to give it back, the pie, too, but Beverly had refused and simply walked away.

Taylor remembered her dad throwing a fit on the way home, insisting it had been Taylor's fault and that she must've said something to make them seem needy. The rest of the ride home had been spent in silence; their holiday mood soiled.

She hadn't touched a drop of that juice or the pie that year, but she'd never confessed what Lucy had said to move Beverly's sympathy. Her little sister was sensitive. Even though she always tried to play the tough girl, she was easily hurt.

Taylor finished searching her side, came up empty, and went to the sheriff.

"Sheriff, I got wind that Amos and Horis Hedgepeth had words recently and it ended badly."

"Over what?"

"Horis' and Amos' property meet up near the creek, and Horis shot a deer on Amos' side about a month ago."

"Uh-oh. Amos wouldn't have liked that. He considered his land a sanctuary."

"Right. He didn't believe in hunting for sport, and Horis is only interested in how many deer heads he can fit on his living room wall. He's not shooting them for the meat." Like the Higgins, Taylor didn't have a problem with hunting in general, not when it put food on the table. She and her sisters had learned to do plenty with a few pounds of venison back in the day. Their dad used to be pretty good about having a deer or two in the freezer.

The sheriff sighed. "Bring him in and work him over, see what he gives you. I'd hate to think it got ugly enough for Horis to do something this heinous, but we must check it out. Weaver, you getting this?"

"Yeah, I heard. We'll get him in. But I've got something over here," he called out.

She and the sheriff went to him.

There was scattered white powder with a partial shoe print. The print was barely enough to make out if it was from a male or female, but since it was on the wider side, Taylor guessed it was a man. Only a couple of inches of the tread style showed, but it could help make a match.

"I didn't see this before," she said.

"Me either. Maybe it got here since then," the sheriff said.

Taylor scanned the area, then pointed to a shelf. "There's cockroach powder up there. I bet that's what's on the floor."

"Taylor, call Beverly and ask her who has been in this garage since the incident. Weaver, you take photos from every angle. One of you ask Danny for all his shoes. If he says no, we'll get a search warrant."

"He won't say no," Taylor said. At least, she hoped he wouldn't because it would only make him look guilty, especially since the discovery about his gambling.

"He'd better not," Shane said, suddenly thunderous. "And Gray, I think you need to be careful with him. I don't want you to try to approach him without backup."

Taylor nearly laughed.

She wasn't a damsel in distress, and she didn't like being treated like one.

"I'll be fine," she said curtly, then walked outside.

Danny would never hurt her, and he wasn't a murderer. There would have to be some damning evidence to convince her otherwise.

That was the bad thing about Shane. He was a great detective, but he was like a dog with a bone when he thought he had his suspect. Taylor felt like he narrowed it down too quickly, but she was only a deputy lucky enough to be involved. He had the detective title, so what did she know?

Shane had left a rose on her truck window that morning, too. It had to be from him. He'd parked beside her. Who else would give her a flower? She hadn't said anything about it yet. While it was a sweet gesture, she wasn't happy he'd done it at the department where anyone could've seen him. The last thing she needed was for her team—or God forbid, Miss Dottie—to find out there was even an inkling of anything more than professionalism between Shane and Taylor.

She went around the garage, searching for more footprints. Over the last few weeks, she'd done a lot of thinking. She'd just about made up her mind to tell Shane that they had to stay just friends. Taylor didn't want to trade her dream of being a detective just to be Shane's girlfriend for a time. She had no doubt, too, that he'd eventually dump her. While he had transformed himself and his life, she was still Plain-Jane Taylor, mired down in Hart's Ridge with no plans to go anywhere else and no desire to improve her looks.

He could do a lot better, and she didn't need the heartache when he realized it. The only thing worse than a department relationship was a department breakup where she'd have to see him every day.

She also didn't need more complications.

Her life was careening out of control these days. Everything had changed. Now that Cate was out and living with her, as well as Lucy and the baby, and Sam was breathing down her neck about

Diesel, she felt like she didn't quite have a handle on things like before.

They were all pitching in to buy groceries, so that wasn't it, but Taylor felt like it was her responsibility to make sure meals were planned and everyone was as comfortable as could be. She was concerned about Cate settling into her new life, and she was worried about Lucy and Johnny, for all sorts of reasons.

Taylor didn't have time to be the perfect host, but she couldn't let go of the worry about it.

"Taylor," the sheriff said, coming from around the corner. "I'm out of here, but you and Weaver head over to the Hedgepeth farm and see what Horis says. Don't let him get agitated because we want him down at the department. Make it happen."

"Gotcha."

Shane joined them, his thumbs dancing on his phone while he walked.

"Weaver, let Gray take the lead with Horis. He's an old country boy who doesn't take kindly to strangers. He probably doesn't even remember you were once a local."

"Okay."

After the sheriff left, Taylor got in Shane's car, pulled her phone out, and searched Horis' wife on Facebook. She scanned through the woman's posts and photos while he drove.

Horis didn't use social media, so the wife was the next best option.

A few pictures of a pure white baby goat were posted on the morning the murders took place. No people in the shots, just the kid and the mama, and a caption that they'd named it Comet.

It was beyond cute.

Taylor had always wanted to get some animals. A few goats, maybe some chickens. A donkey. Yes, definitely a donkey. She was obsessed with them. It was something about their serious countenance and the unpredictability of what they would do at any given moment.

Donkeys were protective, too. They took their jobs as guardians over the livestock seriously. She'd heard many stories about donkeys stomping a coyote or two to save the goats or sheep under their supervision.

Horis himself had come into the Den once telling a story of such an encounter—when one of his donkeys had taken on a coyote. He'd heard it braying loudly during the night, and he'd came out with his shotgun to investigate. He arrived just in time to see his donkey turn and try to kick the coyote, then charge it and chase it to the fence, where it leaped five feet and disappeared into the dark.

Taylor supposed she got her love of animals from Cate. She could see herself having a small variety of them out at her place.

Cate would love it, too.

But animals took money, and that was one thing Taylor was always scrambling for. She couldn't ethically build the small farm she dreamed about if she couldn't afford to take care of its residents as they deserved.

Maybe one day.

Shane glanced over before returning his gaze to the road.

"See anything interesting?"

"Nope."

It was only six or so minutes from the Christmas tree farm to Horis' spread, and they could smell it miles before they got there. When they pulled in, they immediately saw a big truck backed up to a huge pile of manure outside one of the pig houses, a man standing outside with it.

"What is he doing?" Taylor asked, holding her hand over her nose.

"Pumping the manure from the pig pits. The liquid part is squeezed out and used on the land. I'm sure Hedgepeth sells off the solid part. They call it black gold."

"I'm glad I don't live on this side. With the smells coming from the chicken farms and the pigs, it must be unbearable in the summer."

"Agree," Shane said. "But I'm sure you get used to it if you live with it all the time."

They continued, driving past the long pig houses and up to the main house. They could see Horis on a tractor in a distant field.

When Shane laid on the horn, Horis waved, then headed their way.

They got out. While they waited, they both did visual sweeps around the house to see if anything looked out of place. It was hard to tell. Unlike Amos, who kept his property neat and orderly, Horis seemed to have some junkyard blood in his veins. There were piles of abandoned parts and machinery all over, as well as stacks of rotted firewood, old tractor tires, and a hodgepodge of other things.

"I wonder if he'd sell that truck," Shane said, pointing to a rusted old Chevy stepside on blocks to the right of the driveway. Judging by the length of the grass growing under it, it was a forgotten project.

"Ask him," she replied. Sam would like to have it, too. And he knew how to work on it where Taylor doubted Shane could tell a distributor from a dashboard.

There were workers here and there. Most looked Mexican. Some wore face masks and safety goggles.

Taylor felt envious of their masks.

The house itself was fairly big with a nice wraparound porch, but it was also a bit dilapidated, just like the few barns and outbuildings scattered around in no apparent architectural design.

Horis pulled up and cut the motor on the tractor, but he didn't climb down.

"How can I help y'all?"

"Hi Horis, how are you doing?" Taylor said.

When he nodded, the toothpick in his mouth bobbed. "Fine. You?"

"We're good. Just wanted to talk to you about what happened over at the Higgins'. Do you have a few minutes?"

"I already talked to Penner. He took my statement that day. Not much more to say. I didn't hear a thing."

"That's strange," Shane said. "I'd think as close as you are to them, you would've heard the gunshots."

"Nope."

"Well, we'd like to talk to you a bit more about it, if you could come down to the department," Shane said.

"Nah. I gotta lot of work to get done around here."

"Then we'll talk here, but you have to get off the tractor, Horis," Taylor said.

Horis murmured a few colorful words under his breath, then he made a dramatic and clumsy affair out of climbing off the tractor, moaning about his aches and pains.

Once down, he began walking toward the house.

"Well, come on. If I'm on break, I ain't gonna stand around and get more tired. Let's sit down."

He led them to the porch. They all took a seat, choosing from an array of rocking and old wooden chairs.

Taylor chose the one that looked less likely to end with her landing on the floor.

"How's the hog-farming business?" Shane asked.

"Not worth a shit, but that's not why you're here. Get to the point."

The screen door opened. Horis' wife, Cathy, came out. She was as round as she was tall. She had specks of flour in her hair and on her hands, which she rubbed on her apron.

"Well, hello, Taylor," she said, then nodded at Shane. "I didn't know we had company. Horis, did you offer them something to drink?"

"They won't be here that long," he said. "Go back in the house, Cathy. They want to talk to me about the murders."

She frowned and shook her head. "I just can't believe it. So sad.

I don't know what Beverly is going to do without Amos and David. I imagine she'll have to sell that place. That youngest son of hers sure isn't going to be able to help her run it. He has given Beverly so much trouble over the years."

"Cathy, yes, we know. He's about as useful as a screen door on a submarine, but I done told you to go inside," Horis said.

Taylor didn't think they were being fair to Danny, but she let them talk. It was smart to let people talk as much as they wanted while investigating a crime. Give them enough rope to hang themselves, as the saying went.

"I'll see you two another time," Cathy said. "I hope you have a good day."

She went back into the house.

"Horis, there was some talk about you and Amos having words about you shooting a deer on his land," Taylor said.

He leaned back in his chair, crossing his arms over his ample stomach.

Then he nodded. "Sure did. But that was nothing. And as I told him, I shot it on my land. I can't help that it ran onto his."

"Are you sure that's the way it happened?" Shane asked quietly.

Horis dropped his chair back on all fours and leaned forward, glaring at Shane. He looked like an angry toad.

"You calling me a liar?"

"No sir, I'm not. Just trying to make sure you are remembering it like it happened," Shane said respectfully.

Horis laughed dryly. "I'm a bit surprised you're bringing up the deer situation before you do the creek debate. I'm sure Danny told you about that, too, didn't he?"

He hadn't, but Taylor wasn't about to let Horis know that. She and Shane looked at each other over his head.

"He did mention it," she said. "What's your side of the story?"

"It's not a side. It's what happened. The truth of the matter is that our property boundaries are wrong and always have been. The spring starts on my land and goes fifty acres or so before it takes off onto the Higgin's land. It's no secret we've been fussing about that creek for a few decades or more."

"Why don't you just get the land surveyed to find the legal lines?" Shane asked.

"I don't need to pay someone to tell me what I already know. Amos said he didn't either, then he went and got his knickers in a wad because his side ran dry."

"Why would he blame you for that?" Taylor said. "Creeks go dry all the time."

"Because I helped it along, I reckon. Me and some boys built up a dam on my side, which I'm allowed to do because, once again, it's my land." His last words landed with emphasis, as though he was proud of himself.

"What did he do about it?" Taylor asked.

"He bulldozed it down. And I put it right back up. It's not like it was his only source of water. He's got another creek on his property, but he wants all the water around here for his beloved trees. I've got pigs, and I need it, too."

Taylor was going to talk to Beverly and Danny about the creek. See what they had to say. Water rights were a big deal in the country when farming was involved, and conflicts over them could very well escalate to something serious.

Horis pointed his finger at Taylor. "My granddaddy bought this land because of that beauty of a spring, and I can damn well decide where it flows."

"Mr. Hedgepeth, we need you to come down to the department and put all this in an official statement," she said. What they needed was to get him in the interview room to press him, with the camera on.

"Ain't nothing more official than what I say on my front porch," he replied. "This is my office, but now, I need to get back to work. That field ain't gonna plow itself."

He stood.

Shane joined him. "Before you go, what's your hypothesis about what happened on the Higgins property?"

"My hippa-thesis is that I really couldn't say. Amos had his thumb in too many pies. With that comes a lot of secrets. I knew him longer than anyone, and I can tell you that he's slicker than a boiled onion. You never knew what all he had going on because he liked to keep a lot of it under his hat."

Taylor had never seen someone use so many cliché' metaphors in one conversation. Made her wonder if Horis had ever had an original thought.

"You've already told Penner, but tell us again… Where were you and what were you doing the afternoon of the murders?" Taylor asked.

"That day, I was laid up in the house because my ankles swelled so bad that I couldn't get my boots on. Blood pressure was up, I'd say."

Taylor bit back that he might need to lay off the hush puppies and hotdogs she'd seen him often ordering from the Den.

"Oh, did you go to the doctor?" Shane asked.

"Nope. The wife made me soak 'em in Epsom salts and then prop 'em up. Stayed in my chair all day, watching "Bonanza" reruns."

"Did anyone other than your wife see you that day?" Shane asked.

"Yeah, my cousin Baitdigger. Want his number?"

"We have it," Taylor said. His wife and cousin weren't the most reliable alibis. They'd say whatever Horis wanted them to.

"What about your guns? Have you fired any recently?" Shane asked.

"Sure have. Had a pack of coyotes' out here last weekend. Shot to scare them off. Why—is that a crime?"

"What sorts of guns do you own?" Taylor asked.

"All sorts. What kind do you want?"

"Could we take a look at your collection?" Shane asked.

"You sure enough can't. Next question?" He glared at Shane.

"Thanks for talking to us, Horis, but the sheriff may still insist you come to the department," Taylor said.

"He can insist all he wants. If he wants me up there, he'll have to make up the day's pay I'll miss on my tractor."

He said it jokingly, but Taylor wouldn't put it past him to ask for it.

"I'll let him know," she said.

They left him on the porch, then walked toward the car.

"The sheriff is going to have to come out and talk to him if he wants him down at the station," Taylor said. "Horis is only going to get more stubborn."

"And he might lawyer up. I'll talk to the sheriff," Shane said. He looked at his watch. "It's getting late. Want to catch an early dinner?"

"Sorry. I already have a date."

"That grease monkey?"

Taylor was only joking about the date, but his tone and him referring to Sam as a grease monkey bothered her.

"No. With Cecil, if you must know. And Sam's a mechanic, not a monkey. A good one, too."

"I was kidding," Shane said, laughing slightly. "But really, when are you going to go out with me?"

Taylor felt like a wimp. Now was the perfect time to set him straight, but she couldn't do it. First, it would hurt his feelings. Then there was the issue about the chemistry she *did* feel with him.

It was complicated.

"I plead the fifth." She opened the car door and got in, looking straight ahead with a don't-ask-me-anything-else expression on her face.

When Taylor walked into the Den, every guy seated at the bar turned to look at her. Once again, she wished for the superpower of invisibility.

Since she didn't have that, her uniform and badge were the next best thing. It gave her a reason to hold her head high and walk with confidence she didn't feel inside. If they only knew that every time she entered a room full of people, she wished it would swallow her up.

Act your age, Taylor.

She waved at Mabel behind the bar, then nodded back politely to those who nodded at her. Alex, the fire chief, looked away when he saw it was her, and she appreciated that. Her position gave her courage, but it didn't make it any easier to be fake nice. She and Alex would never be polite with each other again, and Taylor had already added him to her list of *those who wished to do her harm*.

He was the only non-arrested person on the list. Everyone else had a vendetta because she'd slapped the cuffs on them for one reason or another. Like it was her fault they chose to break the law.

Suddenly, she remembered Clint McElroy, mentally adding him to the list, too. Her old colleague wouldn't spit on her if she were on fire. She hadn't seen him since he'd been fired, but she'd heard he'd taken a job doing security at the hospital.

She hoped that tiny bit of prestige didn't go to his head. His ego was his worst enemy.

Sissy was seated at the table with Cecil. She had a towel in her hand, but she wasn't using it. Instead, she listened to him talk. Taylor wasn't surprised. Cecil had a way of drawing people in and making them want to hear what he had to say.

"Relationships often fail not because of what was said, but because of the conversations that needed to happen but never did," he was saying as she walked up.

"Hey, that's my date," Taylor said teasingly.

Laughing, Sissy jumped up from her seat. "Well, I borrowed him for a few minutes. But I'd better get back to work before

Mabel catches me loafing. You can have him now. You want some tea?"

Taylor nodded. "Sure. And a chicken salad, please."

"Water and a chicken salad for me, too," Cecil said.

Sissy nodded and took off. Taylor slid into the booth, glad to be off her feet and the clock. It had been a long day with more than a few frustrating roadblocks in the investigation. She needed a break.

"Where's the boy?" Cecil asked.

"Home. I can't have him on the crime scene, so he stays with Cate or Lucy."

"What about Sam?"

"Him, too." She thought about Sam's request to have Diesel live with him again. She hadn't talked to him since; afraid he'd get firm about it. She still didn't know what she wanted to do.

"It's probably good for Diesel to have so much variety in his day-to-day life, I would imagine."

She shrugged. "Maybe. What was up with Sissy?"

"Oh, she was just needing a little pep talk."

"Something personal?" Taylor asked.

He nodded. "Yeah—but she'll figure it out. Tell me what's going on with you. I feel like I haven't seen you in a year. I know the investigation has you hopping. Anything promising?"

Taylor groaned and leaned back. She lowered her voice to almost a whisper.

"Well, there's one lead I'm interested in more than Shane. Someone who had a bit of a back-and-forth with Amos a month or so before the killings."

Cecil nodded. "I'm not going to ask who."

"I know you won't. Also, Shane has his eye on someone very close to Amos and David, based on some of his behaviors related to money. I don't think that one will pan out, but I guess you never know what people will do. As they say, money is the root of all evil."

"I don't believe that. Money can be used for all kinds of good in the world. It's greed that is the root of all evil."

"True. Anyway, I think we're getting closer. Something has to give. Someone is going to say something, or someone will slip up. I can't wait to slap the handcuffs on the coward who did this."

"I'm sure," Cecil said. "But how are you doing? Are you holding up? I know how deep you go. Like in Joni Stott's case. Are you keeping up with your own well-being?"

"I am. Unfortunately, things at home are tense right now. Lucy took off with Johnny, and I'm worried to death about them."

"What happened there?"

She told him about Lucy's request, the boat, and her reluctance to acknowledge that living on the water wasn't safe for a baby, but she did not tell him about Johnny's dramatic beginnings. Taylor trusted Cecil, but the fewer people who knew about 'Jack and Jill' and New York, the better.

"So, you have a decision to make. You can either let her figure it out on her own—and she might move in and then have no contact with you going forward—or you can help her through this to get access to her and Johnny again. I'm not judging… I'm just laying it out there."

"I don't want to keep enabling her," Taylor said.

"Enabling her? Is she doing drugs? Drinking?"

"No—not that I know of, but who knows what she'll do or who she'll have around once she's on her own. I must think of Johnny."

"But if you were around, you could watch for signs of backsliding in her behavior or a bad crowd coming around, couldn't you?"

He made it all sound so simple.

And he was probably right.

"So, let's talk worst-case scenario," he said.

She thought for a minute. "Well, I could help her, and she could still ban me from her life. Also, if I get the place in my name, I'm financially responsible. You know how she likes to take off with no notice."

"I thought you said she has the money to buy it outright?"

"Oh, right. But annual taxes? Slip rent? If she takes off, I'm on the hook."

"Taxes can't be much on a boat that old. And you could always pull it around to your dock and tie it up if you had to. Then sell it."

Taylor sighed loudly, staring at the ceiling.

"How do you always make such good sense out of the crazy notions spinning in my head?" she asked.

He chuckled. "Because I'm not emotionally attached, so I can see things more clearly."

Sissy arrived with their plates, setting them down. "We've got hot apple pie if you want it."

"Thanks," Taylor said. "But I'll pass. If I eat more than this, I'll go into a food coma. I have a lot to do when I get home."

"I'll take a thin slice," Cecil said, smiling up at Sissy.

"I got you. I'll even drop a dollop of vanilla ice cream on it. Taylor, you sure?"

"I'm sure. My hips are telling my lips to say no."

"I hear you on that," Sissy said, laughing as she walked away, though she surely had nothing to worry about when it came to saying no to calories. She was built like a model.

"So have you decided what to do?" Cecil asked.

"I guess so. If I can find her."

"You said the boat was in a slip at the Redneck Yacht Club. I'd start there. Maybe the owner let her move in while she gets everything in order."

That was likely. Lucy said the woman was super nice.

"I'll look for her tomorrow after work. If I can get off before midnight."

He laid his fork down. "What about Cate? And Jackson?"

"That's more drama. Dad traded that old camper for a van and gave it to Cate, but the same day he did, she told him she wasn't interested in pursuing a relationship. Now he's gone silent. I'm going to have to try to find time to check on him."

"He needs to respect that Cate has been through a lot. Trauma doesn't happen to you in a way that you can eventually shake off. It happens in you, and she's carrying her experiences around. It's going to take her a long time to even begin healing."

"Can you call him and tell him that?" she said, winking.

"I'd love to talk to him. I miss my old friend."

He looked suddenly sad.

"I'm sorry, Cecil. You know it's not you. He's ashamed he let you down, and I think he can't stand it that you know he's not sober."

"Oh, I know that, girl. You don't have to tell me about shame. I lived with it for decades myself. Let me tell you a little secret. Shame is nothing more than the fear that you aren't good enough."

She thought about it for a second. "You are absolutely right."

"I know I am, and I'm right about something else, too. One day, he'll lay that burden down. I just wish he'd let me help him carry it until he's ready."

Taylor stared at Cecil, noting the deep crags and grooves in his face, the lines around his eyes and the gray over his ears. She thought of his family, wondering how they could've just dropped him from their lives.

"Cecil, how did you get to be so special?"

He smiled gently. "I'm not any more special than you are, Taylor. We just lucked out when we found each other."

CHAPTER 14

$\mathcal{C}$ate finished spraying down the last of the kennels, then hung the hose on the wall. It had been a glorious morning of being busy, stretching muscles and instant gratification with every kennel she cleaned and food bowl she filled. Even though she hadn't had much of an opportunity to interact with any animals, other than a greeting here and there, she already knew she was going to love her job.

"Cate—next week, I'll have the girls train you to do pet intake, so you'll get a break from the grunt work once in a while," Angela said, coming through the door.

"That sounds good, but honestly, I don't mind the grunt work."

"Now see, that's the kind of attitude you just can't get with the young crowd who come through here like it's a revolving door. You also move like your butt is on fire. But this generation wants a job they can do with one hand and be on their phones with the other."

Cate laughed. She had noticed the girls up front tended to be glued to their phones every chance they got, looking at their profiles and everyone else's they knew or didn't know. Cate didn't understand the draw everyone seemed to have at looking at everyone else's lives on the screen.

"Once we get you feeling comfortable, I'm going to have you help with evaluations since you've got experience in training," Angela said. "Sometimes, the girls aren't brave enough. Then there are the difficult people who come through the door that we must deal with."

"We had a doozy up there this morning," Cate said. Before Angela had arrived to get her started in the kennels, she'd sat up front.

"Oh yeah? What happened?"

"A woman brought in her six cats just to be desexed. Sarah explained to her that she could've gotten it done at a discount at the clinic, and the lady said she wanted it done for free."

"Oh, Lordie," Angela said. "Was it Mrs. Hetrick?"

"Yes, I think that was her name."

Angela rolled her eyes. "She is always trying to do that. She has a ton of cats and can well afford their care. I'm sure Sarah told her she'd have to relinquish them for us to do it?"

"Yes, she did. Then Mrs. Hetrick said she'd just let them all be put down and it would be our fault. Then she flounced out."

Angela chuckled. "She always says that, too, and she'll do no such thing. She loves her cats."

"I figured."

"Believe me, Mrs. Hetrick is a minor personality compared to others who come through here. Just wait—you'll be collecting some stories."

"I look forward to it."

Angela nodded. "Also, I'd like you to keep an eye on the animals as you work, then report to me if you see anything that needs attention, whether health or behavior related."

"Will do."

Angela leaned against the wall and took her phone out, then

scanned through it while Cate filled water bowls. She finally looked up.

"Good job on the clean-up duty. You can spend the rest of the afternoon rotating dogs outside for playtime or walks. Just use your judgment to determine which they need."

"Great. I'll get right on that." Cate couldn't hide her smile. She was thrilled to be able to have some animal contact. Not only that, but it felt surreal and so very good to have someone talk to her with respect. In the prison, she been talked to like a child, but with demands and no manners. Demands to do things differently. Faster. Better.

All under constant watch.

That was behind her, and life was feeling good.

Well, except for the fact that they didn't know where Lucy had gone, and Cate missed her and Johnny. And Diesel might be leaving them.

Then there was the issue of Anna.

Cate was worried about her. She just didn't seem happy.

The girls thought it was only because Anna was living a different sort of life, in another tax bracket than they were, but Cate didn't think that was it. Her Anna was still in there somewhere under the perfect wife and mother that her husband expected her to be.

"Any specific order to the rotation, Angela?"

Angela shook her head. "Just whatever works. I'll talk to you later."

She disappeared. Cate went to the kennel that held Nala, a large black Cane Corso that had been abandoned more than eight months before with no interest from any potential adopters yet. She was a teddy bear, but her size was the first thing that people saw and immediately turned away from.

"Come on, old girl." She slowly climbed off the elevated bed she was napping on and came to the gate. Cate put the leash around her neck. She led her down the galley between the rows of kennels, then outside to a fenced play area where she immediately took the leash off.

Nala looked up at her with a questioning expression.

"Go ahead. Walk around. Play. Sniff and pee all over."

Slowly, Nala began sauntering around. She was depressed. Cate could see it in the way she carried herself, her expansive chest seeming to cave inward and her ears downward.

Angela had told her that Nala had been a puppy when her family bought her from an expensive breeder. They thought they'd known all about her breed, including her eventual size and usual temperament. And maybe they had. The Cane Corso was known to be loyal and even affectionate, but only with their people. They didn't normally warm up to strangers, and they were mostly indifferent to other dogs.

They were intensely protective, too. Once Nala grew from a cute and manageable puppy to a healthy ninety pounds and began to intimidate the family's relatives and the children's friends, it should've been a cue that they were remiss in training her. They'd been a young family with busy lives who said they had no extra time for training.

Instead, they'd decided she hadn't been the right dog for their family.

After the evaluation, Nala had a diagnosis of diabetes, so none of the rescue groups would take her either.

Nala walked up to the fence that faced the highway. She gazed out as though trying to will her people to drive up, say they'd made a mistake, and tell her she could come home now.

It infuriated Cate how people treated dogs—as they would a designer purse or a new car—after a time of trying them out, they'd discard them or trade them in for something else.

Now Nala missed the only family she'd ever known. To make it worse, no one else was brave enough to give her a chance to prove she wasn't vicious.

People were strange.

Sarah had told her they'd once had a customer return a cat she'd adopted over a year ago, stating she only wanted kittens and would like to exchange it. Sarah had asked her what she was going to do when the new cat was no longer a kitten.

That hadn't crossed the woman's mind yet.

And that was the reason Cate would rather spend her time with animals.

In her biggest fantasy, she owned a large piece of land that she could turn into a sanctuary for the dogs deemed unadoptable. A place they could be loved and cared for into their golden years.

Nala returned to Cate and went into a sit, gazing up at her as if asking 'what now?'

Cate looked at her watch, then dropped to the ground and patted her lap. "Now you get five minutes of full-on cuddling. Come on, girl."

When the big dog climbed tentatively onto Cate's lap and peeked up for reassurance, Cate said a prayer of thanksgiving she was getting to be there, at that moment, with that dog, while living her new life.

~

Cate pulled into Anna's driveway, relieved she didn't see Pete's car. Though she'd enjoyed her day at the shelter, she was too tired to deal with being around him and how he'd make her feel. It was clear he didn't approve of Cate being around the children, but she wasn't ready to give up on them yet. Not until she got the same feeling from Anna.

Anna didn't know it, but she needed some motherly advice.

Cate would have to figure out how to give that advice without sounding like she was trying to be that mother.

Anna stepped out the side door. When Cate got out, her daughter wore a grimace.

"What in the world are you driving, Cate?"

129

Cate took that as an indication Anna was going to be somewhat receptive to an unannounced visit, and she proceeded to the porch.

"I know, I know. I told Jackson it looks like a kidnapper's van, but he got it for the right price. Since I need transportation, I accepted."

"Are you seriously going to have that as your regular mode of transportation?"

Anna hadn't yet invited Cate in, so Cate stood there at the bottom of the porch stairs, staring at her daughter. "Yep. At least until I get enough money put back to get a *regular* car," Cate said, laughing over the word *regular*. "Are the kids here?"

Anna shook her head. "No. They rode their bikes down to the clubhouse to play pool."

Clubhouse. The neighborhood was even fancier than Cate thought. "Oh, okay. I thought I'd stop by and say hello. If that's okay…"

"Come on in, I guess," Anna said. "We can chat for a minute, but I don't want to call them in early because it's rare for them to have an evening without structured events."

Cate followed Anna into the side door of the kitchen. It smelled like something Italian was cooking, then she saw a pot of sauce bubbling on the stove. Anna went over to it and stirred.

"You're quite the cook, I hear," Cate said. "Did you take lessons?"

"As a matter of fact, I did. Since I didn't have a mother to teach me, Pete's parents hired a private chef when we got married. For the first year, she let me watch her prepare everything, then during the second year, I let her go and took over myself."

Cate ignored the passive-aggressive comment because she deserved it. She leaned on the breakfast bar. "That's quite an achievement."

"Pete thought so," Anna said. "His parents were a bit miffed that I no longer needed or wanted the chef, but they got over it after they had a few of my meals."

Cate laughed softly. She wanted to tell Anna she was proud of her tenacity, but after the 'mother' comment, it wouldn't feel genuine, so she'd wait for another day.

"Are you feeling okay, Anna?" Cate asked instead.

Anna was dressed well, her hair and makeup done subtly, but she looked fragile.

Cate had noticed it a few other times. That was what she wanted to talk to her about. Giving a bit more to herself instead of to her endless pursuit to be the perfect wife and mother.

"I'm fine. Why do you ask?"

"Oh, I don't know. You seem a bit on edge lately. I know you juggle a lot between making sure the kids get where they need to be, their school stuff, and Pete. I just want you to know if there's anything I can do to help, I'll try."

Anna looked suspicious. "Didn't you just start a new job?"

"I sure did. But I'm not working full-time yet. I have time on Wednesday and Friday afternoons."

"Oh. Well, no, I don't need anything," Anna said, then took a swig of white wine from a glass Cate hadn't seen until that moment.

When Anna saw her look, she laughed. "Kids aren't here so I'm starting on my two-glass limit a bit early. Would you like some?"

"No, thank you. I don't drink wine." Cate slid onto the barstool.

"Would you like a soft drink? Sparkling water? I have just about anything you could want."

"A glass of plain water would be nice." Cate had no idea that water could sparkle, and she wasn't eager to test it.

Anna got a glass from a cabinet, then carried it to the refrigerator dispenser. She filled it half full of ice, then to the top with water. Even their fridge was high-tech—not only did it have ice and water dispensers, but it also had a flat-screen TV embedded in the doors, which now showed the news. Her daughter had sure come a long way from her childhood.

"So, do you like this neighborhood?" Cate asked. She hated that it felt so awkward to make conversation, and Anna wasn't making it any easier.

"Yes, we do. There are paved trails for walking and biking and even a small dog park."

"Oh, do you have a dog?" Cate didn't remember seeing one before.

"No, not yet. Pete says the kids aren't responsible enough yet. But when we do get one, we'll have a great place to play with it."

"You could also do that at Taylor's house, right?"

Anna shook her head. "No. Too untamed. Besides, her dog is probably infested with fleas and ticks."

Cate chuckled. "No, he's not. I've checked. But I guess having a manicured park would be nice, too."

"Pete loves the gym at the clubhouse, too. I mean, we have an exercise room here in the house, but sometimes he likes to have company when he works out."

Cate realized Anna had not yet offered her a tour of the house, even though she'd been there a few times now.

She'd only seen the kitchen and living room.

Like a visitor.

Or a stranger.

"Do you work out with him?"

"No. He says he doesn't like it when a woman has muscles. But I keep in shape by walking with a few of my friends. We go three mornings a week, and I play tennis."

"Well, you look beautiful. I don't think you have to worry too much," Cate said.

Anna raised her eyebrows. "You'd be surprised at the competition around here. I swear, Pete's friends keep marrying younger women all the time. It's ridiculous, and I do not want to be a statistic. Nor a single mother raising two kids."

Cate unconsciously wrinkled her brow. "Is that something you worry about, Anna? Because that can't be good for your mental well-being."

Anna smiled wryly. "No, not really. I just want to continue to look like the woman Pete married. Not pull a bait-and-switch as some wives do."

That was concerning. Anna was going to have to face the fact that no one stayed young. Pete wouldn't stay the same either, not unless he was a vampire. Cate hoped that belief wasn't something he was telling Anna—that he expected her not to age—because that was just absurd. While most couples were first physically attracted to one another, the love for who they were on the inside should grow stronger than who they were on the outside. Beauty faded, after all.

Anna slipped into some talk about the women who went to the country club events with her—who was getting Botox, and who needed it. Every so often, she nervously glanced up at the clock, then back to Cate.

She was hoping Cate would leave before Pete got home.

Cate watched her talk, then had another epiphany. Anna was the most successful and well-set of all four of her daughters, but if Cate didn't know any better, she'd also say Anna was also the unhappiest. Anna could pretend all she wanted to, and probably made others believe she loved the life she'd built for herself, but Cate could see through it, and that broke her heart.

When Anna paused, Cate stood and put her glass in the sink.

"Well, I'd better be going and let you get back to what you need to do."

Anna didn't try to stop her.

"I'll tell the kids you said hello," she said. "Drive carefully."

"I will. Thanks, Anna." More awkwardness as Cate slid out the door and let it close gently behind her. It felt like an interaction with a bank teller, not a mother and daughter.

She went to the van and started it, then slowly backed out of the driveway, hoping it hadn't left an oil spot but too worried to look.

It would've been nice to have had a deeper conversation with Anna, but it just wasn't time. The invisible boundaries her daughter put up glared at Cate, stopping her from putting her foot in her mouth about materialism, the pursuit of perfection, and how it could wreak havoc on one's psyche.

When Cate had first gone to prison, after her family, of course, she'd missed so many *things*. She had never been well off or had expensive items, but even the longing for something like a soft blanket, nice shampoo, or good jeans—it all messed with her mind those first years.

Her worldly possessions consisted of a hard cot, a scratchy blanket, a flat pillow, and a few books. Plus, the few cheap hygiene items she could get from the commissary with the money Jackson put on her books. Sometimes, there'd be enough left for a few cups of noodles a week.

Sometimes not.

Her most prized possessions were the few snapshots of the girls taped on the wall over her bunk.

It was only after she'd lost her desire for things that didn't matter that she finally felt free. Not free of the bars or walls—she'd still been a prisoner without the freedom to live her life or the choice in how to live it—but losing the craving for owning material things made her sentence easier to bear.

Then it was only the craving of feeling her children's arms around her neck or their cheeks against hers that tortured her during her long nights. That was a desire that never left her, even when beyond her reach or attention, they'd grown into adults. She'd still pictured them as little girls—even Taylor, an old soul even as a child—who still needed a mommy.

Cate shook off those thoughts, bringing herself back to the present.

Materialism.

She didn't want it.

Nor social status or recognition.

Everyone else could have it.

She never again wanted to be the person who hoped to own a luxury car, a designer purse, or a big, fancy house in a neighborhood with paved trails.

The parts of herself that had let that kind of stuff go so many decades before were parts she wanted to keep. She'd learned the most important things weren't *things*. They were the moments a mother spent with her children, their arms around her neck or their cheeks next to hers. The loyalty they so easily gave and the trust that was already there.

Until it was broken.

Those were the things she had lost.

Whether she'd ever get any of it back again was a mystery.

CHAPTER 15

*T*aylor went back to the cruiser, got in, and backed out of the driveway. The next house was a few miles ahead. She was glad to be out working alone today. It gave her time to think. Not only about the investigation, but also about Lucy and how to approach her, if she could even find her.

First, though, Taylor needed to get something fresh to bring back to Shane and the sheriff, or she might never get to work on another investigation again.

She had read once that solving nearly any crime depended on something that seemed to bear nothing related to the crime at first glance. Today, she planned to talk to as many neighbors around the Higgin's farm as she could find.

She had already stopped by and talked to a few, driving more than fifteen miles away, asking them to think back to that day and tell her everything they remembered.

Every noise. Every car. Every person.

Every anything.

So far, her notes consisted of mundane things that everyone saw in the country.

Mail carrier and the Fed Ex truck.

Kids on a four-wheeler going by.
Propane truck out for deliveries.
So and so plowing their field, or a neighbor walking their dog.

Absolutely nothing out of the ordinary and no strangers or unrecognized vehicles. Penner had already questioned the mail route carrier and the Fed Ex employee. They'd seen nothing on their routes that day, either.

It was infuriating. They were missing something.

People were still nervous, too. Several had to go through multiple deadbolts before opening the door to her. That was something different for most of Hart's Ridge residents, who prided themselves on not even locking their doors during the day.

Taylor always recommended people lock their doors. Now too many things could happen. All they had to do was turn on the evening news or an episode of "Dateline" to see that tragedy was lurking around every small town.

She pulled into the road next to a mailbox with **Dobbs** written across it in white paint.

The Dobbs were an older, quiet couple. They'd once farmed on their land, raising goats and donkeys, selling them off, but like many of Hart's Ridge's older population, they gave it up once it got too physically demanding. They had children, but the farm wasn't in their dreams to take over and they'd built their careers elsewhere.

Taylor saw Clarence Dobbs occasionally in town at the Den, picking up dinner to take home for him and Lynn to eat. She didn't come out much at all and Taylor couldn't remember the last time she'd seen her.

There were no more animals there and as she drove up to the house, everything was eerily quiet.

She shut off the car and climbed out, looking around to make sure no dogs were coming after her before she shut the door.

All was clear so she went up to the porch and knocked.

Lynn opened the door a crack, then all the way when she saw Taylor. But her eyes were wide with worry.

"What is it, Taylor? Is there another murder?"

"No, no, Mrs. Dobbs. I'm just here to chat for a minute."

"Well, come on in. I've got lemonade if you'd like some. Clarence is taking a nap. Well, another one."

Taylor went in, following Lynn to the kitchen. She smelled mothballs, but everything looked neat as a pin.

"Sit at the table. I'm so glad you stopped by. I want to ask you all about what happened. I've been worrying myself sick over it." She shuffled to the cabinet and got a glass, then to the fridge for the lemonade.

She brought it and a few Fig Newtons from a cookie jar over to Taylor on a flowered napkin, as though serving a six-year-old.

"Thank you, Mrs. Dobbs. There's not much to tell you. It's still an active investigation. But I'd like to hear what you remember from that day."

Lynn sat down. "It was just like any other day. You know, I'm somewhat of a closet detective myself. I love to watch "Forensic Files" and all that stuff on the Investigation channels."

"Really?" Taylor asked politely. She sipped at the lemonade.

"Yes," Lynn said, nodding emphatically. "I watched everything I could find when they were looking for that Gabby girl. What was her last name? I can never remember it. Pettit? Pppp... P-something."

"Petito."

"Right. I said all along that she was in that national forest. They should've gone in sooner. Maybe they could've saved that girl. It's just a tragedy what that boy did. Strangled her, then claimed she hit her head. Her poor parents."

"It was sad. But to be fair, he had killed her long before anyone knew she was missing." Taylor wasn't exactly sure about that fact. It happened a few years ago. The details were fuzzy now, but she never approved of armchair detectives trying to second guess the work of those on the ground doing the investigations. There was a lot that went on behind the scenes that most people didn't know.

She did remember that the boyfriend committed suicide by a gunshot to the head. A cowardly but solid answer to whether he'd killed the girl or not. No one doubted it after that.

"So, were you and Clarence home all day on the day of the incident at the Higgin's farm?"

"Yes. When I heard the news, since we live so close, I knew we'd be questioned and have to recall the details. Hold on a minute." She got up, went to a kitchen drawer, pulled out a notebook, then flipped to a page.

"You wrote it all down?"

"Yes," Lynn said, her eyebrows furrowed. "Why? Does that make me look guilty? Like I'm trying to create an alibi? I never thought of that. Am I a suspect?"

Taylor suppressed a grin. Mrs. Dobbs was into true crime—and as far away from being a suspect as one could get.

"No, you're not a suspect, Mrs. Dobbs. Nor is Clarence. I'm just surprised and pleased you were so thorough."

Lynn smiled proudly. "Did you know I used to work for the IRS? Our jobs depended on being thorough. Old habits die hard."

She took a pen and pecked at the paper.

"It's all here. I got up at seven o'clock and fed the cat, then cleaned the litter box. Clarence was up soon after. I cooked him eggs, bacon, and toast with elderberry jam." She paused. "He doesn't know that jam is good for his immune system. But don't tell him or he won't want it again."

Taylor took a bite of the Fig Newton, suddenly glad she'd stopped by.

Lynn was priceless.

"After I cleaned up the kitchen, I made myself presentable. I don't do a lot, mind you, just a tad of mascara and some lip gloss. Pinch my cheeks to give them some color. I know we've been married forever, but I try to keep myself up for Clarence, even if we aren't leaving the house. There's a lot of old widows in town who'd scoop him up in a minute."

Taylor nodded solemnly. "I understand. Where was Clarence while you were doing that?"

"He was outside stacking the firewood. He gets angry that he can't cut ours himself anymore. We wasted all that money getting his shoulder operated on, but now it ain't worth a darn. Clarence can't even hold his arm up long enough to change a lightbulb, much less chop wood. Chipper gives us a good deal, but he wants an extra ten bucks to stack it and Clarence says at least that's something he can do on his own. Chipper was nice enough to offer again that morning, but my husband is a stubborn old fool."

"Okay, then what?" Taylor was starting to get worried about the time. She couldn't spend the whole day there if Lynn was going to draw it out minute-by-minute. She didn't want to be rude, but she was going to have to wiggle out. Somehow.

Lynn began telling her about all the shows she'd watched, the times and plots, pinpointing every half hour of her day, as well as everything her husband did.

If Taylor didn't know better, it would look suspicious, but Lynn was harmless. Not exactly precise and to the point, but definitely harmless.

"When I walked to the mailbox, that Mundell girl went by. The one who drives that old blue Honda with the green driver's door. You remember, she wrecked it in front of Hardee's last year. She can probably tell you more about who was at the Higgins that day."

"Wait—you saw who?" Taylor was suddenly more alert.

"The Mundell girl that Beverly's youngest boy dates. She's Carol's daughter. Did you know Carol has been married three times and is divorced again?"

"No. No, I didn't." Taylor was only half listening now. "You must mean Stacy."

Carol's other two daughters were married, and Danny used to

have a thing with Stacy. But they had asked him if he was dating anyone now, and he'd said no. She remembered Danny and Stacy had broken up a few years back when Amos stepped in and helped his son get back on track. Word around town was that Stacy was a terrible influence.

That maybe they were back together again was an interesting piece of news.

However, Lynn could be wrong, and Stacy may not have even been to the Higgins' farm. Taylor was going to have to talk to Danny again. And Stacy—as soon as she could get a new address on her. Stacy and her mom jumped rentals quite a bit.

"Then after I got the mail, I came in and called my sister. She moved up to Ohio, and what a mistake. Their winters are no joke," Lynn said. "Last year, they had ten inches of snow!"

It took Taylor forty minutes to get Lynn to wrap it up so she could slide out the door and into her car, so sleepy she wished she could pull over and take a nap. Instead, she checked the monitor. When she saw nothing was pressing, she started the cruiser and headed to the department.

She needed coffee after that marathon.

The last name on her list wasn't going to happen. It was Carlos' wife, but she had asked permission to take the baby and leave the state to stay with her parents indefinitely. They'd had her at the station for a lengthy interview right after the incident, and she claimed Carlos had no enemies and was not involved in anything unsavory. She didn't come right out and say it, but Taylor could feel her resentment toward Danny, as though she blamed him. When pressed, she said she didn't have any reason to think the crime had to do with Danny, but she didn't trust him.

The drive was peaceful, and Taylor wished she had Diesel with her. She wasn't giving him enough attention now, she knew that. He never seemed to mind, though. He was as ecstatic to see her as always, no matter how many hours she was gone. The sadness he'd shown for the first few months had dried up once Sam showed up, replaced with a zest for life.

Right on cue, her phone beeped.

Hi. Come hang out at the old ballfield with me and Diesel. Sam.

He'd have to wait for a response until she stopped, but there was no way she had time for that. First, she needed to check back in with the sheriff and Shane, then dealing with Lucy was next on the agenda.

She drove a few more miles before the phone beeped again, reminding her she hadn't responded to Sam's message. She found herself doing math in her head after glancing at the clock.

Maybe a short detour wouldn't be a big deal. She'd love to see Diesel.

Tapping her nails against the steering wheel nervously, she made good time to the ballfield.

She could see Sam in the pitcher's area, throwing a tennis ball to Diesel, who waited motionless until the ball left Sam's hand, then darted out after it. Joy quivered through every muscle as he ran.

He was beautiful.

She got out, walked over, then slipped through the old gate.

When Sam smiled, warmth rushed through her.

"Deputy! I'm innocent, please don't arrest me," Sam yelled, then held his hands up in surrender.

She laughed.

"One more throw and I'll meet you at the bench," he called. By then, Diesel was back. He dropped the ball at Sam's feet, then practically pranced around as he waited to go after it again.

Sam threw it, then headed to the bench while Diesel's back was turned.

He sat next to her.

"It's a beautiful day. I'm glad you could take a breather and come out."

"It sure is. Luckily, I've been in my car most of the morning going to different places, so I've had the windows open. You don't have work today?"

He nodded. "I have a catalytic converter to put on, but it won't take me long. Just thought I'd give Diesel some exercise."

"You get all moved in?" Diesel ran up, his ears on full alert once he saw her.

"Pretty much. I need a new microwave. The one I had bit the dust."

"Geez. Microwaves usually last forever. Is that all you cook with?" Taylor teased.

"Nope. Pop got me an air fryer last year. Between the two, I can make a four-course meal." He laughed, too.

When they stopped, she looked at her phone. "I can't stay but a minute. They're expecting me back at the department."

Sam got up and sat on the bench in front of her. He swung his legs over, so they were facing each other.

He put his hands on her knees. Taylor's armpits instantly started to perspire.

"Then I'll get right to the point. I want to thank you for helping me bring Diesel back into my life."

"You've already thanked me many times. But you're welcome." She hoped he wasn't going to push her on getting him full-time again. She still wasn't ready to say yes.

He seemed suddenly nervous. "I'm not only glad to have him back in my life, Taylor. I'm glad to have you in it, too. What I want to say is that I care about you."

Now it was awkward.

Taylor hated talking about feelings.

"Um… I care about you, too, Sam."

"No. I like—*care* about you. A lot. Hell, what I mean is I want to ask you out on a date. A real date, not just a hike with Diesel or ten minutes here in the ballpark. I want to spend time with you alone."

His words tumbled out in a rush. He sounded nervous—it left Taylor speechless.

She couldn't feign total surprise. Of course, she'd felt something between them. A bit of flirting, maybe some sexual tension. But her life was so complicated right now she hadn't pursued it, or even acknowledged it, to decide if she wanted to take it another step forward.

So much for him being the shy type.

"I don't know what to say, Sam. Things right now are complicated with my mother coming to stay and the investigation, plus this whole thing with Diesel. It's—"

He held his hand up, then put his finger to her lips gently.

"Shh. Don't turn me down. Just don't say anything right now. Think about it. I know what I want, and I'm not going to rush you. I'll wait. We could go after you tie up this case, or before. Whatever you want. I just want the chance to show you how much I appreciate you."

Her face flamed. *Why would he even want her?*

"I know you need to go. I'll drop Diesel off at your house when I leave so he'll be there when you get home. But just think about it, Taylor," he said, then got up.

"I—yes, I need to go. The sheriff is going to be looking for me." And Shane. She didn't mention him, but he was also waiting. Suddenly, she was in her cruiser, driving away... and she didn't even remember saying goodbye.

CHAPTER 16

"Give me one second," Shane said, barely looking up from his computer as Taylor entered his office and went to the whiteboard.

She took a marker and made her notes.

Lynn/Clarence Dobbs: Mail carrier, Fed Ex, Peabody's Propane, Chipper Dayne, Stacy Mundell

She finished and sat down.

Shane stopped pecking at the computer to see what she'd written.

"We already have a statement from the mail carrier on that route. They didn't see anything out of the ordinary. Also, the Fed Ex guy was questioned. And the propane driver. He didn't stop at the Higgins. Went on by. Who is Stacy Mundell?"

"Danny used to date her a few years back. Lynn Dobbs said she saw her go by when she went out to check the mail."

"They dating again?"

"He said he wasn't dating anyone, remember? It could just be a coincidence, but we'd better talk to him about it."

"I told you he's hiding something."

She shrugged. "We'll see. I'll bring her in, too. See what she says about being out in that area. If I can find her."

Shane nodded toward the board. "Chipper Dayne? The firewood guy?"

"Yep. He brought out a load."

"Wait a minute." Shane slid the crime binder over and started flipping through it. He stopped at a page and ran his finger down it, then stopped and thumped it.

"What is it?"

"Penner took a statement from Dayne last week. He said he was out that way delivering the day before, but not the day of the murders. That day, he said he was working a short-term construction job on the other side of the county."

"Lynn might have her timeline confused," Taylor said. "I'll check on it again, just to be sure. She made a note on her phone."

When she looked up, Shane stared at her.

"Let's get Danny in here again, too. We'll see if we can get him to talk about the girl without directly naming her."

"I'm on it," Taylor said, pulling her phone out. She texted Danny to ask him when he could come. "He might take a while to answer. I know he doesn't want to come back up here."

"Tell him he doesn't have a choice." Shane stood and picked up the binder. "I gotta go. I have a meeting with the sheriff. But close that door for a minute."

Taylor gave the door a slight push, and it clicked shut.

"Come around here and let me show you something," Shane said, pointing at his computer.

When she went around, he moved over a bit to let her come up next to him. The computer wasn't even on.

"What?"

Before she could even react, he put his arm around her and

leaned in, then kissed her on the mouth. It wasn't a long kiss, but it was long enough before she pulled away, both hands on his chest before she dropped them to her sides.

"What are you doing?" she said, backing up until she was against the wall and there was at least a foot of space between them.

"What I've been dying to do for months now. I'm sorry. I couldn't wait another day. Taylor, we need to talk. About us."

"Shane, you can't do that stuff here. If someone had walked in —what if the sheriff had seen you? Please, don't do that again."

She was flustered. Alarmed, too.

"Then when can I do it? Can I see you tonight?"

"No. I have plans tonight with Lucy." She left his office before he could say anything else. She went to the restroom and closed herself in a stall, as though hiding from everyone else so they wouldn't see the evidence on her face. Her heart pounded out of her chest.

Ridiculous. This wasn't junior high.

The kiss wasn't bad, though it had mortified her. Why? She wasn't exactly sure. She had always had feelings for Shane, so this wasn't completely out of the realm of possibilities. He'd already made it obvious he was jealous of her having Sam as a friend.

Speaking of Sam—her face flamed with guilt again. He'd admitted he had feelings for her, but it wasn't like they were dating.

He'd be crushed if he knew about the kiss, though.

Taylor exited the stall. She couldn't hide there forever.

In the mirror, she peered at herself, noting her mascara had worn off and too many hairs had sprung free of the usually meticulous bun she wore. She could use some lip gloss or—well, she didn't know quite what, but something.

What had happened to suddenly make her irresistible? She was still the same serious, plain woman she'd always been. What she did know was that it made her already messy life a whole lot messier.

149

∼

Jo's apartment was small but cute. The sparse decorations were colorful and made it look homey. Jo tended toward the Bohemian style, so colorful throws and rugs peppered the living room and her bedroom. The rips and stains on the couch were barely noticeable with the way she'd artfully arranged the pillows and fabrics.

Peeking out from under the rugs, Taylor could see the carpet had bad spots, probably too far gone to be cleaned. Not surprising, considering the cheap cost of the rent.

In the kitchen was a tiny bistro table with two chairs. A small vase of three faux sunflowers made up the centerpiece. Jo had a thing for sunflowers. She even had a tattoo of one on her back shoulder.

"I got the table and chairs off Marketplace for twenty bucks," Jo said. "A quick sanding down and a can of green paint made it look good, didn't it?"

"Sure did."

"The craft store had those sunflowers for seventy-five percent off, and the vase was a dollar at the thrift store."

"It looks so nice, Jo."

Her sister was talented like that. She could find any old thing and do something to make it usable. When they were kids, it was Jo who found the best pieces in the miles of racks at Goodwill, putting them together to make outfits that were close to what other kids were wearing at school.

Over the couch were framed snapshots of Jo and Levi in different settings. The frames were mismatched, but all painted a glittery silver.

Jo sure knew how to make something out of nothing.

"Come see my room," Levi said.

Taylor followed him in to see it wasn't decorated in any sort of specific theme like most boys' rooms. A navy-and-white quilt covered a neatly made twin bed with a tall bookshelf stacked full of superhero figures beside it. Another colorful, but worn, rug covered the old carpet.

There were a few books scattered among the model cars and other knickknacks on a smaller shelf.

Taylor wondered how Jo was able to provide so much for Levi on the sparse amount of money she made. Somehow, she'd always made it work. She'd proved a single mom could raise a well-adjusted boy.

"Nice, Levi. Glad to see you keep it cleaned up," Taylor said from the doorway.

"Mama does it, usually," he admitted sheepishly, kicking a wad of dirty socks under the bed.

Taylor ruffled his hair. He was such a cute kid. Honest, too.

"You two ready?" Jo called from the living room.

"Coming," Taylor said.

She hadn't planned to pick up Jo and Levi, but after she'd left the department, she'd had an epiphany. Lucy wouldn't lose her temper in front of Levi. Yes, Taylor was using him, but it was all for the good of the family.

Lucy's secrets were safe with her, but Taylor felt Jo would be on her side when it came to the safety of Johnny around water. Mother to mother kind of thing. Maternal wisdom that Taylor couldn't lay claim to.

They left the apartment, heading down to the parking lot.

"Can I ride in the back of the truck?" Levi asked.

"No!" Both Taylor and Jo said at the same time, then laughed.

"Not safe, buddy," Taylor added.

"I knew you'd say no," he replied glumly. "But I get the door, Mom. You sit in the middle."

It was a quick ride to the lake park where Lucy had said the boat was in a rented slip. It had a gate with a code, but luckily someone else was going in so Taylor slid in behind them before the gate closed.

Surprise to Taylor, but the Redneck Yacht Club wasn't so

151

redneck anymore. She hadn't been there in ages, and she noticed it looked as though the two long docks with more than twenty boat slips each had been renovated not too long ago.

The rest of the park appeared upgraded, too. It wasn't at any sort of country club level and wouldn't meet Anna's approval, but it was nice enough. The bathhouse wasn't new, but it looked freshly painted with no trash laying around like most of the boat landing facilities tended to have. The grass was kept short, though a bit of weed eating needed to be done around the edges.

"How are we going to know which boat it is?" Jo asked.

"I guess we just look for Lucy," Taylor said.

She pulled into a parking space.

"There's her car," Levi said, pointing it out a few rows away.

"Good. She's here." Taylor's pulse raced. She couldn't wait to get home and put this day behind her. Close herself in her room and take a long, hot bath. It had been full of stressful situations and anxiety.

She wasn't up for a battle with Lucy, but she'd promised Cecil she'd try. It wasn't easy to admit, but Lucy had a way of reaching the most tender part inside Taylor and leaving her mark. Her off-and-on rejection always left the deepest cuts. Cecil had reminded her that relationships didn't come packaged in perfection—that they only came wrapped with potential—and they couldn't survive if only one half was doing all the work. Meaning, Lucy was going to need to put on her big-girl pants and compromise.

Levi was so excited to get to the docks that she barely had the motor turned off before he leaped out of the truck. Jo followed, and Taylor trailed a bit.

"Which one?" he yelled when he got to the water's edge. He excitedly gestured to the dock on either side.

When Taylor shrugged, Levi chose the left dock. He hit the wood running. A man sitting on the deck of the first houseboat scolded him.

"No running," he said. "You might slip and fall in."

Levi stopped in his tracks, glancing back at Jo.

"You heard him," she said. "Mind your manners."

"Yes, sir," Levi said, then walked with an exaggerated slow swagger.

When they caught up, they saw the man leaning back on a lounge chair, holding a glass of wine.

He nodded politely. "Good evening. Y'all with the new girl?"

Taylor nodded. "I guess so. She's got a baby."

"Don't have to tell me," he said. "The little guy cried for at least two hours last night when I was trying to sleep. I finally walked over there, took that baby from her, and walked one lap to the end of the dock and back, he was sound asleep. She's the fourth boat on the right."

"Um—thank you?" Jo said.

"You work for Sheriff Dawkins?" he asked, eyeing Taylor's uniform, his gaze pausing on the gun at her hip.

"I do."

"Figured." He nodded and looked like he wanted to say something else, but he didn't.

"Have a nice evening," Jo said as they moved past him.

"That was fast," Taylor whispered. "Only Lucy would trust a stranger to walk off with her kid on a dock, surrounded by water. See what I mean? She needs to come back to my house."

"Aw, I think he looks nice. He probably has the grandpa touch. Maybe he'll look out for them."

The boats on either side were of a wide variety. One, in particular, was huge. There was a large bulldog painted on the side, the words **Doghouse** over it.

"Georgia football fans," Jo said. "I bet it gets rowdy here on game night."

The next boat was a pontoon, but in ratio might as well have been a dinghy. Taylor wondered how the owners of the pontoon felt with the big, fancy boat parked next to them.

"Hey, Aunt Lucy," Levi called.

Lucy sat on the covered porch—or deck, whatever it was called—of a very old black-and-white boat. As she'd described, it was vintage, with a long, open upper deck that ran the length of the boat, and a slide that ran down the side.

"Cool," Levi exclaimed.

Lucy had been watching them walk toward her, her arms crossed over her chest in a defensive vibe. She was dressed in a t-shirt and colorful pajama pants, her feet slid into flip-flops.

"Hi, Levi. What are you guys doing here?" She looked at Taylor and Jo.

"Just came to see if you are okay," Taylor said.

"How did you—oh, never mind. I told you where this boat was, didn't I? Well, I'm fine. Johnny's fine. We're both fine."

She was still angry, that much was clear.

"Can I come on?" Levi asked. "This is so cool!"

Yes, little nephew, work your magic. Butter her up.

"Of course," Lucy said. "You can go in and look but be quiet. Johnny's napping."

"Kind of late for a nap, isn't it?" Taylor asked. "He's going to keep you up all night wanting to play."

"I'll worry about that," Lucy said, her tone even. "Just like I did last night, and the night before."

"Lucy, come on. Don't be so rude," Jo scolded softly. "Can't we all just get along?"

"Well, I don't know, Jo. Can we? It's not like you have any trouble getting along because you don't come around much. And when you do, your private life is off limits, unlike mine, which is always up for grabs for anyone who wants to know what I'm doing and tell me how to do it."

Jo was impressive. She never let Lucy get her riled. She was cool as a cucumber as she took the lawn chair opposite Lucy, sitting back and crossing her legs.

"I like this, Luce," she said, diverting the subject. "I mean, how crazy is it you can live out here full-time? On a boat? Do you think you'll get seasick?"

"I doubt it. This isn't the ocean, Jo," Lucy said, rolling her eyes.

Taylor took the other chair. She wanted to peek inside the cabin, but she wouldn't dare without an invitation. Not when her little sister was in this kind of mood.

"I suppose Taylor told you everything," Lucy said, looking first at Jo before glaring at Taylor suspiciously.

Jo shrugged. "She told me you want to buy this houseboat and live out here with Johnny. What else is there?"

Before Lucy could say anything else, Levi stepped out of the cabin, his eyes wide. "Mom, you have to see this! It's even got a big wheel to steer the boat, like on a ship." He looked at Lucy. "Aunt Lucy, Johnny is awake, and I didn't do it. He was laying in there playing with his feet and gurgling."

Lucy sighed. "That was a short break."

"I'll get him," Jo said, hopping up and following Levi inside.

When they were out of sight, Taylor turned to Lucy. "Please come back, Lucy. We miss you."

"I'm not coming back. I bought the boat. I live here now."

"In your own name? I thought you didn't want to be tracked?"

"I didn't. I don't. You wouldn't help me, so I did it myself." She looked defiant, like a sullen little girl. "Su—I mean Jill, she isn't going to come looking for me. I know too much. It's better for her if I stay out of the picture."

"If you know too much, sometimes they want to make sure you are really out of the picture. Permanently."

Lucy waved a hand nonchalantly. "I'll be okay. I'm not afraid of her. Or her Ukrainian family. They aren't going to be concerned with me. I'm not part of their scheming, other than about Johnny. She didn't want him anyway."

"Lucy, I can't keep you safe if you don't let me." Taylor felt defeated. She was worried, too. Lucy had always thought she was tougher than anyone else, but it sounded like the couple she'd met were involved in activities that were way above Lucy's petty experiences.

"I don't need you to keep me safe. I want to stand on my own two feet for the first time. Don't you get that? I can take care of my son."

"But Cate and I love having him there. The house is too quiet without him. Without you."

That was the truth, too. Lucy had her issues, but she also brought a certain level of energy to wherever she was. Now the house felt flat.

Lucy's shoulders relaxed, and she let out a long breath.

"He misses you, too. I didn't say you couldn't see him. I'm still going to need help with him when I work evening shifts at the Den. Mabel isn't going to stay shut down at dark forever. As soon as you catch that killer, she's going to stick me on dinners. I don't want to have to hire a strange babysitter. Margaret keeps him when she can, but she has a women's group thing tonight."

"Looks like you already have a sitter lined up," Taylor said, laughing. "He scared Levi when we walked up."

Lucy smiled. "That's Ellis. He's harmless. He's been living out here by himself for the last three years. He fishes a lot, and he considers himself the security detail in the evenings. He helped me move our clothes in."

"Oh, really? He doesn't look old enough to be retired."

That was suspicious. She wondered why he was isolating himself.

"I didn't say he was. I just said he does a lot of fishing, but I don't know what else. We have internet so maybe he works remotely from his boat."

Taylor caught herself from saying too much. "Just be careful."

"I'm a lot smarter than you give me credit for, Taylor. I'm not who I used to be. Johnny changed me, and I want to give him a decent life. You've got to let me try to do this."

Jo came outside with Johnny in her arms and Levi trailing behind her.

When Johnny saw Taylor, he lit up and leaned so far forward trying to get to her that he almost fell from Jo's arms.

"Come here," Taylor said, taking him and setting him on her lap.

"Lucy, I love it. The inside is much nicer than I thought it would be. You've even got a stereo system, and there's air conditioning!" Jo looked incredulous.

"A big water heater, too," Lucy said. "I can take long showers if I want, though I'll probably take a lot of them in the bathhouse to conserve my tanks."

"Good idea," Jo said. "The gray upholstery on all the benches looks like it's in good shape. We can go thrift shopping to get all kinds of stuff to jazz it up, too. Lots of pops of color are what you need for Johnny. It'll be fun."

"Okay, as long as I don't spend too much. It took almost all I have just to buy this thing."

"I got you," Jo said, taking her seat again. "I know all the best places. We'll have this boat decorated in Lucy-style before you know it. Anyway, what did I miss?"

Levi jumped off the boat. He crouched to peer between it and the dock. "I see a fish! It's a big one!"

"You missed nothing, except Lucy was telling me about Ellis, the guy we passed on the boat He's her *friend*." Taylor put quotes in the air with her fingers. "And he's single. We might need to watch out for him."

"He's welcome to be my sugar daddy if he's got any money," Lucy said.

Taylor and Jo gasped.

"Kidding. Kidding. Jeez, take it easy."

"What's his last name?" Taylor asked, suddenly serious.

"No, Taylor. I don't need you to run background checks on all my neighbors."

Damn. Her sister knew her well.

"According to Ellis, there won't be a lot of us here all the time anyway. Not until summer. I think on both docks, there are only about seven boats with full-timers living aboard. Some of these boats look like they haven't been used in years," Lucy said.

She was right. The boat across from them was covered. Not only with a boat cover, but also a large array of spider webs. Taylor couldn't imagine how many were inside.

A boat went by in the deeper water. Under them, Lucy's boat moved up and down, the wave rocking it gently.

"Feel that?" Lucy asked. "I love it. It's exactly what I've always dreamed of. As soon as I can get someone up here to service the motor, I'm going to take this baby out there and try her out. That reminds me, I need to come up with a name. What about *Lucy's Diamond*?"

"Ooh, I like that," Jo said. "Or Lucy's Lair. Lucy's Love Nest. So many options you could use. I bet Sam would take a look at the motor, don't you think, Taylor?"

"I have no idea. You'd have to ask him." She could be salty, too. The truth was, she didn't like it one bit. Not just the name, but the whole damn thing. No one brought a baby to live on a boat. No one with any sense, anyway. But what was she going to do? Kidnap him?

That was an option, but Lucy was quite the scrapper when she wanted to be. There was a lot of dynamite packed into her tiny body. And stubborn! She was just like their dad. They saw things only their way and dug their heels in, never admitting they could be wrong, or that there was a better way.

It was infuriating.

Taylor hesitated, then came out with what she wanted to say.

"Look, Lucy. If you're planning to stay out here, I'm going to install a camera. One where you can see who's outside your door or on the dock from a phone app. And they have those beeper things that signal when someone crosses in front of it. We can install safety measures at those entrance gates for when Johnny starts walking. In case he tries to get off the boat." Taylor looked around, determining the best places for everything.

"Fine, Taylor," Lucy said. She stood and took Johnny. "If that will make you happy, it's your dime. But I swear, you leave my neighbors alone. No interrogations or background checks. People like us don't like the law sticking their noses around. Don't wear your uniform here again, either. Now come in, take a look."

"Wait," Taylor said. "*People like us*? What kind of people are you?"

"Normal people. The ones who like it better when the law stays out of our business," Lucy said, laughing as she led the way into her new miniature home.

She didn't see the lasers Taylor was staring into the back of her head, but Jo did and waved at her to let it go.

Taylor bit her tongue to keep from saying anything else. Just let them say that when they were in trouble and begging the law to save them.

Who'd be laughing then?

CHAPTER 17

On Thursday morning bright and early, Cate sat in a chair next to Sarah and watched as she quickly entered information from a form into the computer, jumping from one screen to another so fast that it was hard to keep up.

"Once you've finished entering it here, then you also put the name and number in our other database. Just click on this icon," she said, pointing out a small square on the screen. "You'll have a user ID and password. We'll set that up next."

Cate would never be able to do it. It was just too much. Under the desk, she wiped her sweaty palms on top of her jeans.

"Got it?" Sarah asked.

"Uh—yes. I think." No, she didn't.

Not everyone was born with a keyboard in their hands. Cate wished the younger ones would be more aware of that.

Angela had taken a real liking to her. She'd decided she was going to use Cate as a floater in all areas and get her trained up sooner than she'd first planned.

The pressure was on. Cate didn't want to let Angela down, but she had a feeling it was going to happen anyway.

She wasn't completely computer illiterate. She'd used one a bit when she'd headed up one of the greenhouses, but the things she'd done on it were simple. Easy tasks like ordering fertilizer, containers, and new seedlings every year.

When Sarah flipped over a paper, Cate saw *Weldon Gentry, owner & Moxie, dog* written there. The dog's fearful brown eyes flashed instantly into her mind. She remembered how sad she'd felt when he'd driven away, Moxie gazing mournfully from the back of the truck.

It had broken Cate's heart.

The door opened, and a woman came rushing in. She was on the phone, still talking a mile a minute when she approached the counter.

She was very well dressed, all the way up to the gold scarf tied around her neck and the classy wedge shoes.

Sarah stared at her impatiently, waiting for her attention.

"Oh, sorry," the woman said. She put her phone down, then pushed her glasses up higher on her nose.

"Can I help you?" Sarah said.

"Yes, I'm here to pick up my two dogs. Alice and Arlo. Under the name Johnson." She pulled out her wallet.

"That's a common name. What's the owner's first name on the application?"

"My husband said he didn't fill out anything when he came. Can you just tell me how much it is so I can get them and go? It was for two weeks while we were on a cruise. Please hurry, too. I'm a realtor. I have a showing in half an hour, and I must drop the dogs off at home before then, too."

"Oh, sorry, Mrs. Johnson. It's unusual that he didn't sign anything, but do you know who he talked to? I can look it up in the note files we leave for each other."

Mrs. Johnson picked her phone up and dialed, then walked toward the wall of windows and spoke sharply into the receiver, hesitated, then turned back to them.

"He said he didn't come in. He dropped them over the fence

because we were going to be late for our flight, and you all knew they were coming."

Sarah's brow wrinkled. "I'm not sure I'm following."

A red flush started creeping up Mrs. Johnson's neck. It filled her cheeks.

"Where's your manager? What kind of boarding kennel is this to be so complicated to pick my dogs up?"

Cate wasn't following either, but Sarah suddenly looked alarmed.

"Boarding kennel? No, we don't board dogs, Mrs. Johnson. This is the Humane Society. If your husband dropped your dogs over the fence, they were treated as stray dumps."

Mrs. Johnson looked stricken. "Humane Society? I put in the address he gave me this morning. Is this 1109 Bayou Highway?"

Sarah shook her head. "Yes, but he must've taken them to 1109 Bayou Place, in the plaza on the other side of town. That's the boutique kennel for small dogs."

"Oh my God," she said. "I don't think so. He wrote the address down for me. It was this one. Please tell me you still have my babies?"

"What date and what kind of dogs?" Sarah said, tapping at her keyboard furiously.

"Bichons and—"

"Oh no," Sarah said, looking up and interrupting her. "The white toy breeds? Kind of look like poodles?"

"What do you mean, *oh no*?"

"I remember them. I'm the one who came in the next morning and found them huddled in the yard, scared to death. Those dogs were adopted the very next day. They went together as a package, though."

She said the last part on a high note, as though that made everything better.

Cate swore that if the woman had a gun, she'd have pulled the trigger right then and there.

"I knew we should've never moved to this hillbilly town. Who names a highway and a street the same thing? Are you the manager?" she said to Cate through clenched teeth.

"No, I'm not. I'll get her," Cate jumped up from her chair, then briskly walked down the hall to Angela's office.

She poked her head in, and Angela looked up.

"I heard everything," Angela said before Cate could say a word. She held her head like she had a headache. "Idiots. Who thinks a shelter is a boarding kennel? And who simply drops their dogs over a five-foot fence without checking them in? This is going to be a hell of a mess."

"I'm sorry." Cate didn't know what she was apologizing for, but it felt right.

"Well, come on. Let me go talk to her."

Cate followed reluctantly. She'd much rather be outside with the dogs.

At the front, Sarah stood at the window, looking out.

"She said she's calling the police. That we sold her dogs," she said when she saw Angela.

"Well, that's just great," Angela said. "Just what I needed when I'm in the trenches of trying to apply for another grant."

They joined Sarah at the window to watch the woman pacing back and forth behind her car, one hand gesturing wildly as she talked.

"She's livid," Sarah said.

"Yep," Angela agreed. "Might as well not go out there yet then. If the police are already on the way, it might save some drama between me and bat-shit-crazy Mrs. Johnson because I'm going to have to inform her about what sort of idiot she married."

Nobody laughed.

"What will you do?" Cate asked.

"Sarah, pull up the adoption file on the two Bichons. I think they went to a family named Chavez. They'll be so disappointed.

Just explain to them what happened and ask them to bring the dogs back. If they don't want to cooperate, give me the phone."

Sarah went back to the desk.

"This isn't good," Angela said. "The Chávez's were so happy with being chosen for the dogs that they gave us a generous donation. They'll probably want it back, and I already used it to buy a pallet of cat litter. Sometimes, I hate my job."

"I'm sorry." Cate wanted to bite her tongue. All she could think to do was apologize. She felt like an idiot.

Cate saw a sheriff's car pull up and park next to Mrs. Johnson.

"Oh, they're here," Angela said. "But let's wait until they come in for us. Let Mrs. Johnson tell her side first."

Taylor got out.

Even from the window, Taylor looked calm and in control. It was impressive. Cate wanted to declare that it was her daughter, but she didn't know how Taylor would feel about that, so she didn't say anything.

"That's Deputy Gray," Angela said. "If anyone can calm that woman down, it'll be her. She has a way with people."

Cate felt her chest fill with pride.

"One time a few years back, there was a drugged-out meth head who crawled out a bedroom window onto a ledge with her two small children. She was screaming someone was trying to kill them all. Deputy Gray went in and spent three hours talking her into letting the children come back in through the window before she jumped."

"Oh my gosh. Did she die?" Cate asked.

"Nah. Just broke both her ankles, if I remember right. They sent her to a rehab in Florida after her surgeries. But Gray saved those kids. They were too young and fragile to survive that fall without worse injuries or death. I think she should've gotten an award for that, but that I know of, she never did."

Cate watched Taylor talk to Mrs. Johnson through the window, witnessing the antagonistic body language somewhat relaxing right before her eyes. She could easily visualize Taylor saving children from a whacked-out mother. Especially knowing now how she'd cared for her sisters so well.

"I tell you; drugs are going to start taking over this town," Angela said. "Right now, everyone thinks it's just isolated cases and that we're safe here tucked away in our little community. Not true. The drug dealers and the users are here, hiding in all the dark corners like cockroaches, only coming out at night when the good people are sleeping and think they're safe in their beds."

Cate hadn't heard Taylor talk much about Hart's Ridge having a drug problem, but from what she'd seen in the prison system with all the intakes of addicted young women, it didn't surprise her that any town would be facing those problems. These days, no one and no place was safe from what was becoming an epidemic of tragedy. Where once it only touched families from a lower level of income, now it was a rampant part of every community, but the well-to-doers just hid it better.

"Oh, here comes Deputy Gray," Angela said.

They watched as Mrs. Johnson got in her car and pulled away. Taylor walked up to the door, still calm and collected.

Angela held it open for her.

"Hi," she said as she came in, looking from Angela to Cate.

Cate nodded but held back.

"I'm so sorry about this, Officer," Angela said. "What a disaster, but can we tell you what happened? It's their fault, but I'll try to fix it."

"She told me. She admitted her husband made a huge mistake. I explained to her that no one was going to be arrested because no laws have been broken."

"Exactly," Angela said. "Normally, if a dog is surrendered, they are not given back no matter if the party has regrets or if they are now in a better situation. New adopters are never obligated to return animals in that case. But since these dogs technically weren't knowingly relinquished, this is complicated. I'll do what I can to reunite the dogs with her, but she's going to have to be patient while I sort it out."

"I told her that. I also told her that if she got antagonistic with you like I suspect she already has, it will not bode well for a positive outcome. I think she's going to be apologizing."

Again, Cate was impressed by the way Taylor had handled things, diffusing the situation with just a handful of words and a few minutes. She would've made a great prison guard. Not that she'd ever want her daughter in that environment, though.

"Thank you so much, Officer," Angela said.

"Keep me updated. And while I'm here, Angela, did you know that Cate is my mother?"

Cate's stomach squeezed in on her.

Angela looked surprised. "No, I didn't. Cate didn't say anything."

She raised a brow at Cate questioningly.

"I—sorry. I wasn't sure if Taylor wanted me to. I wasn't trying to hide anything," Cate said, suddenly worried.

"No, that's fine. I should've put together the last names, but I didn't even notice," Angela said. "Anyway, thank you again, Deputy Gray. I'm going to get started trying to work this mess out."

She walked away, leaving Cate and Taylor at the door.

"You look natural in here," Taylor said.

"Thanks. I'm not. You should see me trying to learn how to work the computer. But I'm much better back in the kennels."

"Yeah, I'm sure. You love the dogs," Taylor said. "You coming home soon?"

"Yep. I have a few more things to do, then I'll be out of here."

They said nothing for a few seconds. It felt weird seeing each other out in a public setting, both in their professional roles.

"Drive carefully," Taylor finally said. Then with a parting smile, she was gone.

Cate watched her go, wishing they were more comfortable with small talk, or just being near each other without unease. She sighed, then turned back to the desk. She had another half hour of pretending to be smarter than she was, then she could go.

⁓

Cate looked at the photo on her phone and memorized the address, then plugged it into her maps app. She knew she shouldn't even have taken the picture, and she felt bad about it, but all she was going to do was drive by to make sure the dog was okay.

There was still about an hour before it got dark, and she was going to do it while she had the courage.

She tapped the steering wheel nervously as she drove, following the directions that led her to the other side of town. When she got to Grouse Gap road, she turned off. Not too much farther down, she slowed when she saw a farm gate protecting a small dirt driveway.

The mailbox number matched.

She pulled over.

Now what?

She couldn't see the dog from the road because the driveway was too long.

There was a no-trespassing sign posted, too.

Damn it.

She'd come all the way out there, and she knew what would happen if she didn't appease her worry. She'd be awake even longer than normal, obsessing over ignoring her gut to check on Moxie.

It's not your business, so move along.

That was a mantra she'd used so often in the last few decades that it came to her automatically. But in prison, it had been a different story. Getting involved in a situation there could cost much more—like her life.

And there wasn't an innocent dog right in the middle of it.

She weighed her options. If she wasn't seen and didn't touch anything, was it still considered trespassing?

All she wanted was one look. Then she'd go home, and no one would ever know. It was semantics, but it worked.

She got back on the road, driving up about half a mile until she saw a small grove of trees she could pull the van into to keep it out of sight. She eased off the road into it, killed the motor, and got out, shutting the door quietly.

Quickly, she walked back to Gentry's gate and looked both ways, then climbed over it and dropped to the other side. She got off the driveway, then followed the tree line to stay out of sight.

Gentry kept a junked-up property, she noted as she walked by multiple piles of odds and ends. Rotting firewood in a heap with a stack of old fence posts beside it, the barbed wire still wrapped around the lot of it.

An abandoned chicken coop still reeked.

A beam of sunshine glinted off something close to the ground. When she got closer, she was shocked to see a trip wire.

He must have thought everyone was out to steal his massive collection of junk, or maybe his dogs, since he went to the trouble of setting booby traps. That it was an old-school trip wire, though, was impressive.

Carefully, Cate stepped over it.

The house came into view—as pitiful as the rest of what she'd seen of the property. It needed painting. And from the slope she could see, a new roof, too. A lonely wooden rocking chair graced the rickety front porch, and a huge set of antlers adorned the front door.

A few dogs started barking, so she followed the sound, staying as far from the house as she could. As she crept to the back, she spotted wire kennels. She counted eight in total, all occupied. The overturned wine barrels inside the cages were used for shelter.

One of the caged hunters put his nose in the air and sniffed, then let out a string of deep barks.

Another howled.

When she heard a door open, she froze.

"What're y'all raising hell at? Shut up! I'm watching the news."

Weldon sounded as mad as a hornet.

Cate crouched lower to get a better view. He approached the kennels, then picked up a metal rod. Stomping past all the fencing, he ran the rod down the length of chain, making such a racket that the dogs jumped back in fear.

When he got to the last one, he stopped and peered in.

"Where you at, you little bitch?"

Cate couldn't see a dog from her vantage point, but he must have because pulled a key from his pocket, unlocked the padlock, and ducked inside.

He kicked the barrel hard. When nothing happened, he bent and looked into it. "Hey—you dead?"

When he crouched into a squat, Cate thought he was finally going to show some empathy to the dog hidden in the barrel, but he fooled her.

"If you're still alive tomorrow, I'll feed you. By then, you'll be ready to do what I say." After he stood, he used the rod to pound on the top of the barrel.

Cate heard a distinct whimper.

She couldn't see Moxie, but she knew without a doubt it was her. Cate's gut instinct had been right—the dog was in trouble.

Weldon let himself out of the kennel. He reached for the padlock, then dropped it.

"Oh hell, wouldn't nobody wanna steal a wimp like you. You ain't worth the trouble it takes me to keep fishing out my key."

Yes, Cate thought. *Walk away, you bastard.*

He did. Stomping back to the house, he muttered obscenities under his breath. He kicked the door open before disappearing inside.

Cate shook with fury. The man was an idiot for thinking starvation would help make the dog trust him or behave in what he thought was an appropriate manner for a hunting dog.

The fact was that some dogs weren't cut out for what their breeds were known to be bred for. Just like people, they came with different personalities, gifts, and even fears. No matter how much money he'd paid for her—or even the training he piled on her—if she didn't want to be what he wanted her to be, she wouldn't.

Period.

Especially after he'd abused her.

Cate spotted a large trash can with a lid on it near the kennels. It was too clean for it to be for trash, so it had to be the dog food.

As soon as she showed herself, they were all going to sound the alarm, which was a conundrum. She wondered if she'd have time to run out, get a scoop, and toss it into Moxie's kennel before the dogs made Weldon mad enough to come back out.

In all actuality, she should back out quietly and leave. Taylor would be furious if her mother ended up arrested for trespassing.

Her heart thudded so loudly that Cate was surprised Gentry couldn't hear it from inside the cabin. She was terrified, her hands and knees trembling with the fear of getting caught. Or worse—getting shot.

Resolutely, she turned and quietly started heading back to the road, walking like she was on eggshells to keep the dogs from hearing her. She was halfway to the road when she thought of Moxie's brown eyes again.

What if the dog couldn't make it another night?

Damn it.

Her legs were weak now with worry, but she quietly turned around and crept back to where she'd been before.

The dogs had settled down, though a few still lay atop their houses.

Moxie hadn't come out and since Cate couldn't see her, she didn't know how bad off she was or even if she had access to water. Just like humans, dogs could survive quite a while without food, but they had to have water.

Surely, he wasn't that cruel? Moxie was an investment for him, so Cate doubted very much he'd let her get too close to death.

Her phone beeped in her pocket. Cate rushed to get it out and turn off the sound. She'd forgotten about it, but thankfully it was only a text message.

Stop by and see my place before you go home.

It was from Lucy. She'd added her address, too.

Lucy wanted Cate to visit!

Finally, her youngest was sticking an olive branch out and here Cate was hiding in the blasted woods, unable to walk away until she got eyes on a dog who didn't belong to her.

Maybe all that time behind bars had given her brain damage.

Suddenly, she heard music blaring from the house. It was an old song from Hank Williams, and not the junior. One of his hard-rocking loud ones that were irritating at a high volume.

She wondered what Weldon could be doing in there, but she wasn't going to waste the opportunity.

Quickly, she sprinted out of the tree line toward the kennels.

As expected, the dogs began to bark, the sounds escalating with each step she took closer until they sounded frantic. As she ran by each kennel, the dogs snarled and snapped at the wires, trying to get to her as though they were Dobermans on a security team. Cate knew that outside of their kennels, they'd most likely be a lot tamer, but when dogs thought they were protecting a perimeter, they took it much more seriously.

At the last kennel, she looked through the fencing, but it was too dark to see Moxie in the makeshift house.

She hesitated.

The music still blared, so she opened the gate and went in.

"Moxie?" She crouched to look inside the shelter.

Cate could see a ball of fur, but not her face. She took her phone out, turned on the flashlight app, and shined it inside.

Moxie stared at her, but she otherwise didn't move.

A stranger in her kennel and within reach, but no reaction.

Cate saw a metal bowl overturned in the dirt.

Not a drop of water anywhere.

A murderous rage coursed through her, but she reined it back. She called out to Moxie again, using a soothing tone to coax her. Slowly and gingerly, she reached inside until she touched Moxie's flank. She rubbed it gently.

Moxie gave one tiny flop of her tail, then it lay flat.

"You remember me, don't you, girl?" Cate shined the light on Moxie's eyes. They looked sunken back in her head, a sure sign of dehydration.

Suddenly, the music cut off.

Shit.

Cate reached in and grabbed the dog, pulling her out of the kennel and into her arms. She stood, almost losing her balance, but then found her footing.

Moxie struggled for a minute, then gave up and relaxed, too weak to fight.

Even malnourished, Moxie wasn't a light dog to carry, but Cate wouldn't have cared if she weighed a hundred pounds. Moxie needed to see a veterinarian. Cate shut the kennel door, hoping Weldon would be too lazy to check on Moxie again. With the other dogs barking a chorus behind her, she ran for the tree line.

Once she had cover, she adjusted Moxie more comfortably in her arms, cradling the dog's head against her chest like a baby, then she half walked half ran, scanning for the tripwire she needed to avoid as she got the hell out of Dodge.

During Cate's twenty years in prison, she'd never felt like a criminal. She'd lived her life as an innocent woman moving amongst masses of the guilty. She'd held her head high because not once had she ever felt guilty about doing anything wrong. She was a model citizen who had never broken a single law in her life.

That all changed when she hustled to her van and climbed in with Moxie.

CHAPTER 18

Out of her four daughters, Cate knew Lucy would be the most likely to help her figure out how to avoid being arrested and not judge her for the stunt she'd just pulled.

Hopefully, she'd also know an emergency vet, too.

Cate had put the address in her phone and now she drove fast —probably too fast considering she'd just committed what might be a felony, but she wanted to get to Lucy's and then figure out what to do. She doubted Hart's Ridge had a 24-hour animal clinic, but she was banking on Lucy knowing someone who might open the doors for them.

She checked her rearview mirror. So far no one else was on the road.

"I hope he didn't pay more than five hundred bucks for you, girl," she said to the dog. "Under five hundred and it's a misdemeanor. Over, and we might go to jail. Georgia takes larceny seriously."

Moxie didn't react, though she stared at Cate from the passenger seat. Cate hadn't wanted to put her on the floor, so she used a blanket that Jackson had left in the back for emergencies and wrapped her up in the seat.

Come to think of it, even a misdemeanor could mean a fine of up to a thousand bucks. In some states, people could even get a year in jail. Cate felt sick to her stomach.

She couldn't ever go back to jail.

What had she just done? She'd lost her mind!

"We just can't get caught."

Dark had fallen during her run, and Cate was even more nervous driving. She hadn't been behind the wheel at night in decades. She slowed down to watch the sides of the road for deer. It'd be just her luck to have an accident close to Weldon's place, and he'd hear the sirens and come investigate.

Then he'd find his dog and she'd go to jail.

When Moxie coughed, Cate reached over and stroked her fur. "I wish I had water in here, baby. I'm so sorry. We'll be there soon."

Finally, she saw the turnoff for the lake park.

"Almost there, Moxie," she said, leaning toward the windshield to see better. She found the parking lot, pulled into a space, cut the engine, then jumped out and hurried around to the other side.

She opened the door, then picked up Moxie and the blanket. Moxie didn't feel limp yet, so that was a good sign.

Cate held her close as she took off down to the docks.

When she got there, she realized she didn't know which dock Lucy had her boat at. She struggled to balance Moxie in one arm and reach into her pocket for her phone, but nearly dropped her.

"Need some help?" a deep voice asked.

She about jumped out of her skin. "Damn it. You scared me."

A man had walked out of the shadows. He was only a foot or so away.

"Sorry about that. Was just taking my nightly walk around the perimeter to make sure no hooligans are hanging out, smoking dope, or doing worse. They try to park out here sometimes."

"Okay…" Cate looked out toward the boats. She still hadn't reached her phone.

He took a step closer, studying Moxie under the light of the streetlamp. "Hey, your dog looks sick. Is there a problem?"

Cate still hadn't reached her phone. "I-I—yes, but I'm trying to find my daughter's boat."

"Don't tell me—her name is Lucy."

Cate nodded, still a bit afraid but starting to feel a wave of exhaustion come over her now the adrenaline had passed.

He sighed, sounding frustrated. "So much for my quiet existence out here. She's had more company in the last few days than I've had in a year. I'm going to need to find a new slip."

"Oh?"

"Never mind. It's fine," he grumbled. "Why don't you let me take the dog? I'm a friend of your daughter's. My name is Ellis. Ellis Cross."

He didn't look like a weirdo. Ellis stood well over six feet, making her usual complex about being a tall woman shrivel under his gaze. His face was tanned and weathered, his hair thick and dark but short and tousled. A well-trimmed beard framed his strong jawline.

As he hesitated, she realized that if he were out to hurt her, he wouldn't ask to hold the dog.

And he knew Lucy's name.

"Fine," Cate said, handing Moxie over.

The transfer of weight instantly took the pressure off her neck and the muscles that were already sore from a hard day of cleaning kennels at the shelter.

"Are there any injuries? Broken bones? Sprained legs?"

"No, nothing like that," Cate said.

"What's his name?" he asked as he led the way to the dock on the left.

"Her. Mox—I mean, um... Brandy," Cate said, thinking quickly. She'd almost forgotten he was carrying a stolen dog that someone would be looking for. She prayed that by some fluke of irony, Ellis didn't know Weldon Gentry.

"Perfect. She looks like a Brandy with those eyes and her coloring." Ellis carried her like she weighed nothing. He was tall *and* strong.

When they stepped onto the wooden dock, Cate saw Lucy walking toward them. "I thought it might be you," she said. "What's going on?"

"Your mother's dog is sick," Ellis said.

"What dog? Diesel?"

"No," Cate said. "I'll explain in a minute. First, can we get her some water? And do you have any baby food?"

Lucy turned to lead the way to her boat. "Of course, I've got baby food. I have a baby. He's sleeping, by the way, so be quiet."

"Pray to God he sleeps through the night," Ellis said, stepping carefully onto the boat after Lucy.

Lucy chuckled and opened the sliding door, disappearing inside.

Ellis lay Brandy—Cate decided instantly that was her new forever name—down on the deck, then crouched over her.

Cate joined him, petting the dog's flank again.

He opened Brandy's eyelids and peered closely, then pinched the skin covering her spine and let it fall back into place. She stared at him quietly, as though she knew she'd been rescued.

"Not as bad as I thought it was going to be," he said, then stuck a finger in Brandy's mouth and pulled up her lip to look at her gums. "She might be fine if you give her the water gradually. Along with the baby food."

"Are you a veterinarian?" Cate asked.

"No—but I grew up on a farm. We didn't have a vet on call all the time. Had to learn emergency care. Before I went off to college, I had a lot of responsibility with the animals. Mostly for horses and goats, but a few dogs, too."

Cate had thought for a minute that she'd lucked out. Now she worried again. Did he know what he was talking about? Should she try to find a clinic?

"I promise, she's going to be okay." When he made eye contact with Cate, she instantly felt something she hadn't felt in too many years to count—something she'd resigned herself to the idea that she'd never feel again—from a place deep inside her that she thought was long dead.

Butterflies.

A lot of them, too.

The deepest shade of brown, his eyes pierced her with an intensity that seemed to see right through her, His nose was slightly crooked like it had been broken before but never quite healed.

He wore a serious but thoughtful expression. This man was someone she didn't need in her life right now. Or probably ever.

When he smiled, she tried to stand so fast that she lost her balance and fell backward, landing on her butt.

Lucy chose that second to return, balancing a plastic bowl of water in one hand and a jar of baby food in the other. She stopped when she saw Cate sprawled on the deck.

"What are you doing?"

Cate scrambled up, sheepishly dusting her hands off on her jeans. "Nothing. I fell." She took the bowl of water, then sat next to Brandy.

Lucy pulled an infant medicine dropper from her back pocket and handed it to Cate, but when Brandy saw the water, the dog struggled to get up.

"I'll let her lap it up," Cate said. "She wants it badly."

"Just a little at first," Ellis said. "Don't want her to throw it up."

As Brandy drank, Cate stroked her back. She could just feel that the dog had a sweet soul. She'd never want to hunt anything. It wasn't in her.

Ellis reached over to pet Brandy and accidentally put his hand on Cate's arm, causing a firestorm of sparks to run through her fingers, all the way up her arm to her face.

Cate jerked it away, then tried to pretend she'd done it to take her ponytail down and smooth her hair back into it again. She twisted the elastic around it slowly, suddenly feeling silly for even wearing a ponytail. She was an old woman. Not a girl. She had burn scars—patches of her skin were puckered grotesquely, scattered on her forearms and her neck. He had touched one. Surely, he was trying to hide his revulsion.

"Sorry," he said, looking at her strangely. "You okay?"

"Yes—I'm fine. Sorry." She pulled the water away from Brandy, then opened the baby food jar and sucked some of it into the dropper. Cate slowly released it into Brandy's mouth.

"What kind of food is this? It smells funny," Cate said, sniffing the jar.

"Beef and gravy. You're acting weird, Cate," Lucy said. "Are you going to tell me where you got the dog?"

"I found her. On the side of the road after I left the shelter. She must've gotten loose and ran herself ragged before she dropped."

"Aww, poor thing," Lucy said.

Ellis was staring intently at Cate.

Too intently.

Cate averted her gaze.

"Well, you saved her. Why're you looking all nervous?" Lucy asked. "That's a good thing."

"I'm n-n-not nervous," Cate stuttered. "I mean, I almost ran over her. With the van. On the road. It scared me."

She sounded like a robot.

"I thought you said she was on the side of the road?" Ellis asked.

Shit.

"She was—but I was looking at my phone to put Lucy's address in and I sort of went off the road for a minute. When I glanced up, I saw her in my headlights and swerved."

God, she was a horrible liar.

"Well, it was a great coincidence for her to drop right in front of someone who works at an animal shelter," Lucy said. "You going to take her in tomorrow?"

"No! I-I mean, no. I think I might keep her. She seems sweet. Do you think Taylor would mind?"

"I doubt it, not as long as Diesel and her get along. It's not like you're staying there forever, right? You'll have your own place soon."

Ellis rose, then settled into a lawn chair, watching them.

"Oh, you new in town?" he asked.

"Yes." She gave Brandy another dropper of food.

"Where you from?"

"She's from Montana," Lucy said. "Big-sky country. Grizzly bears and bison burgers."

Please, Lucy, do not tell him everything. Please.

"Nice," he said. "I took a group of guys on a fly-fishing excursion up in Billings one time. Big Horn River, I think it was."

Her stomach squeezed at the mention of Billings, and she pretended not to hear him. She gave Brandy another bite. The dog moved closer, not taking her eyes off Cate.

By the time she was done with the whole jar, Brandy had crawled into Cate's lap and gotten comfortable. Cate gave her another sip of water, watching as life came back into the dog's eyes.

"What are you going to do with her tomorrow?" Lucy asked. "Don't you have to work? She might still need supervision for a few days."

"Oh, I didn't think about that." Cate considered whether she should call out of work. She didn't want to, not when Angela already had so much confidence in her.

"I'm not doing anything tomorrow," Ellis said. "I'd be glad to keep her on my boat and tend to her. You could come by after work. If she's feeling better, you could take her then."

"That's a great idea," Lucy said. "I'd offer, but I'm afraid that, with Johnny, I might not be able to watch her close enough."

They waited while Cate hesitated.

"Is there some reason you don't trust me?" Ellis asked, raising his eyebrows at Cate. "I mean, I have been helping care for your grandson, and, so far, he's still kicking and screaming, with heavy emphasis on the screaming."

"Ellis, stop teasing. You know he's not that bad," Lucy said, laughing.

"Only after midnight," he replied, but he laughed, too.

"Okay. I don't want to impose, but that would be nice of you," Cate said, noting the easy camaraderie between them. "But I promise, it'll just be for one day. I'll pick her up tomorrow."

He shrugged. "It will be nice to have company. I bet she's quiet, too."

"Okay, Ellis," Lucy said. "Now you're giving me a complex. Get off my boat and take the dog. I'm going to show Cate my house, then she's going to get going, too, so I can get a few hours of sleep before the boy wakes up."

Relief washed over Cate.

She was going to be okay.

Brandy was going to be okay.

Maybe eventually, and with enough time, everything else would be okay, too.

CHAPTER 19

$\mathcal{J}$t was hard to tell the difference between shame and anger because both could crush a person, whether they deserved it or not. Taylor wished she had a crystal ball that would tell her if Danny were guilty of anything that had to do with his father's and brother's deaths.

He hadn't wanted to come back in for another talk, but Taylor told him if he didn't, they'd find a way to make it mandatory. He wasn't aware of it, but the girl, Stacy Mundell, was in another room, waiting her turn.

Taylor had already studied Stacy's social media the day before. Stacy wasn't a frequent poster, and there'd been nothing new on the day of the murders or the days around it. There also wasn't any indication she and Danny had been communicating online. No new photos or comments had been shared between them.

That didn't mean anything, but it was noted.

Stacy had come willingly, but, according to Penner, she looked scared half to death.

Taylor watched Danny carefully, searching for any clue. He still looked like hell, his clothes rumpled and his eyes bloodshot.

"Have a seat," Shane said, gesturing to the chair on the other side of the table before taking his.

Taylor was already in place. Shane hadn't wanted her to have any additional contact with Danny that wasn't necessary since he saw her as a friend more than a law enforcement officer.

"Yeah—I know the drill, and no, I don't want anything to drink. Ask what you want to ask so I can go home," Danny said. "There's a murderer out there while you two keep wasting time looking at me. I'm over it."

"I fully understand how you could feel that way," Shane said.

"Oh, do you? Have you had two of your closest family members slayed literally yards away from you where you could've done something but didn't because you didn't know what was going on?"

Looked like guilt to Taylor.

Maybe not guilt for committing the crimes, but guilt for not keeping the murders from happening. And that was sad.

"No, can't say I have, Danny. Let's get this done, why don't we? Do you know a Stacy Mundell?"

Danny glanced between Shane and Taylor like he was confused. "Yeah, we used to date. Why?"

"When was the last time you had contact with Ms. Mundell?

Danny hesitated. "What does that have to do with anything?" he finally asked.

"Just answer the question," Shane said.

"Maybe I should *just* get a lawyer before I answer any more of your questions," Danny said.

"That's your right, and it would surely tell us something," Shane said.

They had a ten-second stare-down before Danny turned to her.

"Taylor, what is this shit? Are you seriously going to let him try to pin this on me? You know me." He gazed at her imploringly.

"Danny, just answer the questions. That's all we want," Taylor said.

He leaned back in his chair, crossing his arms over his chest. "Fine. I saw her that morning."

Taylor could see the excitement when it hit Shane, even though he tried not to show it. Under the table, his leg shook next to hers.

"Before or after?" Shane asked.

"Before, obviously. And no, she didn't have anything to do with what happened."

"What was she doing there?" Taylor asked.

"She just stopped by for a minute. We aren't dating or anything like that."

"Is that so?" Shane asked. "Because your father didn't approve of her?"

"No. We broke up a long time ago. I have no interest in picking that back up again. We aren't on the same path."

"And that path is what?" Shane asked.

Danny dropped his chair back down on four legs. "Look, I smoke a little weed now and then, just to keep my anxiety down. Stacy brought me some of her stash. I asked her to because I didn't want any of my old suppliers to know I dabble a little again. Don't need them hitting me up, trying to make money by selling me the harder stuff."

Taylor was disappointed to hear he was smoking pot again. With his type, a little pot was never enough. It always led to more. Something bigger and scarier. Just like he said.

His confession also did nothing to help him look innocent.

"A little weed, huh?" Shane said. "How are you paying for that little bit of weed? From what I hear, most of your money is sucked down slot machines. Sounds like you have a drug problem… and a gambling problem, to boot. Both could mean you needed money fast."

Danny's face went white, and Taylor could see a muscle ticking in his jaw.

"Let's play out this scenario," Shane said. "You and little Stacy-

Hotpants-Mundell were seeing each other on the sly because your father didn't approve of her or the person you were when you used to date her. You were afraid of being disowned from the family business because of it. You two were getting closer, and she was feeling vindictive because your relationship had to be a secret. Women don't like to be a secret, Danny Boy. So, you told her there was a way for you to have a load of cash and run off together."

"Bullshit," Danny drawled, pretending to be bored.

Shane tapped his pen on the table. "You planned the robbery for when your dad was away, but surprise—he wasn't gone. You didn't know that when you were trying to get into the safe and your brother came up on you. You shot him, then your dad ran out and you led him back inside where you shot him, too. Then, just to make it look good, you called 'ole Carlos up there, and boom—he was gone, too, because no one would ever suspect you'd kill your best friend. Then, you texted Stacy to come over."

Danny was shaking his head back and forth, getting madder by the second.

"She came, but she wasn't expecting a triple homicide. She thought it was just going to be a robbery, so she took off and left you shitting yourself in the woods, trying to figure out what to do next. Lo and behold, Taylor—our fine deputy here—drove up and gave you the perfect way to discover the bodies and look shocked."

"How dare you get into my business?" Danny asked. "I don't have a drug or a gambling problem. So, I play slots, so what? I do what I need to do to stay out of trouble, and if it isn't something you and your straitlaced buddies do, then excuse the hell out of me. But I did not—and let me repeat it again—did *not* kill my brother, my best friend, or my father. Now I'm done. If you have anything else to ask me, ask my lawyer instead. I'll forward his information to *Deputy Gray*."

He rose from the table, then opened the door. Before he left, he said, "And by the way, you both can kiss my ass."

Then he was gone, using about a hundred and sixty pounds of force to slam the door.

He was going to be even madder when he saw Stacy's car in the lot.

Shane turned to her.

"That went well, don't you think?"

～

They took an hour's break after Deputy Kuno led Stacy to the interview room—to make her wait a bit before they joined her. It was good to let her sweat. Taylor also needed to shake off some of the stress from the interview with Danny. She'd planned to just sit in her truck with the window open and listen to some tunes alone, but Shane had found her there half an hour into her respite.

He got in with his handy-dandy notebook, wanting to talk strategy.

"One of them will stumble," he said. "Then we pounce."

Thankfully, he didn't try to kiss her again, but she felt awkward because of what had been left unsaid between them. Taylor had dated before—somewhat successfully—without looking like an idiot. But now that she had two men saying they'd like to date her, it made her feel like an awkward high school girl who couldn't say no but also couldn't say yes.

She'd rather just stay focused on work, to be honest.

Now here they were, and her assigned role was to stay mostly quiet and look for clues that Stacy was lying.

"Tell us about your relationship with Danny," Shane began.

Stacy was biting her lip hard enough to make it bleed. Just in a few spots, but Taylor squashed the urge to get her a tissue. This was a case interview, not an outreach program.

"There's nothing to tell, not really. We used to date, but we're just friends now. Basically, that's it," she said. "I have a boyfriend. It's not Danny."

"Then tell us how it all began, way back in the beginning," Shane said, his tone even and friendly.

For now.

Stacy started talking. Within a few seconds, Taylor could tell Stacy was still in love with Danny. Her eyes shone when she talked about their early days when they were an official couple before it went bad.

They'd met at a bonfire near one of the lake landings, as so many did. Danny had been dating a friend of hers, but they'd fought. He came to Stacy looking for advice, maybe comfort, and then it was on.

"What about the trouble you two got into?" Shane asked.

Stacy raised her brows as though she didn't know what he was talking about.

"Two counts of breaking and entering," Taylor cited from her notepad. "And you caught a few drunk and disorderly charges. Possession of controlled substance. Not only with Danny, but you've also got charges you've picked up with a few other guys around town. I have it all here, Stacy."

She looked worried now. Her eyes darted back and forth, and her voice trembled when she talked. She seemed ready to cry at any minute.

Taylor could see why Danny had a thing for her. She was a tiny girl, no more than five foot two, her petite frame making her appear innocent and feminine. She poured on the makeup, but underneath it, you could still see she had nice features, big brown eyes, and a pert nose. Lucious lips, even. It was sad that her reputation was so sullied, not only from her behavior, but also from that of her mother. Taylor hated it when someone was judged by their family's misdeeds, but, in this case, it appeared the apple didn't fall too far from the tree.

The only thing Stacy could do now was leave town and start over somewhere far away, where no one knew her or her family members.

If she weren't guilty this time.

If she were, her reputation would hopefully follow her to prison to give her some street cred. Life was tough in there for small women.

"I swear, I had nothing to do with any of what went on up there. Okay—I went there to bring Danny a tiny bit of weed. That was it." She looked from Shane to Taylor, then back to Shane. "I'll take a lie detector test."

He wrote that down. "Where did you go after you sold him the weed?"

"Straight to work at the Purina plant. You can check the time-cards. I had to swipe in with my badge. I was there all day until five o'clock when I clocked out."

"What's your boyfriend's name?" Taylor asked.

"Carter. Carter Anderson."

The name sounded familiar, then she remembered. Taylor had delivered a court notice to his beaten-down trailer the year before. She'd handed it over to his mother, who was a treat in her own right. The woman had left a lasting and unwelcome impression.

"Are you going to talk to Carter?" Stacy asked.

"Possibly," Shane said.

"Oh, God. Can you please not tell him that I met up with Danny or that I sold him weed? He'll freak out."

"That depends. What else can you tell us about Danny? Has he mentioned to you that he needs money? Any more than usual?" Shane asked.

"He's not hurting for cash. His dad pays him well. I wouldn't ever spot him on the weed. He always pays me up front."

"What about his gambling? How often does he go to the casi-no?" Shane asked. "Do you ever go with him?"

"He goes to the casino? Since when? He didn't when we dated, not that I know of, and no—I've never been to a casino in my life. I don't have the first clue how to do that stuff."

Shane kept Stacy talking, asking more questions until she was visibly shaking. Taylor got the feeling that the only thing the girl was guilty of was being a dumbass for selling weed, but some people knew how to lie convincingly. Until her alibi checked out, she'd stay on the suspect list.

Finally, he took down her supervisor's phone number, then cut Stacy loose by telling her not to leave the county. She practically ran out of the room like a scared rabbit.

"What do you think?" he said, turning to Taylor.

"I don't think she had anything to do with it."

"That's what you think about Danny, too."

"No—I haven't formed a complete assessment on Danny. But if he did do it, I don't think Stacy was involved or knew about it. I'll talk to her boss to confirm her alibi, but I think it'll be tight."

He looked at his list, nodding. "Also want you to talk to Chipper Dayne again. The firewood guy. See what day he was out there. Maybe he saw something he doesn't even know he did. Pick his brain."

"Yep, had that on my list to do today, too. Are we done here?"

His leg was still bumped up against hers. She wanted to move hers, but she didn't want to be too obvious about it.

"I don't know. Do we have anything else to talk about?" He raised his brows.

Now was as good a time as any. It had to be done.

"Well, yeah. Just quickly, Shane. I'm glad you came back to town. I missed you—"

"—Uh oh, I sense a *but* coming…"

She swallowed hard. "But I think it would be too complicated to date someone I work with. If you were at a different department or something, well maybe. But not with us both here."

He looked crestfallen.

"No one has to know, Taylor."

"Yeah, but you know how things have a way of getting out. The guys already believe I get special treatment from you and the sheriff. I just don't want things to escalate."

"Things meaning you and me?"

"No. Things like harassment. It's a real thing, Shane. I've dealt with it my whole career. Dating someone in an upper position could mean trouble for me. I know you understand. That goes for doing things like leaving that rose on my windshield. If someone saw you do that, it would spread through the department like wildfire."

"What rose? I didn't leave a rose."

"You didn't?" She scrutinized his eyes, searching for the lie. She didn't like game-playing.

"No, I didn't. Who else in here has a thing for you?" He glowered.

"No one. I don't know who could have left it, then."

He cursed under his breath.

"Probably someone's idea of a joke," Taylor said. "Like the time they stuck a maxi pad to the windshield."

He ran his hand through his hair. She could tell he was struggling to keep his cool.

"How about we table this discussion for now?" he asked. "When we close this case, we can revisit it."

It sounded like he was planning a quarterly financial meeting or something, not the possibility of being romantic partners. But that was something she liked about him. He was serious, not all mushy and romantic.

At least, she thought she liked it.

"For me, I'm not going to change my mind," she said, then held her breath, shocked at her bravery.

He smiled slowly.

Gorgeously.

Something about him *did* pull at her—something that could get them in all sorts of trouble.

"We'll see," he said, then winked.

CHAPTER 20

*C*ate used the hose like an expert now. What had at first taken her three hours to do now took less than one. When she finished the last kennel, she hung the hose up and started the feeding rotation.

The newest resident, a black-and-white juvenile husky named Charlie, grumbled at her, but his tail was wagging back and forth at the sight of the food bucket. He was one of their most vocal dogs, as was common with his breed, who communicated with a lot of so-called talking.

"Yes, I know, you're always hungry. Might be why you're here, you know? Maybe they couldn't afford your healthy appetite?"

That probably wasn't true. Many of the bigger dogs were there for behaviors such as destruction or barking, which was ironic because those usually stemmed from dogs being bored and not having enough exercise or socialization. Dogs couldn't be tied up or left alone outside—or inside, for that matter—for endless hours or days. They craved interaction with humans, and they needed to expend their energy with exercise.

Cate stood outside his kennel, closed her eyes, and put her

finger to her lip, making her wish before touching it to his nameplate.

She had started a routine of closing her eyes and wishing the animals a short stay. Every time she interacted with the dogs, she made the wish and sealed it with a kiss. It was silly, and she wasn't usually prone to such superstitions and woo-woo, but leaving them each day to spend the nights alone in the shelter pulled at her heart. She wanted them to find homes as soon as possible. If she had to be a little weird to help push it along, no one had to know.

Quickly, she gave Charlie his portion of kibble, then moved on to Apollo's—a black lab whose whole body quivered in a greeting —kennel.

She made her wish and fed him, then moved on again.

Today, she was only in the kennels. For that, she was grateful. She was glad not to have to struggle with the computer.

Sarah and Angela were up there together, working on the details of their next fundraiser. They were hosting a charity event at the local golf club.

Putt-Putt for Paws.

Cate wondered if Pete would be there. She was glad Angela had said Cate wouldn't be needed that day. Instead, Angela said she expected Cate to help with the next fundraiser, a country-music festival at one of the lakeside restaurants in town. Cate was fine with that. It was more up her alley than a stuffy country-club setting.

Being in the kennels for the day also meant Cate hadn't had to talk to strangers, and she'd had more quiet time to immerse herself in thoughts about Brandy, which had led to more thoughts about Ellis.

She looked up at the clock.

Five more minutes.

Normally, she hated leaving her job. Today, though, she looked forward to getting back down to the boats. A mix of anticipation and nervousness filled her, and she couldn't help but wonder more about Ellis.

It was so kind of him to take care of Brandy for her.

Still, Ellis was a mystery. Not yet old enough to retire, and he carried a sense of sadness about him, too. Probably because of losing his wife, but Cate felt there was something more, a silent burden he carried, just like she did.

As soon as the hand hit five o'clock, Cate signed her timecard and left, hurrying to her van. The ride to the lake park was fast. Within fifteen minutes, she was walking briskly down the dock, looking for Brandy.

Lucy met her first, Johnny on her hip. She was dressed in black pants and a polo Cate hadn't seen before.

Lucy looked completely stressed out.

"Hi," she said. "I'm in a bind. My babysitter didn't show up, and she must have her phone turned off. Can you watch Johnny for a few hours?"

Cate was nearly speechless with surprise. "I-I, yes. I can. What do I need to know?"

Lucy handed Johnny to her. "Nothing special. He's tired so he'll probably fall asleep super early, but just let him. If he gets too fussy, there's a pre-made bottle in the fridge. Nuke it in the microwave but be sure to test it first to see if it's too hot before you give it to him."

"Okay. Where are you working? That's not what you wear to the Den."

Lucy pulled her keys from her pocket, then grabbed her purse from where it sat on the patio table. "Yeah, it isn't. This boat cost most of my savings, so I took another job as a cashier at Ingles. I'm scheduled until nine. If it's slow, they might let me off early. I gotta go."

She leaned in and kissed Johnny, then hurried up the dock to the parking lot.

Cate watched her get in her car and leave. She jostled Johnny around to keep him from crying.

"Hey over there," Ellis called from his deck. "Brandy saw you come up and wagged her tail before she went back to hiding. Come on over. Let me see the little guy."

Johnny heard his voice and got excited, so Cate walked over.

"Come in. Let's sit at the table so you can see Brandy," Ellis said, opening his gate to let her walk through. He led her inside.

Cate slid into the booth, then propped Johnny on her lap. He slapped the table with both hands. Down by her feet, snuffling alerted her to the fact Brandy lay there, staring up at her.

"Dababababa," Johnny said, making them both laugh.

"Hold on, I have something to keep him busy." Ellis opened a drawer, then took out two sets of colorful nesting measuring spoons. When he brought them to the table, Johnny immediately lit up and reached for them.

"Love it. That's old-school stuff."

"Yeah," he said. "I'm not a believer in handing your child a phone or tablet the second they can push buttons."

"I've wondered about that myself."

Ellis slid into the seat across from them. "Giving them electronics too early can have lasting effects on their ability to learn to read faces, and their short-term memory. Just not good. How did work go?"

He sounded like an expert on child development. She was impressed.

"It was okay. Worked my muscles. How is Brandy doing?"

"Much better today. She's coming along."

"That's good. I know it's going to be a while before she's feeling stronger, as malnourished as she is."

"Yes, but you'll be surprised at how she bounces back. Listen, I'd like to show you something," Ellis said. "But it's out on the lake. Want to take a short ride? Don't worry about Johnny. He'll think you're rocking him like a baby."

"Out there?" Cate stared at the water in the distance.

Johnny had stopped playing with the spoons to lay against her chest. She had his little butt resting on the table in front of her to help take the weight off her shoulders. He was a big baby—soon to be a wandering toddler. Time was moving fast.

Ellis chuckled. "Yes, out there. Haven't you ever been on a boat ride before?"

Memories flooded her. Long-ago days spent on the lake with the girls when they were little. Laughter. Splashing. Sunscreen and sandwiches.

Fun days before their family had been ripped apart.

She hadn't let herself go back there in decades.

"Yes, I have. It's been a while."

"Is that a yes?"

She looked at Brandy, who cowered under the dining table. Cate wasn't ready to leave the dog yet anyway. And Johnny now had his face nestled in the curve of her neck. She could feel his hot breath tickling her skin and smell the mild scent of baby shampoo in his hair. It was heaven. She was so glad she'd arrived in time to step in as a last-minute babysitter while Lucy went to work. She was only going to be gone four hours, but it was the first time she'd agreed to let Cate handle him alone.

It felt like a pop quiz.

Ellis watched her patiently.

"Yes. I guess it would be fine." She hoped Lucy wouldn't mind.

He stood, then stepped onto the dock. Going around to all the rope ties, he unfastened them, then went to the console where the steering wheel and all the electronics were.

It looked like a complicated affair. Cate stayed where she was, letting him concentrate. When the motor started, she expected to hear a loud rumble, but it was smooth and somewhat quiet.

Ellis stood at the wheel, his body strong and proud as he guided the boat, his shoulders broad and upright.

Cate enjoyed the feel of the boat gliding across the water. She felt herself relaxing, the tension from the day and the nervous anticipation she'd held melting away.

"Go sit out on the deck," he called from the wheel. "You can see better."

She opened her eyes, surprised she'd nearly fallen asleep while sitting at the table.

Brandy was still under the table, but she was alert and looked curious at the sound and movement.

"Want to come?" Cate offered, holding out her hand.

Brandy slunk back a little farther so Cate left her there. She wouldn't force her.

Cate balanced Johnny as she slid out of the seat.

When he stirred, she hushed him back to sleep by murmuring a nursery rhyme in his ear.

"Baa, baa, black sheep.. have you any wool…"

She considered taking him to the bedroom to lay him down, but she didn't want to waste a single moment of him in her arms, so she took him out to the deck with her.

When she went past Ellis, he smiled.

She smiled back, then went to the deck and took a chair at the front, turning it into the breeze. Settling herself into it, she maneuvered Johnny into a more comfortable position across her stomach and chest.

Cate was struck by the scenery around them—the mountains in the distance and the clear sky above. The fading sunshine sent little sparkles of diamonds glittering across the surface of the water, and the gentle hum of the engine provided soothing background noise.

A flicker of movement caught her eye. Brandy crept up beside her, her body hunched and hugging the deck floor.

She paused at Cate's chair, then kept going until she was at the front of the boat. Brandy's body relaxed, and she lifted her face to the wind.

Cate turned to look at Ellis.

He smiled again, winking. "That's what I wanted to show you. She loves the water. It eases her anxiety."

He was right about that. The cowering and frightened dog from minutes before was gone. Now, Brandy appeared totally at peace. As though knowing she was the subject of conversation, she turned and gazed at Cate for a second or two. It felt like a message passed between them before the dog turned back to the water.

Brandy had been expressing her gratitude. Cate felt a sense of accomplishment she'd never felt before. She thought back to her run through the woods, the listless dog in her arms, and the thought of an armed man just yards behind her.

The whole incident had been terrifying for so many reasons, but Cate had pressed through and let her heart take control, pushing past the fear of getting caught, being arrested, and bringing shame to her daughters, especially Taylor.

With it, she'd made a difference.

It might be with just one small creature, but it was something. She'd put her well-being aside to give Brandy a better life and a chance to learn that all humans weren't bad.

Would Cate break the law again if given the same choice?

For Brandy, yes. But Cate wasn't planning any more escapades that could jeopardize her freedom or her already-shaky relationships with her family.

Ellis went a bit farther, then cut the motor.

He bumped around behind her before joining her, a bottle of wine and two glasses in his hands. Ellis sat, crossing his legs, and leaning back before letting out a long sigh.

"These are the moments I live for now," he said. "Oh, and this wine pairs well with the sunset you are about to see."

"I don't drink."

"Oh, I'm sorry. You don't ever drink alcohol? Is there a reason why?" He poured wine into one glass, swirled it around, sniffed it, then took a sip.

It was red.

That was the extent of her wine knowledge.

"Not really, other than my first husband was an alcoholic. It turned me off the alcohol."

She kept her gaze on the top of Johnny's head, feeling embarrassed that she was so uncultured.

"Well, that's understandable. But occasionally drinking a glass or two doesn't mean you'll become addicted. Also, I doubt your ex even knows or cares that his illness brought on your no-alcohol pledge. But I respect you for your stance."

Cate stared out at the horizon.

Ellis was right. Jackson had no idea she didn't drink because of what he'd put her through—what he'd put them all through. If they were still together, he might have—maybe even acted like he cared or pretended to—but even that was doubtful. Jackson wasn't known for giving too much thought to anyone's needs but his.

"I think I will have a glass of wine," she said, the sudden words surprising herself at how easily they slipped out.

He raised an eyebrow, his expression serious. "Look, I don't want to be a bad influence or pressure you into something you don't want to do. I'm fine with getting you some juice or water. It's not a big deal. Truly."

"No, I want wine. I've never tasted it before, and this is the perfect time to try it." She gazed at the scenery, the sun setting in beautiful reds and pinks that spread across the horizon. It wasn't only the perfect setting, though. For some reason, she wanted the new experience to be with him. Someone who didn't know anything about her or her past.

Cate would never again underestimate how nice it felt to sit in someone else's company and be at peace, not having to question their motives or actions like she'd been forced to do for the last twenty years.

In her arms, Johnny shifted and began to snore.

It was a light snore, but it proved he was comfortable in her arms, that he felt safe enough to relax. A feeling of such intense love moved through Cate that she thought she might cry. She knew she would do anything to protect him from the world, including giving her own life if it came down to it.

Ellis was busy pouring the wine.

When she cleared the tears from her eyes, she watched him with a mixture of curiosity and hesitation.

"What should I expect?" she asked.

He looked up when he finished. "This is a cabernet Sauvignon. It's a rich wine with strong flavors of dark fruit, like blackberries and black currants."

"Want me to take Johnny?"

She didn't want to give her grandson up, but her neck and arms were beginning to ache quite a bit, so she nodded.

Ellis stood and reached down, easily pulling Johnny into his arms without so much as a flicker of effort. He settled back in the chair, and looked like a professional of holding babies.

Johnny never stirred.

At the front of the boat, Brandy did a few circles, then settled down with her tail tucked under her legs and her muzzle resting on her front paws. It was the most relaxed Cate had seen her yet.

"Ready?" Ellis asked, pushing the glass closer to Cate.

She picked it up, but she had no intention of making herself look like an idiot by mimicking his earlier swirling technique or by sniffing the wine.

"Sip slowly, then hold it in your mouth for a few seconds," he said. "Tell me what you taste."

She took a sip, surprised at how flavorful it was, then swished it in her mouth before swallowing. "I can taste the fruit as you said. But there's a hint of vanilla and spice, isn't there?"

He nodded. "Yes, there is. Good job."

She took another drink and repeated the exercise, letting the flavor linger on her tongue as she tried to discern what it was.

"I swear I taste chocolate. Just a little."

Ellis laughed. "Some people do. You also might feel a bit of a kick at the back of your throat. That would be the tannins. It comes from grapes. It gives the wine its structure and complexity."

Cate thought about that, visualizing rows and rows of grapes in the background of a beautiful vineyard. She'd never seen one in person, only in some of the castoff magazines she'd read in prison. The pictures always showed tables set romantically in the forefront, white flowers and tablecloths, and models toasting each other with love in their eyes. Images from a fairytale sort of life… when her reality couldn't have been further from what she saw on the pages.

Then there were the family magazines with articles about the 'ten best vacations to take with your family,' and 'fifty activities to do with your kids during summer,' and on and on, snapshots of mothers and children enjoying their lives.

Eventually, she'd stopped looking at magazines.

"What do you think?" he asked, pointing to her glass.

"I'm not sure. I can't say I love it, but I don't hate it either. It's just different than anything I've ever had."

"Wine is usually an acquired taste. Once you get used to it, you'll develop a palate for it and be able to understand the many nuances and flavors a good bottle can offer."

"I doubt I'll get there. Wine isn't really on my grocery list of things I can afford. I'll probably stick to juice."

"One day, you might decide to try it again. You know, they say a moderate consumption of red wine has health benefits, too."

She drank more this time, seeing the bottom of the glass through the small amount that remained.

It had gone quickly.

A warm, cozy feeling spread through her body, along with a lightness in her head. Suddenly, she was having a hard time remembering what she'd been so stressed about earlier. It was easy to see how people could become addicted to a magical potion that could erase all their worries.

It was kind of scary, to be honest.

"Would you like more?" he asked.

"No. No, thank you. I have to drive home."

"Is that a hint? You ready to turn back now?" He looked sad at the thought.

"No—let's finish watching the sunset." She didn't want to tell him, but the wine also made her feel easier in his presence, less on guard about him judging her.

She wanted to savor the feeling in case she never had it again.

"I'm curious, Ellis. What do you do for a living?"

He was in the middle of lifting the glass to his lips, but her question made him pause in mid-air. Then he took a sip and set the glass down.

"I don't do anything now, but I used to be a doctor."

"Used to be?" she asked. It made sense now why he'd been so good with Brandy in that first meeting.

"Well, technically, I still am, but I don't practice anymore."

She thought it must be nice that he'd been able to make enough money in his career to retire early. She would probably be working until she could barely get out of her rocking chair to hit the time clock.

On the other side of the coin, she didn't think she'd be happy not working. She'd at least want some sort of responsibility to wake up to.

"Do you have regrets about leaving your job?"

"Funny you should ask that, Cate. I've been thinking a lot about regrets lately."

"Do wish you still worked?"

"Not exactly." He drained his glass and poured another, then took a long sip. "It's a bit of a complicated story."

CHAPTER 21

*I*t felt like one of those moments that weighed a
thousand pounds as Cate waited for Ellis to say more.
Complicated stories were something she knew well, not only for
herself and her family, but also from the many women she'd met
over the last few decades. The telling of those stories could be done
in a variety of ways, but the deepest and most important had to be
approached carefully. Cate had learned there was a time to ask
questions, and a time to shut up and listen.

He finally spoke.

"I lost my wife in a car accident a few years ago. It was four in
the morning when a woman in critical condition was brought in.
The patient had been hit by a car while riding her bike. After I
scrubbed up, I approached the table, only to realize it was my wife
lying there, her body badly broken in many places."

The water continued to ripple gently around them, a soothing
lullaby that contradicted the hard things they talked about.

"They expected you to work on your own wife?" Cate asked,
imagining the horror of staring down at the woman he loved as she
took her last breaths.

He spoke slowly and methodically as if the words were physically painful. "It had to be me. No one else there that morning was qualified to perform the surgeries she needed. But despite my best efforts and more praying than I've ever done, I couldn't save her."

Cate was at a loss for words. She didn't want to say the wrong thing, so she stayed silent and let him talk.

"It was the worst day of my life. The person I loved more than anything in the world lay on my table. I had become a doctor so I could give her and our kids everything they'd ever want. Yet, I couldn't save her. I felt so powerless. And then, a few days after her funeral, I found her journal. She'd written about how lonely she was, and how she wished I wouldn't work so much."

"I'm so sorry, Ellis."

"Me too. Reading her journal made me realize I'd been so focused on my work and building my bank account that I'd neglected the most important things—my family and our time together. I felt like the shallowest human on the face of the earth. She basically raised our children by herself."

"It wasn't your fault," Cate said, reaching over to put her hand on his. "That's what people do. They get married, have a family, then spend most of their lives providing for them. You only did what you thought you were supposed to do. You can't blame yourself."

"But I do. And it's the hardest lesson I've ever had to learn. My kids were in college and they're adults now, but they know it, too. They realize everything I provided for them cannot make up for the time lost as a complete family. The memories they made without me."

"Do you see them?"

He nodded. "They come to check on me occasionally, but they're busy building their own lives now. My daughter works for a fancy law firm in Atlanta. She's just as ambitious and driven as I was, even though she doesn't see it. My son is taking life slower, learning how to appreciate the little moments more. He rents a cheap little studio in Maui, works various jobs to pay his bills, and refuses any help from me, of course. Likes to surf and is a hell of a spearfisherman. Amazes me how deep he dives, holding his breath the whole way, then still comes up with a fish for his dinner every time."

"Sounds like a wonderful life," Cate said.

"Yeah, I'm happy for him. What about you? Want to share your worst day ever, since I just exposed my guilty soul?"

She froze.

When she'd left the prison, she'd pledged to never, ever speak of the fire again. If Ellis thought he carried a lot of guilt, he'd seen nothing yet. If she had only been in the same room where Robert had slept, or woken up sooner, or managed to climb in through the window before they'd pulled her back.

Losing a spouse was hard, she knew that. Probably worse than she could imagine. But losing a child? And so tragically?

No, she wasn't ready to see the question in his eyes, the wondering if she might be guilty. Taylor said the reports said he'd been gone before the fire got him. She had to keep telling herself that or she would drive herself crazy.

"I'm sorry, Cate. I can see I touched a nerve. Please, just forget I asked. How rude of me."

He tripped over himself trying to apologize. Cate wondered if Lucy had told him anything about their past. He'd seen her scars. As a doctor, he would know they were from burns.

"It's fine. Really. Maybe I'll tell my story when I can have more than one glass of wine," she joked, trying to lighten the moment.

He looked relieved. "Thank you—for letting me off the hook and for listening to my tragic tale. I haven't talked about it in years, and I'm surprised I did tonight. You have a way with people, Cate."

"I do?"

He nodded. "Yes. You know how to listen. That's a gift many don't have these days. It invited me to talk, and that's something I don't do much."

"I'm glad I could help."

Johnny stirred in Ellis' arms.

The sun had set during Ellis' confessions, the moon taking over lighting the water before them.

"We need to get back," Cate said. "Lucy might return home early since this is my first time keeping Johnny alone."

He handed her Johnny before heading to the controls.

Brandy rose and took her stance again, her face in the wind.

As the boat turned around to head back to shore, Cate fell into a comfortable silence, content to simply soak in the beauty of their surroundings and the peacefulness of the moment.

When he glided them expertly into his slip, Cate could see that Lucy's boat was still dark except for the one light she'd left on.

Ellis cut the motor and moved around the dock, tying the lines before he took a seat again. Brandy came and dropped down at his feet.

"Look at her," Cate whispered. "She's not going to hide under the table."

"Yeah, she's been coming out when it's just me. I'm glad she's trusting you, too, now. She's made me want to take the boat out more and enjoy some coves I haven't seen in a while. It's nice to show her a different side of life. Something she enjoys."

Cate was happy, too. When she shifted Johnny a bit, he stirred.

"Want me to carry him over there for you?"

Cate had been thinking about Ellis' story and how touched she was that he'd chosen to share it with her.

She turned to him. "You shared your tragedy with me, and I feel like I need to do the same."

"No, you don't have to."

"I want to."

He relaxed back in his seat. "Okay. I'm listening."

She took a deep breath. Eyes on Johnny's sweet face, she steeled herself to say the words.

"My little boy died in a house fire."

"Cate, I'm so sorry." He started to lean forward like he was going to touch her arm.

She held her hand up. "No, wait—there's more. Let me get it out. I was charged with murder by arson, and I served twenty years in a Montana women's prison before I was exonerated recently."

She waited for his pity to change to suspicion. Or anger. Maybe hatred or revulsion.

It didn't.

"I'm so sorry," he said.

Now that the initial words were out, it felt easier. Like she could breathe. "Me too. He was the apple of my eye, and I miss him every day. He was such a special little boy."

"Will you take me through it? Tell me what happened? I think it might be therapeutic for you."

Cate hesitated for a moment. She wanted him to know, but it would be hard to talk about it. "I woke up to find the house filled with smoke and fire. Robert slept in a room I couldn't get to through the flames."

"Do you know how it started?"

"Faulty wiring. I woke up coughing and saw the fire, but the flames blocked me from Robert's room. I ran outside, around to his bedroom window, and I shattered the glass. By then, someone had called the fire department after seeing the smoke from the road. I almost made it into the window before someone pulled me back and held me down. They say I would've died in there with him. And I wanted to." She stared down at her feet. "Some days, I still wish I had."

"Please don't say that, Cate. If you'd died, you wouldn't have met or held your grandson. Did a fireman try to go in?"

Cate shook her head. "Yes, but it was too late. Robert was already gone."

"I can't imagine what that must have been like for you."

"Just like with your wife's accident, it was the absolute worst day of my life. I was burned badly and in the burn center when they told me he was gone. Then, while I was still in the hospital, I was arrested. A few crooked, so-called investigators looking for fame and glory sealed my fate with their false testimony and faulty tests. The jury convicted me. I went to prison for a crime I didn't commit, and I had to leave my four daughters to be raised by an alcoholic father."

She didn't tell him that they thought she had died, too. It was already an overload of tragedy, and she wasn't ready to confess that mistake to him.

"I'm so sorry, Cate. What an injustice."

"It is, but, after a few years, I learned to get past the anger and bitterness so I could do my time and get out. It ate me up inside. But the guilt—I still have it. Not only for not saving Robert, but also for my girls and the childhood they had without me. So much wasted time where I hadn't been there for them. In a way, like you think you weren't there for your children."

He searched her eyes.

"Thank you for sharing that with me. I swear to never talk about it to anyone else. I feel like you need to hear you can trust me."

It was nice of him to say, but she already knew that. She felt it deep in her bones. Ellis was a good man.

She stood, rearranging Johnny against her chest to make it easier for her to walk. "I'm going to go now. Thank you for a wonderful evening, Ellis."

He rose and gestured to Brandy. "Come on, girl. Let's get you over there. You'll be going to a new home later."

Brandy didn't move a muscle and a sudden look of fear came into her eyes. She didn't want to leave him.

Cate couldn't bear to cause her more anguish. "Let's hold off on that, Ellis. I think she's good right here with you for now. You're helping her heal."

She couldn't see his face in the dim lights, but she felt his gratitude. What she didn't say was that she was pretty sure Brandy was also helping *him* heal.

CHAPTER 22

Carter Anderson was avoiding them, but Taylor had a lead on where to possibly find him. She and Shane were headed there now. Thankfully, Shane was keeping their talk to work-related topics.

The sheriff had reamed them out that morning, and he said they'd better bring back a solid lead on the murders before the day was out.

Horis Hedgepeth was off the hook after talking to the sheriff at length and showing his gun collection. Treating him informally had proved to be the best approach, so the sheriff had taken on that task. Horis was of the good 'ole boy generation who didn't take kindly to modern-day investigative processes.

The search on Danny's apartment had also yielded nothing. His phone records were good, and no gun residue had been found on his person. To Taylor, that was enough evidence to clear him of any involvement in the murders, but Shane wasn't ready to take him off the top of their list.

Yet, they still had to investigate every other possible suspect. That meant Stacy had to be looked at closely because of her connection to Danny, and Carter Anderson was going to be the next stop. They were banking on her boyfriend spilling something useful.

"Lynn says she didn't have her timeline confused, so, after this, I want to go talk to Chipper Dayne," Taylor said.

"That's a long shot, but we'll do it. Maybe he'll remember something he saw. Something he thought was not important. Someone has to have seen something out there."

"You would think so."

"My money is still on Danny. I think Stacy is hiding something, and we'll just see what her little boyfriend has to say about her meeting Danny that day."

The pressure was on, and it was affecting them both.

She'd looked in the mirror that morning, horrified to see blemishes on her face, a sure sign her nerves were shot. She'd used some makeup to cover it and hoped Shane didn't comment on her unusually made-up face.

When she realized she was bellyaching about her skin when a murderer was walking around on the loose, she felt disgusted with herself.

"Turn here," she said.

She'd wanted to drive her squad car because she liked being behind the wheel, but Shane said it would be better to go in undercover, so he'd won that one. It always felt weird riding shotgun with him. Like they were a couple. It didn't feel that way with the sheriff or any of her other peers, but, for some reason, it did with Shane.

He slowed down, creeping past a few abandoned trailers. This was the ugly side of Hart's Ridge, and it was an embarrassment to the county.

As Shane pulled up to the designated house, they didn't see any cars or evidence that anyone was there. They watched for a minute, and Taylor saw a tiny movement of the shred of a curtain that hung on the front window before it went back into place.

They exchanged a glance. Both had seen their fair share of trouble, but something about this situation seemed off.

"Be careful," he said, putting his hand over his revolver as he exited the car.

Taylor did the same.

After they approached the door, Shane raised his hand to knock. But before he could make contact, they heard a loud bang from inside the house.

"Gunshot," Taylor shouted.

Without hesitation, they both drew their weapons and Shane kicked down the door. Inside, the scene was chaotic. Two unknowns scrambled to flee out the splintered front door while Carter bolted toward the back.

Shane pointed at Carter, then turned to chase the other two out the front door.

Taylor went after Carter. They ran through the living room and into the kitchen, then she caught up and tackled him just as he reached the back door.

She pinned him to the ground while he struggled, cussing and kicking.

"Why were you running?" she demanded, securing him until he stopped struggling, but she still held him there.

Carter's eyes darted around nervously, and he hesitated before speaking.

"I-I don't know what's going on! I didn't do anything!"

He was high. She could see it in his eyes.

"Who shot the gun? Where is it?" Taylor asked, worried for Shane.

"I don't know. Not me, I swear."

She pulled him to his feet and pushed him up against the wall, using her leg to spread his feet apart. She frisked him quickly, finding a very sizable baggie of meth in his pocket.

"Oh, here we go," she said, tossing it to the side before searching the other pocket.

In that one, she found a pipe. It was still warm.

"Seriously, Anderson? Can't you just get clean? What would your mama say?" Taylor asked. She wanted to slap some sense into him. He was too young to throw his life away.

"Damn, I just got out on probation from Gwinnett county," he moaned.

"And you're an idiot for telling me that. I hope you like the nice aroma of desperation on the mattresses in the county lockup. That's where you're going today. I'm sure it'll be a while before you get sprung this time."

She cuffed him and led him to the car, opening the door and shoving him inside before slamming it shut.

Adrenaline still pumped through her veins while she called for backup.

Shane came running back.

"They're gone. I couldn't catch them."

"You didn't call in their last coordinates?" she asked.

"No—I'm telling you, they just disappeared." He bent over, his hands on his knees while he heaved in big gulps of air. "Just some tweakers, anyway. You got who we were after."

Shane wasn't as in shape as she'd thought.

"You okay?" she asked when he kept his head down. Then she saw movement behind one of the overgrown bushes on the side of the house.

She quickly signaled to Shane, and they drew their weapons again.

"I got this," she whispered.

"Come out with your hands up," he shouted, ignoring her last comment.

His voice echoed through the empty streets, and no one moved.

Carter shouted from the car, a muffled message that was intended for the suspect, because a figure emerged slowly.

"I'll do it, I swear," Stacy said, holding a gun to her own head.

"Let him go or I'll pull the trigger."

"Let me handle this," Taylor hissed at Shane through her teeth.

"Stay back," Stacy yelled. "I mean it."

Taylor could see her hand shaking as she held the gun, and she prayed the girl didn't accidentally pull the trigger.

"I told you there was more to her story," Shane said.

Taylor ignored him. There would be time for I-told-you-so's later.

"Stacy, just stop. We aren't even here for you. We just wanted to ask Carter some questions." She slowly slid her gun back into the holster, ignoring Shane's quiet demands to take it back out.

"Damn it, Gray. You're going to get shot," he hissed.

"You're lying. You were going to tell him about what happened at the farm," Stacy shouted, tears running down her face. "You want to break us up!"

"No, Stacy. That's not true. None of it. Just put the gun down so we can talk about this." Taylor slowly began to inch toward her.

"If she makes one move of pointing that gun at you, she's a goner," Shane whispered.

"I heard that. I'm a goner anyway," Stacy shouted. "You're going to put Carter in jail, too."

"Not necessarily," Taylor lied. "It was a tiny bag of dope, Stacy. Nothing major. He'll be out by the afternoon. Don't you want to be there for him when he gets out?"

For a moment, it seemed like Stacy was considering Taylor's last question, but then she pulled the trigger. The blast reverberated through the air.

Taylor ducked, but when she looked up again, she saw the shot had missed Stacy's head.

Taylor reacted quickly, tackling her to the ground before Shane came and helped get her up. As Shane cuffed her, Taylor couldn't help but feel a sense of relief. It had been a close call, but they had managed to keep her from blowing her head off. Now to get them both to the department and find out what the hell was going on.

CHAPTER 23

*I*t was late afternoon before Carter and Stacy had been processed and finally led into the interview room. Taylor felt defeated after they'd finished and sent them back to the holding tanks. Now they were going out to Chipper's property in the hopes of salvaging the day.

"Nothing. An absolute waste of time," Shane said. "We couldn't even get out of them who the other two were who fled the house."

She drove this time and she thumped the steering wheel with her thumb, trying to think. It had been a long day, and she was tired. Tired in her body but also in her soul. It always depressed her to see people throwing away their lives.

"Just kids, though," she said. "It's a shame they're in so deep with these drugs. Stacy's mother was crying and making calls to try to find a free rehab with a bed. She's finding out the waiting lists on the free spots are miles long."

"Yeah, well, that girl will probably detox on her own because she's going to sit in jail until we see if she wants to give us anything. It's not purely a coincidence that they hooked up again after all these years, not on the day of the murders."

"She says they've been talking for months, but I see what you're saying. I'm just glad she didn't point the gun at us, or she'd be facing all kinds of charges. I made sure they put her on suicide watch, but I don't think she wanted to kill herself."

After it was all over, Taylor remembered seeing Stacy tilt the gun slightly up right before she pulled the trigger. The gun wasn't even hers. They suspected it belonged to one of the two who had gotten away, but the serial number was filed down too far to read.

Chipper lived out on Bode Weevil Road. Once they were on it, his driveway was just another quarter of a mile. Taylor drove down the bumpy dirt road, dust billowing up in their wake.

Next to the driveway was a handmade sign advertising firewood and delivery. Taylor kept on until the house came into view.

The house had seen better days, the roof sagging and in need of repair. The yard was overgrown, and a broken-down truck sat on blocks off to the side.

It was about what she expected, considering he only sold firewood and did some handyman projects now and then. He also took a few construction jobs when he was hard up for money. His wife, Vera, stayed home for the most part, but she also sold Avon and a few handmade quilts here and there.

They were both active in the church. Vera was a Sunday school teacher, and Chipper was an ordained deacon. Taylor had gone to their church a few times, at the invitation to accompany Della Ray for Easter services, and she'd seen them there, both dressed to the nines as though they came from a better part of town and not dusty Bode Weevil Road.

After Taylor parked, they got out and climbed the rickety porch steps. Shane led, only because he always insisted, and he knocked.

They heard a couple of locks being disengaged.

A small dog erupted into high-pitched barking. Vera opened the door, pushing the dog back with her foot. She was already in her pajamas, her feet in matching pink house slippers.

"Deputy Gray," she said, smiling, then nodding at Shane.

The dog kept yapping.

"Hello, Mrs. Dayne," Shane said, raising his voice over the racket. "I'm Detective Weaver with the Hart County Sheriff's department. We'd like to talk to your husband."

She looked worried. "He's not here right now. Is there something wrong?"

"No, we just have a few questions for him. Nothing's wrong."

"We haven't had another murder, have we? I'm just so nervous out here by myself. Are you coming to tell us something bad?" She still had not invited them in and, with her foot, she blocked the dog from getting out.

The dog decided it wasn't going to get any farther, so it turned and disappeared deeper into the house.

"No, of course not," Shane said. "But speaking of the tragedy, do you mind if we ask you some questions?"

"That's fine, though I don't know anything that can help," she said, opening the door all the way to let them in. She held her arms to her chest, as though covering her bosom. "Should I go put on some other clothes?"

"No, you're fine," Taylor said. "I can't wait to get in my own nightclothes."

"Just wait until you're an old lady like me. You'll never get out of them," Vera said, chuckling. She led the way to the kitchen and had them sit at the table.

The inside of the home was much nicer than the outside, obviously from a woman's touch. The kitchen chairs were covered in yellow-flowered slipcovers that looked homemade, and the room was spotless.

"Coffee?" Vera asked.

They both refused, and she sat down with them. She was barely in the chair before the little white blur of fur streaked in and made a flying leap onto her lap.

"Biscuit, behave yourself," she said, pushing it to sit.

"Mrs. Dayne, do you remember May seventeenth?" Taylor asked.

She nodded emphatically. "Yep. I'll never forget it. Beverly is a friend of mine, and my heart just aches for what she's going through. She and I were in a quilting group together last year. Amos was a good man, and I'm pretty sure his son, David, was too. Just a shame."

"Where were you that day?" Shane asked.

"Right here. All day."

"And your husband?" Taylor asked.

"I can tell you exactly. He was doing a job in Jasper for a contractor he knows. Chipper works for him occasionally when he's in a bind or his crew is short. I don't like it because I think some of the projects are too hard for Chipper and should be done by younger men. That day, he hung some drywall to make some extra money."

"Did he know what had happened?" Taylor asked.

"Not for a long while. He was so busy when it came over the news that I couldn't get him on the phone until he was on his way home. I was pretty shaken up, as you can imagine. He had his hands full with me when he got here."

"I understand. It was very shocking to us all," Taylor said. "Did he say if he'd seen anything at all out of the ordinary that day, on his way out of and back into town?"

She shook her head. "No, I don't think so."

"Do you have the name and number of the contractor he was working for?" Shane asked.

Vera got up and went to a drawer, pulled it open, and brought out a small spiral notepad. She flipped the pages.

"Here it is. I make him give me emergency numbers in case he loses his phone, and I can't get him. JD is all I know him by, but I have his number from a few years ago when Chipper helped him on a roofing job. You ready?"

"I'm ready," Taylor said. She had the notes app on her phone out. When Vera called off the numbers, she put them down with JD beside it.

"Do you know where your husband is right now?" Shane asked.

"He's out on deliveries," Vera said. "Probably won't be home until later tonight."

"Would you mind calling him and asking him where he is and if he could swing by for a minute?" Shane said.

"Sure, but I don't know how close he is." She went to the counter near the sink and picked up her phone, then dialed. She walked into the other room to talk.

"What do you think?" Taylor asked Shane. "Picking up any vibes?"

"Nada. I think we're wasting our time."

From the hall, Vera's tone changed as she talked. They couldn't tell what she was saying, but she sounded exasperated.

She returned, but now her smile looked forced.

"He said he won't be home for hours, I'm afraid."

Shane stood. "That's fine, Mrs. Dayne. We'll head out, but do you mind if we look around your property? We've been asking everyone just in case the suspects may have hidden out around here and left any clues behind."

She covered her mouth. "Oh, heavens. Do you think they were on our land? With me right here in this house?"

"I doubt it," Shane assured her. "But it doesn't hurt to check. If you don't mind."

"Oh, I don't mind at all. I'm sure Chipper would be happy to know you've done your jobs. Our property is always open to law enforcement. You can even check our camper."

"Is it out there?" Taylor asked.

"Oh no, it's down at the Cripple Creek campground. Maybe that's too far now that I think about it. I'm sorry. Sometimes my mouth gets ahead of my brain."

"No problem. We'll put it on the list. If any reason comes up to check out there, we'll know we have your permission. What site is your camper on?"

"BA16. It's a mess because we haven't been out there to clean it up for the season yet." She led them to the door, opened it, and held it open. "You two be careful poking around. Like Chipper keeps telling me, there's a madman on the loose and he doesn't care who he takes down."

"Yes, ma'am," Taylor said. "Don't forget to lock this door behind us."

"Oh, you can bet the farm on that," Vera said. "Chipper put me another deadbolt in after what happened and I'm all about making sure it doesn't get rusty."

CHAPTER 24

$\mathcal{T}$aylor felt like the day would never end, but she couldn't hold anyone else responsible because it was her idea to go look at Cripple Creek while they had the time. It was a place they hadn't thought of, which was embarrassing, as they should've checked every campground in the county for suspicious activity after the crime.

They pulled out of the long driveway and back onto Bode Weevil Road. Her car was going to need a wash when they got back. Hopefully, she could bribe Penner into it. She wasn't a fan of washing cars, especially when they didn't belong to her.

"Let's just do it all and knock him off the list, other than his statement," Shane said. "Give me that number."

Taylor handed him her phone. He pulled up the number Vera had given them and dialed it on his phone. Someone picked up on the second ring.

"Hello, this is Detective Shane Weaver with the Hart County Sheriff's department. We're investigating a recent crime. I'd like to ask you a few questions about someone who works for you."

He stared ahead intently at the road while he listened.

"Thank you. I appreciate it. The man's name is Chipper Dayne, and he was on-site working for you in Jasper on May the seventeenth. I just need you to verify that—let me know what time he arrived and left there."

A long pause.

"Are you sure? May seventeenth." Shane looked at Taylor, a surprised expression on his face.

Another pause.

"What about in that week? Or when was the last time he worked for you?"

When he hung up, he shook his head. "We have a problem. Mister Contractor JD says Chipper hasn't worked for him for at least six months."

"No way," Taylor said.

"Yep. Now we can thank sweet little Vera for permitting us to look at their camper, though it's still a long shot that anything is going on."

"I agree. I can see Chipper lying to his wife about where he was because he tries to be quite the charmer. He may very well have a girlfriend around the county somewhere. But I doubt we're going to dig up any deeper dirt than that."

"That's what I thought. It'll be one more to check off the list, but we'll need to get a statement from him, too."

"Agreed."

Just before the turn-off to the Cripple Creek campground was a country convenience store that had been there for ages. It only had four pumps, and they weren't the computerized type either, but there was a truck pulled up to one, getting gas.

"Pull in there. I've got to grab something to eat," Shane said. "Want a hot dog?"

She grimaced, but she pulled in. Many of the country stores around the county sold hot dogs or BBQ sandwiches with pickles and slaw, but Taylor could visualize the rolling wiener-holding tank and all the grease involved.

"I'll pass. But I'm coming in, too. I want a bottle of water, and I'm going to ask them if they know Dayne."

They got out and went in, Shane heading to the food counter and Taylor taking a shortcut to the coolers. She grabbed a bottle of water and went to the check-out counter.

The woman behind the counter looked like she'd just stepped out of nineteen-ninety-five. Overly permed and bleached hair piled atop her head and dark blue eye shadow. Before Taylor even looked at her fingers, she knew they'd be stained from nicotine and would have one-inch nails.

"Hi," Taylor said as warmly as she could.

"Well, hello there." She typed a price into the cash register carefully with the tips of her nails.

No scanning of barcodes or computerized checkout for them.

All old school. Antique, as Levi would say.

The clerk told her the price with tax, and Taylor handed her card over.

"We don't take those here, honey," the woman said, giving her a pitying look.

"Oh—I—"

"I got it. I've got cash," Shane said, coming up beside her, a hot dog and a can of coke in his hands.

"Well, look at you," the clerk said, her voice heavy with a suddenly deeper Southern drawl. "Paying for her drink and all that."

She fluttered her eyelashes at Shane, practically salivating. Taylor tried not to laugh at Shane's sudden uncomfortable body language.

"Um, Miss… I'm sorry, what was your name?" he asked the clerk.

"Melanie." She rang up his hot dog and coke and told him the price of everything together. He dug out his wallet, then handed her a ten-dollar bill.

"Were you working on May the seventeenth, Melanie?" he asked.

She squinted her eyes, looking at the ceiling like she was trying to remember.

"It was the day of the tragedy down at Hart Valley Farms," Taylor said.

Melanie's face changed quickly to one of horror.

"I sure enough was, honey. I remember because my cousin lives not too far from there. When she heard the sirens, she went over and checked it out, then called me. I was here, working alone. I got so scared that I locked that door until my husband could come and finish the shift with me."

"Did you see anything or anyone strange that day?" Shane said.

She shook her head. "No, can't say that I did. Thank goodness, I mean."

A man came up to stand beside them at the counter.

"I came in here that day, too," he said. "Well, I come in just about every day. For the hot dogs. But I'll never forget that day. So sad what happened to that family."

When they turned to him, he apologized.

"Sorry, I need to pay for my gas. Overheard you talking." He gestured out the window to the truck parked at the pumps.

"Did you see anything out of place?" Taylor asked.

"Nah. Just the same old people. You might want to ask Phil Pearman. He was in here, too. Sat down with me. Had a sandwich and a bag of peanuts. We were talking about what happened. Oh, and Chipper Dayne was outside getting gas when we left. He might've saw something."

Taylor felt Shane stiffen beside her. She bumped his arm.

Don't blow it.

Then she stepped closer to the man.

"Are you sure it was Chipper Dayne?" she asked.

He nodded. "Yep. Matter of fact, I remember Phil saying 'well, here comes Chipper D,' but then we saw he was in a hurry."

"Why do you think he was in a hurry?" Shane asked.

"Don't know, but he had dirt and leaves all over him so I 'spect he'd been in the woods cutting. Probably wanted to get cleaned up and rested."

"Oh, I saw Chipper, too," Melanie said. "I didn't think nothing of it since he's not a stranger."

"About what time do you think it was?" Taylor asked.

Melanie hesitated, but the man answered. "Lunchtime! I was here for my hot dog."

"Yes, I'm sure it was around eleven or so," Melanie agreed.

"Thanks so much," Taylor said.

She pulled out her notebook and flipped it open. "Can I get your name and phone number in case we have any more questions?"

"Sure, I'm Brett." After he gave her the rest of his information, they left the store and got into the car.

Shane unwrapped his hot dog and took a big bite.

"Well, what do you think about that?" Taylor said, breathing through her mouth to keep the nauseating smell of the hot dog away.

"I think it's good we're going out to the campground," he said, his mouth full. "Step on it."

CHAPTER 25

Cate led the big white dog out to one of the play yards, then took him off the leash. He was a stoic one who was always cooperative and resigned to whatever it was they asked him to do. He didn't bark or try to chew his cot. He was the model inmate, as they'd say in the prison.

"You're a good boy, Gilly."

She rubbed his head, and he smiled at her in a way only a dog could, then began to investigate the parameters of the yard, lifting his leg at every corner.

Gilly was a favorite, simply because of his quiet and stoic demeanor. He was found wandering a highway and was miserable in the shelter, that much was clear. As a Great Pyrenees, he was born to be in wide open spaces. The breed was known to be guardians of their pack, and members included their humans, livestock, and other family pets.

He missed having his freedom, but Cate was sure he missed his job more. Dogs like him needed to feel useful. To have responsibilities.

She'd taken him on several long walks through the woods that ran along the backside of the property, and he had enjoyed it.

The door opened and Sarah came out, leading a couple.

Gilly came back to her side, looking for support at the sight of strangers.

"Cate, this is Melissa and Michael, and they're interested in meeting Gilly."

They all approached the gate and Cate opened it, letting them come in. They appeared to be in their late fifties and looked lean and fit.

"I'll leave them with you. Show them back when they're done and have decided if they want to adopt him," Sarah said, then headed back inside.

"Hi. Nice to meet you." Cate held her hand out to shake with them both.

Melissa bent and petted Gilly, talking to him in a voice that bespoke experience with bigger dogs.

"You sure look strong and healthy," she said.

"He's a hoss," the man added.

Cate was starting to be able to tell when an interested adopter had only had small dogs before, as they tended to talk to the dogs in baby voices. Those who were used to talking to big dogs used a deeper and more adult tone.

"Can you tell me a little about your family and your home, or the environment a new dog would be living in?" Cate asked.

"Yes," she said. "We're empty nesters and have five acres in the country around Clermont. It's completely fenced in, and I just started raising chickens. Will he chase chickens?"

They both looked suddenly concerned.

"We haven't tested him with chickens, but if he does, he can be trained not to, but I think he's probably a good boy."

"Okay. We also have a few goats and a donkey, too. The coyotes are getting to be bad around us, and we feel that having a dog like this might help keep them away."

"You don't plan to leave him outside all the time, do you?" Cate asked.

"Well, yes," she said. "I told the girl up front that, and she said this is the one we should meet."

"They were originally used in the Pyrenees mountains to protect their livestock from wolves and bears, I'm sure they can handle a mild Georgia winter," the man said.

Cate nodded. "They can, but you will still need to make sure they have adequate shelter to get into in bad weather. A barn or an insulated doghouse. Over the years, the dog breed has gotten softer, as they were introduced into homes more and more. Not to say he won't want to be outside all the time. He probably will."

"Oh, we'll have a good shelter for him," Melissa said. "Does he like to hike?"

"He does. I've taken him on several long walks, and he loves it. He knows a few commands, too."

She held her hand over him, then put her palm down. "Sit, Gilly."

He immediately sat.

"Oh my gosh, he's so smart," Melissa said.

"Down," Cate said, bringing her hand down slowly until Gilly dropped his belly and then his muzzle to the ground. "He also knows the commands *drop it* and *leave it*. He would probably prefer a home without small dogs as their yapping gets to him."

"How do you know that?" Michael asked.

She smiled. "I can tell. I'm pretty good with dogs."

"What about with kids? We are expecting to have grandkids eventually if all goes well," Melissa said. "And my sister's kids visit a lot. Would he be okay with them?"

"He's great with kids. A few played with him here just the other day. He's very patient and tolerant. Most Pyrenees are." She still remembered how sad Gilly looked when the family with the kids left. The parents had decided he was too big for them.

"That's good. Could we take him on a walk? Outside of here?" Michael asked. "We'd like to see how he handles on a leash."

"Of course. You can go right out that gate. There's already a trail through those woods that we've been using. You probably won't see anyone on it, but if you do, don't worry. Gilly will be a gentleman."

She hooked the leash to his collar before handed it over to Melissa. The least strong of the couple needed to determine if she could handle a big dog. Gilly was a good one for her because though he liked to lead, but he didn't pull.

They headed out. When they disappeared from sight, Cate realized she was nervous. They looked like a great option for Gilly, and she wanted him to be free so badly.

Please be good, Gilly.

She turned and went back inside, beginning another round of cleaning. She felt nervous and excited about her evening plans. She'd promised to go out on the sunset cruise again with Ellis and Brandy. This would be their third time.

Ellis was calling it dog therapy.

Cate wasn't sure if the therapy was for her or Brandy, but she told herself that was all it was, and that she wasn't interested in him other than as a friend.

A very attractive and interesting friend. One that was way out of her league, but she tended to try to forget about that detail.

She turned and looked down the galley, toward the window. It felt like Gilly and his prospective new pet parents were gone an excruciatingly long time, but when she heard the gate outside, she glanced at the clock and saw it had only been half an hour.

That wasn't long enough to fall in love.

Her shoulders dropped, and she let out a long sigh.

Gilly was going to have to wait a bit longer for his forever family.

She went out the door. Both Melissa and Michael were sitting in the grass, Gilly between them with his head on Melissa's legs.

"Can you make sure they get the paperwork ready?" Michael called out. "We want to make sure he doesn't spend another night in that kennel."

Cate couldn't help the joy that filled her, and she clapped her hands and laughed, a sound she rarely heard come from within her. "That I can promise you a hundred percent will be done," she said, then turned to go in and get Sarah right on it.

Her week was made.

Gilly was going home.

CHAPTER 26

*T*aylor drove slowly past the rows of neatly spaced-out tents and campers, and a few big RVs. The campground was ramping up now that it was almost Memorial Day weekend, people claiming their spots with some coming early to stay through to the holiday.

"I'd love to have a spot to camp on, but not here squeezed in among all these people," Shane said. "It's bad enough in my condo."

"Me, either. I like to be secluded when I go on vacation. I'm around people enough doing this job." She noted the numbers on the campsites. When she saw BA16, she pulled up and stopped.

They got out, then approached the faded red-and-white camper. It had a metal awning stretched over a patch of dirt that held a picnic table, serving as a patio. A smattering of folding chairs and a rusted grill were scattered around the area.

The evening was moving in quickly, and the sound of crickets was already a backdrop to the dropping temperatures.

Shane walked to the end of the camper where there was a lawn chair next to what appeared to be a fire pit. He bent and used a stick to move some of the charred pieces around.

"Look here," he said, holding up a tiny piece of metal.

Taylor headed over. "What is it?"

"Grommet. Goes over the eyelets on a boot. Sometimes, they call them speed hooks. You know, the things the laces go through. I'm going to get an evidence bag from my trunk."

He retrieved one and came back. They poked around again and found a few more, then Taylor found a metal snap, like what was used to fasten a pair of coveralls. It was getting dark, and she couldn't make out the brand, so she shined her flashlight on it.

It read *Dickies*.

She'd seen Chipper in gray Dickies coveralls too many times to count.

"He wears this brand, but why would he be burning them?" she said, trying to piece together what she was seeing.

"If they had blood on them, he would. Let's look inside."

They went to the door, and Shane tried the knob. "It's flimsy, but I can pop it in two seconds."

He hesitated.

"She gave us permission," Taylor reminded him.

He pulled a credit card out of his wallet. He was right—it took him two seconds before the door opened.

They stepped inside.

The interior was cramped and smelled like mothballs. One side held a kitchenette and the other a bed built into the end, a window above it covered with red-and-white checkered curtains and torn blinds.

Just before the bed was a small door.

"Must be the shower," Taylor said.

Shane opened it and peeked in. "Yep. Tiny in here. I couldn't use it."

He moved out of the way, and Taylor went in. She opened the shower door to run her hand along the wall.

"Someone's had a shower in here not too long ago," she said.

Shane squeezed into the room with her, making it feel uncomfortably close. He looked at the ceiling.

"No ventilation. You take a shower in here, and it's going to take a long time for the water to completely evaporate, especially in May."

"You think the shower could've been taken weeks ago?" Taylor asked.

"It's possible. Remember, Vera said they haven't been up here in months. That water got in here somehow, and I don't see any leaks in the ceiling."

"There's a towel, too." She pointed at the towel hanging on a hook beside the shower. She touched it, but it was dry. She picked it up off the hook to smell it. It smelled mildewy. "I would think they'd have washed everything up when they closed it for the season."

"I agree. Vera wouldn't leave a dirty towel hanging up here through the winter," Shane said.

Taylor's head was spinning, trying to put the pieces together.

"Let's take a closer look outside," she said.

They went out. After looking around the camper, and again in the firepit, they walked over to the bathhouse.

Taylor went into the women's side and Shane took the men's, both going over every inch to search for any evidence.

They met back outside.

"Nothing," he said.

"Same." Taylor shined her flashlight out over the campground, spotting an outbuilding in the distance. She stopped her light on it. "What about that shed? Think we can get in?"

"Probably where the groundskeeper keeps his things. Let's go look."

They went to it and tried the door, but it was locked, so they searched around it, going to the back of the building.

It was an old structure and still set on large concrete blocks with at least a foot of space underneath.

Taylor crouched to shine her light under it. There were some old railroad timbers slid into one side, and a rusty small animal trap that might've been used for raccoons.

Shane crouched beside her and leaned down, his palms on the ground so he could peer under with his light.

"I don't see anything useful," he said.

But something was niggling at Taylor. She felt a current running through her. The kind she'd gotten before when she was close to an important discovery. She wasn't ready to walk away. Not until the tingling stopped.

"I'm going under there," she said.

"What? Why? Don't do that, Taylor. It's snake season."

"Because I want a closer look," she said, then laid flat on her belly and army-crawled in. She checked every inch as she went to make sure she didn't wake up a grouchy snake.

She went to the timbers first, but she couldn't tell if they'd been moved.

"Be careful," Shane called, sounding worried. "I don't like this. I don't have a snake kit in my car. Come on out, Taylor."

As she moved around to the other side of the timbers, she could see marks in the clay mud that looked like something or someone else had been under there recently.

A coyote or a stray dog possibly, depending on the size. She shined her flashlight around, looking for paw prints, but found none.

What she did see was a small mound that looked fresh.

She crawled over, putting her hand on it.

Yes, it was fresh.

"There's something buried under here," she called out to Shane.

"Something big? Like a body?" He sounded excited.

"No, something small. I'm going to try to dig it up." She kept her flashlight on, but she used the end of it to move the dirt aside and dig deeper.

It was hard going the farther she dug down as the clay was packed in tight, but she wasn't giving up.

"Can you see what it is?" Shane asked.

"Hold on." She put the flashlight down and pointed it at the spot, then dug with her hands, ignoring the pain that streaked through her fingertips.

She hit something hard.

Using the light, she saw what appeared to be a cigar box.

She dug around it some more until she could lift it from the hole. It wasn't a cigar box, after all. Just a plain wooden box.

"I got it," she called. "It's a wooden box."

"Shit, Taylor. It's probably where someone buried their pet frog or something. Come on, get out of there."

Taylor opened the box, then shined the light into it.

The tingling stopped immediately.

Because she was looking at several rolls of cash laying atop a 44-magnum pistol. She shut the box and crawled out with it, then held it out to Shane.

He opened it, shined his light inside, then turned to her.

"Looks like we might have something here. I guess Danny has just been demoted and is no longer my prime suspect."

CHAPTER 27

*S*hane was on the phone with the sheriff, getting him started on an emergency search warrant while Taylor drove, racing back to Chipper's property. They wanted to be there when he got home in case their visit had spooked him and he planned to hide any potential evidence.

Taylor prayed Judge Crawford would come through, and she was confident he would. He wanted this case solved as badly as anyone. He'd also been good friends with Amos.

"He's on it," Shane said, putting the phone down. "He can't believe we found that box. What luck. But listen, when we get to Dayne's property, we'll just go in and talk casually. Go over questions again while we wait for the sheriff to call. I don't want things to escalate before we get our hands on his guns."

"Agreed." With Taylor ignoring the speed limits posted and blowing out the dirt road so fast it looked like a sandstorm chasing them, they made it back in record time and pulled into the driveway.

Chipper's truck still wasn't there.

It was dark, and a porch light came on.

They got out and went to the porch, then the door.

Taylor knocked. "Mrs. Dayne, it's me again. Deputy Gray."

The curtain moved, then dropped, and Vera disengaged the locks and opened the door. "What's wrong?" she asked, clutching a housecoat closed over her pajamas.

Shane turned on his smooth detective charm.

"Nothing's wrong, Mrs. Dayne, but we forgot we need to check that all your husband's guns are accounted for. Just to make sure one wasn't stolen to commit the murders."

Her eyes widened. "Oh. I see. Chipper called and said he was going to pick up a truck from a guy in Florida. He does that sometimes. Buys them cheap and flips them for more money. He won't be coming home tonight after all, but I guess it's okay."

Yes, keep going, Shane. You got her.

Taylor didn't say a word, but she set her phone on record, furtively turning it in Vera's direction. Now the tingling was crawling up her hands to her shoulders.

"Are you giving us permission to enter and search the premises, Mrs. Dayne? And to check your husband's guns?" Shane asked.

"Why, sure. I want to help however I can." She looked at him as though she wondered why he'd even ask such a thing.

"Great, can you show us where he stores his guns? Gray, can you make a call and let the department know we'll catch up with Dayne later?"

He gave her a knowing look and she nodded, then walked outside and called the sheriff.

"He's running," she said when he picked up. "Supposedly headed to Florida to pick up a truck."

"I'll call the U.S. Marshals in Florida right now. They'll set up surveillance and get him when he crosses the state line," the sheriff said. "Just hope he doesn't off himself like a coward. I want him back."

"Okay. Also, his wife is permitting us to search the house, so we may not need the search warrant."

"I'll have it in an hour anyway," the sheriff said. "Good work, Taylor. Keep at it."

His praise shot through her like adrenaline.

"Just back here in my laundry room," Vera said, then led them through the kitchen to the back of the house into a room that held her washing machine and dryer, as well as two large gun safes across the opposite wall.

"Do you have the keys?" Taylor asked.

"Oh, no. I don't think so. But I'm sure they're around here somewhere. If we can't find it, I'll call Chipper again."

"No, it's fine. He's driving," Shane said. "Let's look for them."

Vera opened a few drawers and cabinets, and Taylor ran her hand over the top of the doorframe. She felt the keys laying end to end.

"Got 'em," she said, handing them to Shane.

He opened the first safe, looked through the rifles in the rack, and shut the door. Then he opened the second safe and stood back.

"Gray, get your gloves on."

Taylor was preoccupied with a rod of clothes hanging from the ceiling. On it hung two pairs of gray coveralls for drying. She saw they were Dickies brand, too, but she turned to the gun safe and looked around Shane.

She saw the 22-magnum rifle they were looking for.

Bingo.

"What is it?" Vera asked.

"Is this your husband's gun?" Shane said.

"They're all his guns. I've told him that one man doesn't need so much artillery just to do some simple deer hunting, but he likes to collect them. Why?"

"Do you mind if we take this one?" he asked, sidestepping her question.

Vera immediately looked suspicious. "Something's not right here. Are you thinking my Chipper might be a suspect in those murders?"

They hesitated. Taylor would let Shane handle that question.

"Because if you are, that's so ridiculous that I'll let you take whatever you want to, just to prove he had nothing to do with that mess. I know my husband, and he's not a killer, thank you very much."

She was indignant but so foolish. Thankfully, Taylor had turned the video option back on and got her statement of consent.

"I'm sure you're right," she said to Vera. "Danny and a few others had to provide a lot of stuff, as well. That's how we eliminate suspects. I hope you understand."

"I sure do. And when he gets back, we'll get this all squared away," she said. "Take what you need."

~

At the department, they all took turns pacing the floor of the conference room. The sheriff was the most agitated, constantly checking his phone to make sure it was still working.

"If he's driving to Florida, it's going to be at least three more hours and that's if he doesn't stop anywhere," he said.

"He'll probably stop and dump his truck in the swamp," Taylor said. "Then walk out. You know if he did this, that truck has DNA in it. He left a bloodbath behind at the Higgins, and he had to have transferred something to the vehicle when he took off."

"Absolutely," Shane said. "I'd like to go looking for him myself, to tell the truth. I'd find him, though I can't promise he'll be breathing when I bring him in."

The sheriff shook his head. "No. You both are staying right here. Let the marshals do their job. They're excited about this. Not too often can they put collaring a triple murderer on their resume. If he crosses that line, they'll get him and bring him to us. Don't you worry about that."

Taylor leaned back in her chair, taking another sip of coffee. It was lukewarm, but it kept her awake. The sheriff had let Penner and Kuno go home at midnight, though they'd wanted to stay. He said they needed to have someone with some energy the next day in case the town turned upside down.

Though it felt like that was what was happening now. Taylor was stunned at the turn of events. She'd just finished typing everything up, cataloging every detail from the moment Lynn Dobbs had mentioned Chipper Daynes, to talking to Vera, to the campground discoveries.

It appeared to be open and shut. At least until Chipper had taken off.

However, no case was ever easy no matter what evidence they collected. A good defense attorney could turn what they'd found so far into nothing. He could say it was all circumstantial.

She prayed the gun came back from testing with good news. Hopefully, one of them at least would have DNA on it, but, if not, they needed to be able to match the casings they'd found.

If none of that panned out, they needed a confession.

Actually, they needed that anyway. But to get that, they had to get Chipper's ass back to Hart county.

Taylor thought about the last few days. Lynn Dobbs, bless her sweet soul, had no idea that her observation and statement about Chipper coming out there that morning had turned the case upside down. If she hadn't paid attention and didn't even know he'd been there delivering wood, they'd still be trying to determine who their prime suspects were.

That made her think of Danny, and she felt a rush of guilt. Shane had already marked him as the killer. Taylor's gut had told her Danny was innocent, but the way it was going, she was starting to question her instincts. Shane was persuasive.

If this all came together, Taylor couldn't wait to give Danny the news.

"It's one-thirty in the morning!" The sheriff cursed, leaving the conference room in a huff.

Shane hit the wall with his fist, and Taylor jumped.

"What the hell is wrong with you?" she scolded him.

"I'm going nuts in here," he said, then began pacing again.

"Then go outside. Don't act like a damn fool. This isn't some high school locker room." She fought the urge to kick out at him from her chair, which would make her look like a juvenile, too.

He glared at her. "Fine, I will."

"Good. Go." She pointed at the door.

"Don't forget, Taylor. When this is over, you and I are going to talk about us."

Even that sounded angry. Why did men have to go all testosterone when they were frustrated? If he thought acting like a caveman was going to win points in their relationship, he was dead wrong.

He grabbed the door handle at the same time the door opened, and the sheriff returned.

"They got him."

Relief flooded through Taylor as she jumped up. Shane threw his arms around her and spun her around.

"Hell, yes!" he shouted.

CHAPTER 28

The lake was calm and clear, the sun just beginning its descent toward the horizon with warm hues of pink and orange as Ellis guided them out. This time, it was just the two of them, as Lucy was home with the baby and had sent them off with a wink and knowing smile that had embarrassed Cate.

Ellis, ever the gentleman, pretended not to see it.

Brandy was in position again, their little mascot at the front of the boat, her body language even more confident than the last time as she looked out over the water. She was already starting to fill out, too, her coat beginning to shine because of the good food Ellis was giving her. She had come a long way both physically and mentally, and she hadn't even cowered when Cate came onto the boat this time. She'd run up, her head just a bit lowered but her tail wagging furiously at the site of her rescuer.

Cate already loved her so much.

On their last cruise, Ellis had told her that he knew her story wasn't true, that she hadn't found Brandy on the side of the road. He said when she was ready to share, he wouldn't judge because Brandy needed to be taken out of whatever situation she was in.

"How did you know I wasn't telling the truth?" she'd asked him.

"She wasn't wearing a collar. If you found her on the side of the highway, you wouldn't know her name."

Her face still burned at getting caught in a lie.

The wind picked up and moved through her hair, lifting it off her neck in a deliciously relaxing way. She leaned her head back and closed her eyes, relishing the peaceful moment.

Ellis had brought her a glass of Chardonnay, he called it. She was waiting for him before testing it, as she knew it would taste better with him there to explain it, and to look bemused at the expression on her face as she sipped it.

She was determined to learn about wine if only to have something in common with him. They came from such different worlds that she wondered how long their friendship could last.

He navigated the boat out toward the center of the lake, the mountains looming large in the distance, then he cut the motor and joined her.

They settled into a comfortable silence, both lost in their thoughts, watching the sun dip lower and lower as they sipped a tangy white wine.

She liked that about him, that he didn't have to fill every second with conversation. She'd spent so many years alone, her thoughts her only company, that she'd become comfortable with silence.

Finally, Ellis turned to her. "Cate, I need to tell you something. Since my wife died, I haven't dated anyone, nor did I ever think I would. But lately, I find myself thinking about you all the time. There's something about you that is different from anyone I've ever met. You are an old soul, but a kind one, too."

Cate felt her heart skip a beat. She'd been fighting with her own conflicted thoughts, and his words sent a rush of emotions through her.

"I know what you mean," she said softly, finally breaking the silence. "I've been thinking about you, too. I never thought I'd feel this way again. But being with you, it's like the sun is rising on a new day. A new chance."

Ellis reached for her hand.

Cate's heart raced as he got down on one knee, the light of the setting sun illuminating his face.

"Please don't be afraid," he said as she looked at him in terror. "I'm not asking you to marry me, not yet. But I would like to ask for permission to court you, to take you on dates, and get to know you better. I want to see where this goes."

Cate felt tears pricking at the corners of her eyes. It was a beautiful moment, and the sunset was the perfect backdrop. As she looked out at the fading light, she knew that her life was about to change, in the best possible way.

She'd never been courted, either. Jackson didn't count. They were rebellious teenagers who hadn't had a clue what they were doing. They'd been in lust, not love. Then the kids came, and they were her everything. Yes, there was loyalty and commitment built between her and Jackson, and he felt she belonged to him—but there was no love.

And no courting.

"Yes," she whispered, her voice barely above a whisper. "I would like that very much."

He got back into his chair, but he didn't let go of her hand and she didn't want him to. She didn't worry even once about him touching her scars.

As they watched the sunset make its final descent, she couldn't help but feel like it was a metaphor for their feelings—a beautiful ending to one chapter, and the promise of a new beginning.

CHAPTER 29

*T*aylor entered the interview room and sat down across from Chipper Dayne. Shane followed and took a seat, too, slapping his notebook on the table without having to even fake his anger. It had been building for two days and was tinged with exhaustion, just like hers.

Waiting all night for the Marshals to bring Chipper in from Florida was torture, but honestly, the extradition happened faster than normal. Still, it was almost five in the morning after he'd arrived and was processed, then taken to a holding cell.

She and Shane had stood aside, watching every second.

Dayne hadn't said a word through all of it. Not a denial or an affirmation. He didn't look afraid, either. It was as though he had shut off his emotions while going through the steps of the arrest.

Taylor and Shane hadn't left the department since the afternoon before and though they were excited to get their chance at Dayne, they were running on fumes.

Well, fumes and coffee. Lots of it until they finally got him into the interview room.

Now Dayne sat slouched in his chair, a friendly expression on his face. He looked alert, as though he hadn't just traveled seven hours handcuffed in the back of an official van, then spent another couple sitting in a jail cell.

"Mr. Dayne," Shane began. "We have some serious allegations against you. Do you know why you're here?"

Dayne said nothing, but his smile slowly disappeared.

"We have evidence that places you at the scene of the crime out at Hart Valley Farms," Shane continued. "We have witness statements and DNA. We also have a video of you on that road about the time of the murders. It's all very incriminating, Mr. Dayne. What do you have to say about that?"

Taylor nodded as though everything Shane said was accurate, though some of it was bluffing.

Dayne remained silent, but his eyes darted around the room, taking in his surroundings.

"Look, Dayne," Shane said, leaning forward. "We know you did it. We just want to know why. What could drive a man to commit such heinous crimes?"

Dayne shrugged. "I don't know what you're talking about."

"You can stop lying," Shane said. "We have a mountain of evidence against you. You're going to get the death penalty unless you cooperate with us. Tell us why you did it."

Dayne leaned back in his chair and crossed his arms. "I want a lawyer."

Shane sighed. "Fine. We'll get your lawyer. But know this, Mr. Dayne. You can run, but you can't hide. The truth will come out eventually."

Shane's phone rang. He stood up and left the room, leaving Taylor alone with Dayne. She changed tactics.

"We got you, Chipper," she said softly. "You're only going to make this more difficult for yourself. What would your wife say? Wouldn't she want you to do the right thing? Give the Higgins family some closure? And Carlos' wife? Think of those poor children, now fatherless."

"Taylor, you know I could never do something like that." He looked at her beseechingly.

She shook her head, disgusted.

Not only at him, but at herself. How had her gut not told her a long time ago that he wasn't who he said he was? What kind of detective was she going to make if she hadn't picked up that he was a cold-blooded killer in all the times she'd been around him? So much for the so-called instinct she'd always been proud of.

"JD said you weren't working for him that day, and he hasn't seen you in months. So, your alibi is shot all to hell. Think about that."

He didn't respond, just looked at her as if he felt sad or sorry for her ignorance.

Shane returned and sat down. "You don't have to say a word until your lawyer is present, but I can talk all I want."

He flipped open the binder, then pointed to a report.

"Your guns were tested. You wiped them clean, so no DNA there, but the casings had the same markings as the ones left at the scene. Perfect match. It's confirmed that your guns were the ones used in the murders."

Chipper stared at him, his eyes devoid of emotion.

Taylor remembered the day months before when he'd stopped and helped her with Mr. Diller, how friendly and accommodating he'd been. He always whistled, too, everywhere he went.

People liked him. They talked about how his name matched his personality, always chipper. They trusted him in their homes, carrying in firewood or doing small handyman jobs. The pastor of his church had defended him, outraged to find out he was a suspect. Chipper Dayne had fooled her. He'd fooled them all.

He was a chameleon.

And a psychopath.

Taylor slapped her hand down on the table. "After you left Amos, David, and Carlos laying in their blood, you went straight to the campground to clean up. Your wife said the camper has been closed off since last summer, but the shower there doesn't have proper venting and still had droplets of water that hadn't dried up."

"Your truck was seen going east in the direction of the campground just after the murders, and then you were at the country store right there on the corner, pumping gas. Three witnesses to that, too. But you said you haven't been anywhere near the campground in months," Shane said.

"There's a video of you there," Taylor added. "Can't refute that."

They didn't have a video, but they had Brett and Phil Pearman. And Melanie with the frizzy hair and blue eyeshadow. It was going to be interesting seeing her on the stand, giving testimony. It would probably be the most exciting thing to happen to her since her prom night and, no doubt, she'd be just as dramatic.

Shane flipped the page, thumping a photo stapled to the next report. It was of the fire pit close to the camper. "Yep, you took your clothes and boots off and set them on fire right there. See that? Those are the charred remains of the eyelets off the boots. Also, the snap of your coveralls. Same brand as another pair we found in your closet. A pair your wife eagerly handed over because she thinks you're innocent."

Taylor thought she saw a barely perceptible flinch at that.

"Last but not least," Shane said. "Guess what that call was a few minutes ago?"

Chipper didn't respond.

"We got the truck, Dayne. You didn't hide it well enough. You should've sunk it in the marsh, not just left it for us to find."

Taylor felt excitement surge through her. Tingling started at her fingertips and worked its way up her hands into her arms.

"You want to take a guess what we found on the truck's tailgate?" Shane said. When he tapped his pen slowly against the tabletop, it sounded like a bomb ticking.

Chipper looked worried now.

"Burgundy paint," Shane said, letting the two words drop like a bomb.

"It all makes sense now, Chipper," Taylor said. "You put down the carpet squares to keep from leaving distinguishable tire tracks, then backed your truck to the safe. You tried to slide it up onto the bed, and that's how you transferred some of its burgundy paint to the tailgate. The safe was too heavy and you were struggling when you saw David approaching. You shot him first."

Taylor continued after taking a breath. She had a lot more to say. "Amos heard the shots and came out to see what was happening. He surprised you because he wasn't even supposed to be there that day. Beverly had told you he was going to be out of town when you called her about delivering firewood. Amos ran out to the driveway when he saw David lying there, and you came around and forced him back toward the house at gunpoint, where he lost his slippers along the way. Before you could get him into the house to find the key to the safe, he wasn't being compliant enough or he was telling you that you were as good as caught. You panicked and shot him in the garage."

Chipper stared holes through her as she spoke.

"He begged you to let him tend to his son, didn't he?" Shane said. "When he wouldn't keep moving, you killed him execution-style. You're a monster, Dayne."

Taylor leaned forward and locked eyes with Chipper so that he could see the fury that ran through her. "With them both incapacitated, you went inside and found the key, and was back out there emptying out the cash when Carlos came up for the gopher traps."

Shane spoke next. "You hid from Carlos. He saw David, then Amos, and ran inside to get help. You grabbed another gun from your truck and followed. You killed him, then you took off for the campground, but you were almost out of gas, so you had to stop at the country store. After that, you went on to the campground and burned your boots and your coveralls, then took a shower. You told your wife you were working in Jasper."

"Then yesterday, when Vera called to tell you we were at your place, you knew we were onto you so you ran for Florida," Taylor said. "You didn't think we'd figure it out, did you?"

They were done telling him the details, and they let the silence fall around them.

Chipper let out a long, troubled sigh. "Damn it. It wasn't supposed to happen like that." He lowered his head into his hands, speaking through his fingers. "I was only going to take the safe and go. Just a burglary. In and out. I never wanted to kill anyone."

Shane turned to Taylor. "You want the honors, Gray?"

"Damn right I do." She stood and took her handcuffs off her belt, then went around the table. He was already in custody, so the cuffs weren't necessary, but it was the symbolism that mattered.

She made him stand and put his hands behind his back.

"Chipper Dayne, you are under arrest for the felony murders of Amos and David Higgins, and of Carlos Rodriguez."

CHAPTER 30

*T*aylor parked her truck in the driveway and got out, then walked up to the porch, admiring what she saw. Sam had been working hard to clean up the old Langston property because everything was freshly painted and now the house that used to be a rusty, faded red was a crisp new white with black shutters.

The porch floor was painted black, too. Something Taylor had never thought about doing, but it looked sharp. The house looked completely different than the last time she had seen it. There was now a wooden swing with fluffy cushions and some potted flowers lining the railings.

She'd never known a man who potted flowers. It made her smile to imagine Sam with his hands, which were usually entrenched in grease and auto parts, in rich soil and blooms.

The sun was setting, and a warm golden glow cast over the yard. As she approached the front door, she knocked, but there was no answer.

When she heard Diesel barking in the backyard, she made her way around the side of the house and leaned over the fence to watch. Just like the front yard, the back was cleaned up and neatly trimmed. He'd spread mulch around a few trees and a bed of pansies, and the colors popped against the dark wood chips.

Sam had just thrown a ball for Diesel and was waiting on him to bring it back. He didn't look impatient or in a hurry. He looked happy to be living in the moment with his dog.

With *their* dog.

"Hey, Sam," she called.

He turned, a wide smile spreading across his face. "Taylor! Hi. I thought you'd never get here. Come on in and play with us for a minute."

She found the gate and entered. "Wow, the place looks great."

"Thanks, I've been working on it."

Diesel brought the ball back and dropped it so he could greet her. She knelt and hugged him, then rubbed his head. She grabbed the ball and threw it, and he was off again.

"I heard about Chipper Dayne," Sam said quietly.

"Yeah. Finally got him."

He put a hand on her shoulder. "I know this has been hard on you, Taylor. I'm glad it's over."

"Thank you. I'm exhausted. I think I'll sleep for two days. The sheriff is going to let me have the rest of the week off."

The case was over for their part, but for Beverly and Jenny, and even Carlos' wife, it wasn't. They still had a lengthy trial to prepare for, and they had to learn to live without the men in their lives.

Taylor felt a lump form in her throat as she thought about how much they had lost. Beverly was going to have to live her twilight years without her soulmate. And Jenny might remarry one day, but David's girls would never know their real father. They were so young they'd probably forget him.

She and Shane had gone to the farm earlier and gave Danny the news first. He deserved that, as well as the apology Shane added to it. Danny had barely looked at her. He'd probably never forgive her for not defending him more.

Simultaneously, the sheriff had arrived at Jenny's to give her and Beverly the update. He'd wanted to do it himself, in honor of his friendship with Amos.

Taylor didn't think the sheriff would ever get over this one.

Sam was right—it had been a tough case, one that had hit close to home for a lot of them. They'd all realized how hard it was to remain objective in an investigation when you knew the victims.

Sam studied her. "It's okay to feel what you're feeling, Taylor. You did your best, and justice will be served. That's all anyone can ask for."

She looked up at him. For a moment, she forgot about the sadness that had been weighing her down. She took a deep breath for what felt like the first time in a month. He had a way of doing that to her. She suddenly felt relaxed in his presence, and it was as though nothing else mattered.

"Let's go inside," Sam said. "I want you to see what I've done in there."

"Okay, but I can't stay long. I just came to get Diesel if that's okay. I feel like I need him tonight."

"Of course," he said, then led the way to the back porch. Diesel followed, then went around them in a beeline for his water bowl. He began slurping it up and splashing it everywhere.

Taylor laughed. "Good to see it's not just my house he does that at. Do you hide your toilet paper, too?"

Sam laughed. "Sure do."

As they stepped into the house, she was greeted with a much cozier and inviting atmosphere than she was expecting for a bachelor pad. Candles were burning, and the air was filled with the aroma of clean linen, her favorite scent.

He led her around, showing her the bedrooms and a small office he had set up, then to the living room.

"It's all used furniture, but I think I did pretty well."

"You did great," she said, meaning it. His decorating skills were surprisingly on par with Jo's. A lot of cozy and colorful accents to style up older stuff.

"Have a seat. I'll get us something to drink." He disappeared into the kitchen.

Diesel joined Taylor and flopped down at her feet, panting as though he'd just run a mile.

The couch was a sectional, and she could see where Sam had tucked a nice throw over the soiled cushions. On a bookshelf near the fireplace was a framed photo of Sam and Diesel next to a set of Harry Potter books. She couldn't imagine Sam sitting down with a thick novel, but it was heartwarming to picture it, though maybe they were from his teenage years.

Another framed photo was of him and his father, their arms around each other in a friendly embrace. Next to it was a photo of his father with what must be Sam's mother, because he looked just like her.

He returned with two Cokes and put them down on the coffee table, then sat next to Taylor. He left a bit of space between them, enough for a whole person, then he went into a story about a customer he'd had come to him that week to look at her car.

"She said there was a loud clunking sound whenever she stopped the car, and then it would sound again when she'd pulled away. I was able to repair it for free."

"And what was it?"

"A bowling ball loose in her trunk," Sam said, laughing.

Taylor liked how he told the customer the truth and didn't try to make up some sort of fake repair to charge her something.

Sam relayed a few more funny stories. He had her laughing and forgetting her previous somber mood, but then he got quiet.

"Taylor, we've known each other for a while now."

Uh-oh. Here it comes again.

She could feel the sudden tension in the air.

"So, I'd like to invite you over for a Memorial Day cookout. Some of my friends are coming to see my new place. And my dad."

Relief flooded through her. A cookout she could handle.

"That sounds fun," she said. "Can I bring Adele, my grand-mother? She's flying in for a short visit."

"Absolutely. Your sisters and mom are invited too. So that's out of the way. But I also just want to tell you how amazing I think you are. You put everyone in your life first. Your sisters. Your parents. Even the people of Hart's Ridge. I don't think you know how special you are."

He looked genuine, and it warmed her heart. Broke it a little, too. She'd thought she was out of the woods, but now she saw where the conversation was headed and needed to shut it down.

"Sam, I know what you're about to say and I just don't know if I can do this. My job takes a lot out of me, and you need someone who can give you more than I can. Someone to be the kind of girl-friend you deserve."

Sam looked at her, his eyes filled with warmth and sincerity. "Taylor, I don't need anything from you except for you to be your-self. I don't care that your job takes up a lot of time. And your family, too. I just want to be here for you, and to be with you. Just like you are."

Taylor felt her resolve crumbling as she gazed into his eyes. She had never had someone like Sam in her life, someone who cared for her without any ulterior motive or without putting demands on her time and affection.

"What are you thinking about?" he asked. "You look lost."

A sense of understanding flooded through her. Since someone had broken into her home and assaulted her, she'd been so busy building walls to keep the bad guys out that she had lost sight of the good ones.

The ones she needed to let in.

"I'm not lost."

Then she leaned in and touched her lips softly to Sam's. He took the invitation, then control of the situation, pulling her onto his lap.

First, the only thing Taylor could think about was absolutely nothing but the heavenly feel of his lips. Then she realized she'd been trying to dream of this moment for a while but hadn't let herself quite go there in her imagination.

It all felt familiar. Not like it was their first kiss.

She'd never been one to feel feminine, and she'd always compared herself to those who did more to be pretty, with their perfect makeup and snazzy hair. Cute clothes that enhanced their figures. But here, in this minute and on Sam's lap with his arms around her, she could feel his heart pounding and his attraction to her.

And it made her feel like a woman.

Also, a bit out of control.

It had been a long time since she'd been with a man, and she'd thought that after the rape, all her passion and desire had been snuffed out forever. But when Sam guided her back onto the couch, her body allowed it—even begged for it—and her brain miraculously went along too.

She pulled him on top of her, their lips never dividing.

When his hand cupped the back of her neck, then began to travel down, Taylor's pulse raced. Heat filled her body until she thought she'd melt right there in his arms.

Then her phone rang.

Sam kept going, but the phone continued ringing.

Taylor pushed against him, freeing her lips.

"I'm sorry, Sam," she murmured. "I need to see if it's an emergency. It might be work."

He groaned and rolled off her.

Taylor pulled her phone from her pocket and looked at the screen. It was Margaret, Sissy's mom.

She never called. Suddenly, Taylor was terrified that something had happened to Johnny. Margaret kept him while Lucy worked at the Den sometimes. She sat up and put both feet on the floor, holding the phone to her ear tightly.

"Hello, Margaret? What's going on?"

"Taylor, is this you?" Margaret sounded like she was crying.

"Yes, it's me. What's wrong?"

"It's Sissy. She didn't come home last night and hasn't called. Her phone goes straight to voicemail. She'd never do that to me, Taylor. She always comes back to Hayley. I need you to come right now. Sissy is missing."

The End

Are you ready for more Hart's Ridge? Do you want to help find Sissy and return her to Margaret and her young daughter? What about Taylor's other sisters? They have their own stories, too. You can get book Four, BORROWED TIME, now at the following link and read further down to *grab a bonus scene* of the home invasion in the Banfield Hudson Bay home for *free*! Find out what really happened to Ian and Suki.

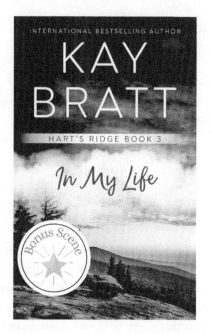

[DOWNLOAD BONUS SCENE HERE]
Or go straight to the next book in the series!
DOWNLOAD *BORROWED TIME* HERE

People don't want to hear the truth because they don't want their illusions destroyed.

Every minute counts when a long-time friend of Deputy Taylor Gray's comes up missing. This one is personal and if Taylor doesn't want the State Police to solve the case first, she is going to have to step up her game to find the wolf that mingles among them in sheep's clothing.

With the Hart's Ridge series, you will find Deputy Taylor Gray, a young woman carrying the world on her shoulders as she does her best to solve mysteries (each inspired by a true crime), as well as fight to piece her fractured family back together.

Borrowed Time is book four of the new Hart's Ridge small-town mystery series, written by Kay Bratt, million-copy best-selling author of *Wish Me Home* and *True To Me*.

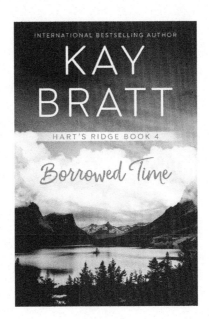

DOWNLOAD *BORROWED TIME*
Please join my monthly newsletter to learn more about myself and the Bratt Pack, and to be notified of new releases, sales, and giveaways! JOIN KAY'S NEWSLETTER HERE

A NOTE FROM THE AUTHOR

Hello, readers!–I hope you enjoyed In My Life, the third book in the *Hart's Ridge* series. The true crime wrapped into the fictional town of Hart's Ridge and its fictional characters was loosely inspired by a tragic triple murder referred to as the Christmas Tree Murders.

In 2009, Frederick Phillip Hammer of Crumpler, NC pleaded guilty to five counts of capital murder and one count each of robbery, breaking and entering a building with the intent to commit larceny while armed with a deadly weapon, and grand larceny and use of a firearm in the commission of a felony. Hammer worked as a handyman for the owner of the farm and was also known to deliver firewood to the locals. Just before his sentencing, Hammer said, "What happened that day should not have happened, and I'm sorry," Hammer told the victims' family members in court just before he was sentenced. "I went there with the intention of doing a burglary…. It was going to be in and out."

Later it was determined that Hammer was also a suspect in other unsolved murders from the past, in different areas he had lived in. He subsequently confessed to more than seventeen killings from the time he was a teenager to adulthood. My deepest condolences to the Hudler and Miller families involved in this case.

Are you ready to read *Borrowed Time*? Fasten your seatbelt because someone you have come to know and love is missing and Taylor is desperate to find them before it's too late. You'll also get to know more about Taylor's sister, Anna, who possibly isn't what she tries to portray to others.

Lastly, I invite you to join my private Facebook group, Kay's Krew, where you can be part of my focal group, giving ideas for story details such as names, livelihoods, etc. to this series. I'm also known to entertain with stories of my life with the Bratt Pack and all the kerfuffle's I find myself getting into. Please join my author newsletter to hear of future Hart's Ridge books, as well as giveaways and discounts.

Until then,

Scatter kindness everywhere.

ABOUT THE AUTHOR

PHOTO © 2021 STEPHANIE CRUMP PHOTOGRAPHY

Kay Bratt is the powerhouse author behind over 30 internationally bestselling books that span genres from mystery and women's fiction to memoir and historical fiction. Her books are renowned for delivering an emotional wallop wrapped in gripping storylines. Her Hart's Ridge small-town mystery series earned her the coveted title of Amazon All Star Author and continues to be one of her most successful projects out of her more than million books sold around the world.

For more information, visit www.kaybratt.com.